Hippocrene U.S.A. guide to
Exploring the
AMERICAN WEST
A Guide to Outdoor Museums

Gerald L. Gutek
and
Patricia A. Gutek

HIPPOCRENE BOOKS
New York

To our daughters,
Jennifer and Laura,
our favorite traveling companions

For information, address
Hippocrene Books, Inc.
171 Madison Ave.
New York, NY 10016

Gutek, Gerald Lee.
    Hippocrene U.S.A. guide to exploring the American West : a guide
to museum villages / Gerald L. Gutek and Patricia A. Gutek.
    ISBN 0-87052-793-2
    1. Historical museums—West (U.S.)—Guide-books. 2. Historic
sites—West (U.S.)—Guide-books. 3. Villages—West (U.S.)—Guide
-books.   4. West (U.S.)—Description and travel—1981–   —Guide
-books.   I. Gutek, Patricia, 1941–   . II. Title.
F595.3.G88   1989
917.804′33—dc20   89-15582
                                                        CIP

Library of Congress Cataloging-in-Publication Data

Printed in the United States of America.

Contents

Introduction

Yes, you can still see and discover American Western history. The Old West is there despite large urban centers like Denver and Los Angeles, the Disneylands and ski resorts, the modern highways and housing subdivisions. The oft-repeated comment that America destroys its past instead of preserving it simply isn't true. You can explore sites that have carefully preserved every phase of American Western heritage.

What will you find? You'll see archaeological sites scattered throughout New Mexico, Arizona and Colorado that rival those in Greece and Rome. They display and interpret the physical culture of prehistoric Indian groups including the Anasazi, Mogollen and Hohokom. Ruins of multi-storied, masonry houses with hundreds of rooms built 1500 years ago are mind-boggling discoveries. Cliff dwellings, towns built in large caves on the sides of sheer cliffs, attest to the creativity and imagination of the early inhabitants of our country. Visit these ruins at Mesa Verde, Colorado, Chaco Culture, New Mexico, and Montezuma Castle, Arizona.

You'll see remnants of the influence of the Spanish who conquered Mexico and then established New Spain in the Southwest and California. The Spanish conquistadores and the Jesuit and Franciscan missionaries who accompanied them were on a quest for gold and souls. They didn't find gold, but Spanish priests stayed to Christianize thousands of Indians. The Spanish culture made a strong imprint on the West which remains today. Spanish padres built exquisite churches in the Southwest, many of them adjacent to large Indian pueblos. Some mission churches are still operating while others can be viewed as ruins. Mission sites include San Xavier del Bac in Arizona, Salinas National Monument in New Mexico and San Juan Bautista in California.

Even the Russians were involved with Western history as their fur-trading activities in Alaska crept south into Northern California. Fort Ross on California's northern coast is a rare gem.

Crossing the continent were adventurous prospectors drawn to the West by the lure of fortunes to be made in gold and silver. The prospector's frontier is preserved and interpreted in outdoor museums that depict mining camps and towns such as Jerome State Historic Park in Arizona and the South Park City Museum at Fairplay, Colorado.

An important and colorful part of the West's history was the presence of the U.S. Army, the infantry and cavalry units that garrisoned the string of forts erected along the westward trails. The military history of the West is preserved and comes alive at Fort Vancouver National Historic Site, Vancouver, Washington, and at Fort Laramie National Historic Site in Wyoming.

Exploring the American West: A Guide to Outdoor Museums, is a guide to some of the finest outdoor museums portraying the rich history of the West. The focus of this book is the outdoor museum because it successfully captures the mood and flavor of the West. Its buildings and artifacts are located in mountains, deserts, and valleys, the natural settings characteristic of the region.

An outdoor museum is defined as an excavated, restored, or recreated assemblage of significant dwellings, buildings, or archeological ruins located in a usually contiguous fashion, in a site that is open to the public, either free or for an admission charge. We exclude historic districts where the buildings may not be open to the public, indoor museums, isolated historic buildings, and historical markers which designate places where important historical events occurred but where physical historic remnants no longer exist.

Our book is intended to be a usable guide to significant outdoor museums of the American West. It is designed to help you plan your travel, to provide an accurate historical interpretation of the site, to identify and describe its major buildings, and to supply information about accommodations along with places of interest, or side trips, near the site.

This volume of *Exploring the American West* contains four sections: the Far West (California), the Southwest (Arizona and New Mexico), the West (Colorado and Wyoming), and the NorthWest (Oregon and Washington). This regional organization plan will help you incorporate visits to historical sites with your trips to other places of natural, scenic, or cultural interest in the West.

We provide the information that you will need to plan a visit to a particular outdoor museum including address, telephone number, location, days and hours when open to the public, and admission fees. In addition, we indicate if restaurants, shops, and other facilities are available on the site.

Since travelers may wish to stay near the site, information is provided on overnight accommodations in nearby inns, hotels, motels, and campgrounds. Although we have made every effort to keep this information current, some changes may have occurred since the publication of this book. Call ahead if you have questions.

As is true of any kind of travel, knowledge about the place that you are visiting will enrich your experience. Historical traveling enables you to be a traveler in time. Outdoor museums, in particular, provide a kind of total immersion in the past. For each outdoor museum in the book, we include a section on its history that will orient you to the site. We comment on the persons and the important events that took place there. We also briefly comment on the process of arch-elogical excavation and/or historical restoration or recreation that was used to develop the site into an outdoor museum.

In addition to reading our history of the site, we suggest that you take advantage of the orientation programs available at the site. Many sites, especially those that are National Parks and Monuments, have good slide or video presentations. Spending a few minutes viewing such a presentation is a great help in understanding and appreciating the history and significance of the site. Maps and detailed guidebooks may also be available in the visitor's center which should be your first stop.

After you have oriented yourself to the site and its history, the book's section called the "Tour," will take you through the major buildings found in the particular outdoor museum. Here, we describe the building, identify it by type and struc-ture, tell you who lived in it, describe its interior and relate it to the whole village, town, or community. While some of the outdoor museums have guided tours or docents to explain the buildings and artifacts on the site, most of them rely on the self-guided tour. The tour that we provide gives you the essen-tial information that you need for the self-guided tour.

We would like to thank and commend the United States National Park Service that has been primarily responsible for protecting and preserving Western history. Too much praise can not be given to this department which provides tourists with the finest vacation destinations America has to offer, our favorites being those extraordinary sites that combine incredi-ble scenery with fascinating history.

We have written *Exploring the American West* so that you can join us as time travelers in re-experiencing a fascinating and important part of our country's heritage. We hope that our book will help you to enjoy America's Western heritage as much as we have.

—Gerald and Patricia Gutek

PART I

FAR WEST

1

CALIFORNIA

Columbia State Historic Park

Restoration of a California gold rush town, 1850–70; National Register, National Historic Landmark

ADDRESS: P.O. Box 151, Columbia, CA 95310
TELEPHONE: (209) 532-4301
LOCATION: 135 miles southeast of San Francisco; 80 miles northwest of Yosemite National Park; 4 miles northwest of Sonora on S.R. 49 and Parrotts Ferry Road
OPEN: Daily, 8 A.M. to 5 P.M. except Thanksgiving and Christmas
ADMISSION: None
FACILITIES: City Hotel, restaurants in City Hotel and Columbia House, picnic areas, craft shops, stagecoach rides, horseback riding stables, summer theater, handicapped accessible
MOTELS/HOTELS: Gunn House, 286 S. Washington St., Sonora

95370, tel. (209) 532-3421; Sonora Towne House, 350 S. Washington St., Sonora 95370, tel. (209) 532-3633

INNS: City Hotel, P.O. Box 1870, Columbia 95310, tel. (209) 532-1479; Fallon Hotel, Box 1870, Columbia 95310, tel. (209) 532-1470; Jamestown Hotel, Main Street, P.O. Box 539, Jamestown 95327, tel. (209) 984-3902; Sonora Inn, 160 S. Washington St., Sonora 95370, tel. (800) 321-5261

CAMPING: Marble Quarry Resort, 11551 Yankee Hill Rd., Columbia 95310, tel. (209) 532-9539; 49'er Trailer Ranch, Box 569, Columbia 95310, tel. (209) 532-9898; Moccasin Point, S.R. 120, Chinese Camp, tel. (209) 852-2396

History

Most of the large numbers of settlers who pushed America's frontier west were farmers and their families who wanted to better their economic situations by acquiring land in the new territories.

Others, mostly men who made their living by trapping, hunting, exploring, or trading, were often migratory and didn't establish permanent settlements in the West. By the mid-nineteenth century, the large influx of farmers had ended—stopped by the Great Plains, which many called the Great Desert.

In 1848, when gold was discovered in California, a new wave of tens of thousands of men of all occupations migrated to California to make their fortune in gold, thus pushing the western frontier to the Pacific coast.

Gold was accidently discovered in January 1848 by James W. Marshall, a Mormon hired by John Sutter to constuct a sawmill in California's Coloma Valley. The gold ore found by Marshall had washed down from what came to be known as the Mother Lode of California, a huge lode of gold-bearing quartz more than one hundred fifty miles long in the western foothills of the Sierra Nevada.

When word of the gold discovery got out, thousands of

prospectors traveled to California. Towns grew up overnight. One of those gold rush towns was Columbia, where, in March 1850, Dr. Thaddeus Hildreth and a small group of prospectors found gold. Within a month, a town called "Hildreth's Diggings" had materialized with a population of six thousand. The name of the town changed twice: first to "American Camp," then to "Columbia: Gem of the Southern Mines." The town consisted of tents and shanties quickly erected by the gold seekers, who didn't want to waste time.

Placer mining was the mining method employed by these inexperienced prospectors. Water had washed away parts of the Sierra Nevada's Mother Lode and deposited chunks of gold-bearing quartz into the beds of streams. Using a washing pan, the miner, who often stood waist deep in an ice-cold stream, would throw a few scoops of raw earth into the pan and twirl it until water washed the dirt away and left the heavier grains of gold at the bottom.

Another simple mining tool used by the prospectors was the cradle, a crude box which would be rocked with one hand while dipping earth and water in with the other. The debris would wash out while the gold particles settled in the cleats. Prospecting for placer gold was monotonous and back-breaking work. Although some miners struck it rich, most received meager rewards for their work and quickly became discouraged.

The water needed for gold mining became a serious problem when the only gulch stream dried up in 1850. The problem was solved by digging a ditch that brought water from Five Mile Creek to Columbia and nearby camps. The creek was reached in mid-1852 but was inadequate. The Tuolumne County Water Company had to continue to the south fork of the Stanislaus River.

Once Columbia had an adequate water supply, gold production improved dramatically. However, miners were charged $6 a day for water. In March 1855 miners asked for a lower rate, which was denied. The miners then formed their own water company, the Columbia and Stanislaus River Water Company, and began building a ditch and flume system which drained from the middle fork of the Stanislaus River. The ingenious water system winds over sixty miles and took over three and a half years to complete.

Eventually placer gold mining was exhausted. More sophisticated and expensive methods using heavy equipment to drill into rocks were needed to obtain more gold. Most individuals could not afford to employ those methods nor did they have the expertise or equipment. For most people, the gold rush ended as abruptly as it began. They moved on leaving nearly empty "ghost" towns behind.

By 1860, Columbia's mining and population declined, leaving a town of about five hundred. Eventually some vacant buildings were torn down to mine their sites. However, a large number of the red brick buildings survived, making Columbia one of the best-preserved examples of a gold mining camp of the 1850s.

In 1945, California's state legislature passed a bill creating Columbia State Historic Park, administered by the Department of Parks and Recreation. Over twenty-one buildings have been carefully restored to their original appearance during the 1850 to 1870 period. Several restored buildings have been leased to private businesses and are operated as stores. Furnishings in the buildings are original or antiques appropriate for the period.

Tour

Columbia has preserved the atmosphere of a western town of the mid-nineteenth century. The town's location in a somewhat isolated ranching area in the foothills of the Sierra Nevada lends a sense of timelessness. Although Columbia is a living town, its sparse population is distributed mainly on the outskirts of the restored area.

The well-preserved red brick buildings with iron doors and

window shutters are used as either museums or businesses selling reproduction items. They line both sides of Main Street for about four blocks. The town's atmosphere is rough and ready rather than pristine and well manicured. Tours are completely self-guided. Museums have either printed signs identifying and explaining the exhibits or audio narration.

A good place to begin your tour is at the **William Cavalier Museum,** which has exhibits on virtually every aspect of Columbia's history. There are exhibits on early mining methods, the water supply problems, gold nuggets and flakes, gold panning, prominent citizens, Chinese artifacts, prospectors' kits, guns and rifles, banking, gambling, school days, and even a photograph of the town's prostitutes whom I mistook for a class of high school girls.

As in every gold rush town, Columbia has a **Wells Fargo Building.** Built in 1858, from $55 to $90 million in gold was brought here, weighed, and shipped. The original scales, which are said to be so sensitive that they could weigh a signature on a piece of paper, are on display.

Next door is the **Wells Fargo Stage Office.** Schedules of stages to Sonora, Farmington, and Angel's Camp are posted; and the baggage room is filled with trunks. At the **Assay Office,** located behind the stage depot, is displayed equipment used to determine the value of ore samples. Gold was molded into bars here.

The **Mining Equipment Display** has examples of early mining equipment, including a pelton wheel, and stamp mill.

The **Franco Cabin** exhibits the utensils and sparse furnishings of a miner's cabin of the 1860s.

A **dentist's office** contains dental instruments, a red plush dental chair, tooth molds, and a huge, frightening-looking foot-pumped dental drill.

Drs. McChesney and Parsons began the **Columbia Drug Store** in July 1856, and it is well stocked with medicines and elixirs, including "Dr. King's New Life Pill," "Foley's Kidney Remedy," and mandrake root.

At one time there was a sizable Chinese population living in Columbia. In addition to an oriental temple, there is a **Chinese Herb Shop,** which has been restored. Medicines, herbs, and pharmaceutical cabinets with drawers bearing Chinese symbols are found here.

Fire fighting was important in the fire-prone mining camps. After Columbia suffered great losses from fires, the town prepared for fire fighting by storing large water cisterns beneath the streets. The **Columbia Firehouse** contains the hand-operated fire engines which would pump the water, including the Papette, a two-cylinder fire engine with leather buckets which was built in Boston in 1852.

Several organizations that have museums in town include the **Independent Order of Odd Fellows, Native Sons of the Golden West,** and the **Masons.** The **Columbia Justice Court** is still a working court.

The **Fallon Hotel/Theater,** which was owned by Owen Fallon and his son James, dates from 1857. Today's structure incorporates three buildings: the hotel, the barroom which the Fallons purchased in 1863, and the theater which was built in 1886. Combining the hotel and barroom created a splendid dancing hall where dances were held until the 1920s. Touring acting groups used the theater to perform for the miners. Restored as a Victorian hotel, the Fallon Hotel reopened in 1983. Since 1945 the College of the Pacific has presented summer theater there.

A short walk from Main Street is a two-story, red brick **schoolhouse** built in the 1860s. California's oldest schoolhouse was the town school until 1937. School children contributed funds for its restoration. The second story is a good place to view the surrounding countryside.

The **cemetery** was established in 1855 and contains many headstones dating from the 1850s. Overly enthusiastic prospectors mined the earlier cemetery.

The **City Hotel,** begun in 1857, was once known as the "What Cheer House." It is restored with Victorian furniture and used as an inn for overnight guests. The City Hotel's dining room is open for lunch and dinner; the barroom with the original cherry wood bar that was shipped around the Horn in 1856 is known as the What Cheer Saloon.

Side Trips

Nearby is **Yosemite National Park**, P.O. Box 577, 95389, tel. (209) 372-4461 or (209) 372-4605. Twelve hundred square miles of valleys, waterfalls, rivers, cliffs, glaciers, gorges, granite domes, giant sequoias, alpine meadows, wilderness areas, and Sierra Nevada peaks are in this popular national park. Accommodations include cabins, lodges, and campgrounds while activities include hiking, climbing, horseback riding, fishing, swimming, rock climbing, backpacking, and alpine downhill and cross-country skiing. Daily vehicle entrance fee is $3.

Fort Ross State Historic Park

Restoration and reconstruction of a Russian fur trading post and fort, 1812–41; National Register, National Historic Landmark

ADDRESS: 19005 Coast Hwy. 1, Jenner CA 95450
TELEPHONE: (707) 865-2391
LOCATION: 75 miles north of San Francisco; 12 miles north of Jenner on Coast Hwy. 1
OPEN: Daily, 10 A.M. to 4:30 P.M.; closed Thanksgiving, Christmas, and New Year's Day
ADMISSION; $3 per car
FACILITIES: Picnic area, Interpretive Center with gift shop

HOTELS/MOTELS: Fort Ross Lodge, 20705 Coast Hwy, 1, Jenner 95450 (one mile north of Fort Ross), tel. (707) 847-3333; Salt Point Lodge at Ocean Cave, 23255 Coast Hwy. 1, Jenner 95450 (six miles north of Fort Ross), tel. (707) 847-3234; Timber Cove Inn, 21780 N. Coast Hwy. 1, Jenner 95450, tel. (707) 847-3231; Timberhill Country Resort, tel. (707) 847-3258
INNS: Historic Gualala Hotel, Gualala, tel. (707) 884-3441; The Old Milano Hotel, Gualala, tel. (707) 884-3256
CAMPING: Salt Point State Park, 20 miles north of Jenner on Coast Hwy. 1, Jenner 95450, tel. (707) 865-3221; Sonoma Coast State Beach: Wrights Beach Camp Ground, six miles north of Bodega Bay on Coast Hwy. 1, Bodega Bay 94923, tel. (707) 865-2391

History

A Russian fort in California? Hard to believe, but true. The Russians had settlements on the northwest coast of North America before either the Anericans or the Spanish. The Pacific coast had been claimed and the southern portion, Baja California, had been settled by the Spanish prior to the establishment of Fort Ross, the Russian fur trading fort. However, the settlement of the coast north of Mexico, Alta California, was Spain's response to the Russian presence in Alaska and Oregon. California was the last of the Spanish colonies in North America.

North America was the site of European exploration and settlement both before and after the United States gained its independence from England. For centuries, Spain was the dominant European nation in the southeastern and southwestern parts of North America. The Seven Years' War in Europe ended in 1763 with an agreement to expel France from North America. Spain acquired France's Louisiana Territory, and England advanced to the Mississippi and north into Canada. Spain began to fear that the English could drive through

Canada to the Pacific Ocean and then move south along the California coast. Russia's claims on the pacific coast, from Alaska south to Oregon, also worried Spain. Fear of further Russian expansion prompted the Spanish to colonize California in the late 1760s by establishing missions. By the time Russia decided to move into northern California in 1812, the Spanish had reached as far north as San Francisco Bay.

Russia's interest in North America, which revolved around fur trading, began with the two voyages of exploration led by Vitus Bering and Aleksei Chirikov in 1728 and 1741. They explored the strait, now known as the Bering Strait, and discovered the Alaskan mainland and the Aleutian Islands, both of which they claimed for Russia. The survivors of the expedition returned to St. Petersburg with a large quantity of furs and pelts. In the next half-century, forty Russian fur trading companies sent ships to the Aleutian Islands and Alaska.

In 1799, Tsar Paul I of Russia chartered the Russian-American Fur Company, giving the company a monopoly on the fur trade in Alaska, the Aleutians, the Kuriles, and other North Pacific islands. The charter also authorized the trading company to use the coastal facilities of North America from Alaska to 55 degrees northern latitude and the right to explore and colonize unoccupied lands to the south. No wonder the Spanish were worried.

The Russian-American Fur Company established a permanent Russian settlement at Sitka, Alaska. Several trading posts were established, including some in the Oregon Territory. Food for the Alaskan base had to be brought in by supply ships from Siberia, which were often late.

When Nikolai P. Rezanov, chief executive of the Russian-American Fur Company, visited the Sitka colony in 1805, he found the settlers dying from malnutrition and scurvy. He sailed to San Francisco Bay in 1806 to obtain food from the Spanish in exchange for furs. Although Spanish ports in California were officially closed to trade with foreigners, Rezanov's mission was successful. On his return to Sitka, he urged Alexander Baranov, the company manager, to utilize an unoccupied stretch of California north of San Franscico Bay as an agricultural and hunting base.

In 1812, Fort Ross was established eighty miles north of San Francisco Bay by ninety-five Russians and forty native Alaskans. This fur trading fort was Russia's southernmost outpost in the New World. Building began in the spring, and the base was dedicated on August 13, 1812, as Fort Rossiya, a name derived from the Russian word *Rus*. Located on a cliff-top plateau seventy feet above the ocean, Fort Ross occupied about one square mile. The quadrangular stockade wall was 276 by 312 feet, and both the fence and the buildings were made of redwood. Two hexagonal-shaped, two-story blockhouses defended the walls and were originally mounted with eight cannons.

Inside the walls were the commandant's house, officers' quarters, barracks for Russian employees, a chapel, storehouses, and offices. The Aleuts lived outside the wall in redwood huts. Other buildings outside the wall included a windmill, farm buildings, granaries, a tannery, blacksmith shop, cooper shop, carpentry shop, and bakery.

The Kashaya Pomo Indians, a tribe of hunters and fishermen who lived in villages, had occupied the land where the Russians built their fort. The Russians contracted with the Kashaya for the land for the fort. Originally the land given to the Russians was accompanied by an exchange of gifts. To prevent Spanish claims, the Russians decided to formalize their title with a deed of cession signed by the Russians and the Indian chiefs in 1817. The treaty is the only one known to have been executed between Indians and Europeans in California.

Good relations existed between the Russians and the Indians, many of whom were employed as farm workers. The Russians, Aleuts, and Kashaya developed a cooperative three-way culture at Fort Ross that included intermarriage.

No more than four hundred peoople inhabited Fort Ross at any one time. In addition to seal and otter hunting, the Russian settlement engaged in farming and raising livestock. Farming was not as successful as hoped since there was little level land in the area, too much coastal fog, and serious rodent problems.

The Spanish protested the Russian intrusion into California but were unprepared to take action against the heavily armed fort.

The American government also viewed the Russian settlement with alarm, which was heightened in 1821 by the announcement by Alexander I that Russian claims on the Pacific coast of North America extended south to the 51st parallel. John Quincy Adams, the American secretary of state, attacked the Russian claim. In 1823, President Monroe declared to Congress that the United States opposed further European colonization in the Americas—the Monroe Doctrine.

Opposed by Spain and Mexico and with England supporting the American position, Alexander I bowed to the pressure and gave up his claim. In an 1824 treaty with the United States, the southern limit of Russia's claims on the Pacific coast was set at the 54° 40′ line. The treaty also provided that trading and fishing in the North Pacific be open to both the United States and Russia.

Less than a decade after the establishment of Fort Ross, the seals and sea otters in the area were almost exterminated. The quantity of skins hunted by the Aleuts totaled about 40,000 in 1812 but was under 400 by 1819. Despite the virtual end of fur trading, the fort remained a viable community which produced tools, farm implements, and household wares which were then traded with the Mexicans. The settlers also raised cattle. Through trading, they obtained food which they were able to ship to the Russian settlements in Alaska. Fort Ross even had a shipyard.

The managers of the Russian fort realized that a move inland to better agricultural and grazing land would be the only way to increase the profitability of the economically marginal operation. When negotiations between the Russian-American Fur Company and the newly independent Mexican government for the acquisition of more land broke down, the managers of the Russian-American Company asked permission of the Imperial Government to leave Fort Ross and the other Russian settlement at Bodega and return to Alaska. That decision was approved by the Russian tsar on April 15, 1839.

Peter Kostromitonoff, a Russian-American Fur Company agent, was put in charge of selling the Fort Ross and Bodega properties. After failed attempts to sell to the Mexican government, a deal was struck with John Sutter from Fort New Helvetia, who had recently visited Fort Ross. In December 1841, Sutter purchased Fort Ross and Bodega for $32,000, $20,000 of which would be paid in wheat and other products and the remainder in cash. The debt would be paid over a four-year period.

This was a considerable price for that time. For the first two annual payments, each valued at $5,000, Sutter would have to supply the Russians with 1,600 bushels of wheat, 160 bushels of peas, 40 bushels of beans, 5,000 pounds each of soap and suet, and 6,250 pounds of tallow. Through the transaction, Sutter acquired items he badly needed at his fort, including lumber, plows, rakes, hoes, horses, mules, 3,500 head of cattle, harnesses, carts, wagons, a forge, cannon, muskets, ammunition, a gristmill, cooperage and tanning shop equipment, and the *Constantine*, a twenty-ton schooner.

In January 1842 after thirty years on the northern California coast, the Russians returned to Alaska. Sutter dispatched a party to drive cattle from Fort Ross to New Helvetia. By 1844, Sutter had removed everything he considered salvageable from Fort Ross and Bodega. He then leased the land to a former employee, William Benitz.

Although Sutter's debt to the Russian-American Fur Company was supposed to be paid off in four years, Sutter still

owed $19,000 seventeen years later. When the company tried
to attach Sutter's property at New Helvetia for repayment,
Sutter transferred title to the property to his son, John Sutter
Jr.

The Mexican government, who had never acknowledged
the Russian claim to the California properties nor their right
to sell them to Sutter, appropriated the property in 1845. It
was then included in a 18,000-acre land grant given by the
Mexican government to Manuel Torres. Benitz and his partner, Ernest Rufus, purchased Fort Ross and its adjoining
17,500 acres from Torres in 1847. The Benitz family lived at
the fort for twenty years during which it became the headquarters of a large cattle ranch. In 1874 the G. W. Call family
purchased the fort and ranch.

Preservation of the Russian fort began in the early 1900s
when local citizens purchased the fort and a few surrounding
acres from the Call family and donated it to the state for a
park. Twenty-seven days after Fort Ross officially became a
historic site of the State of California, the massive earthquake
of April 18, 1906, struck and caused structural damage to all
the fort's buildings. The state began restoration of the fort in
1916 and subsequently acquired additional acreage now total-
ing 350 acres. Fort Ross State Historic Park is administered by
the California Department of Parks and Recreation.

Tour

Fort Ross's setting is as dramatic and unique as its history
and architecture. Driving on Highway 1 north from Jenner to
Fort Ross, there are no communities or settlements to intrude
upon the breathtaking vistas of the Pacific coast, with waves
dashing against jagged rocks, and the dozens of sheltered bays,
inlets, and tidal pools. Early morning mists merge with dashing waves. Herds of cattle and sheep graze on the deep hills

and slopes, occasionally wandering onto the highway. Against this background, standing on top of a cliff on this isolated wind-swept coast, is the nineteenth century wooden Russian fort complete with Siberian-style architecture.

Because of Fort Ross's remote location, time, not people or progress, took its toll on the fort's structures. Another major factor affecting the structures at Fort Ross was the earthquake of 1906, which damaged the fort and, in particular, the Russian Orthodox chapel.

The modern **Interpretive Center** serves as a museum, has a small gift shop, and has a ten-minute slide show which gives the background of the fort. There are exhibits on the Kashaya Pomo Indians, the Aleutian Islanders, and the Russians at Fort Ross. Visitors can use narration wands, which are included with admission, on their self-guided tour of the fort.

Only one original building still stands at Fort Ross. The **Commandant's House** is a one-story log building built in 1836 for Alexander Rotchev and his wife, Princess Helena Gagarin. It was the last building constructed at the fort. Restored after suffering some damage in the 1906 earthquake, the house is a modified rectangular shape with an off-center entrance. The sparsely furnished interior is divided into seven small rooms. In the corner of one room are several religious icons, something typically found in Russian homes.

The remainder of the fort buildings and the stockade have been carefully reconstructed on their original foundations. The twelve-foot-high **stockade fence** is made of 8-inch-thick redwood timbers that enclose a quadrangle 276 by 312 feet. They are held together by a complex system of mortised joints locked by wooden pins.

The two **blockhouses,** one of which has seven sides while the other has eight, are built of heavy, hand-hewn timbers laid horizontally. Sentries were posted in these two-story blockhouses, which were equipped with muskets and cannon. Fort Ross was never attacked.

The **Russian Orthodox Chapel,** which is considered one of

the unique architectural structures on the Pacific coast, was built in 1828, collapsed in the 1906 earthquake, and was reconstructed in 1917. The present chapel, which is an authentic reconstruction, was built in 1973 after the 1917 chapel burned down. The small redwood building has a cupola and a bell tower with a Russian cross on top of it. Inside there is a small vestibule, and the main portion of the small church seems surprisingly large because the high ceiling extends into the cupola. Outside the chapel hangs a replica of the Russian chapel bell.

The **barracks** were the quarters for the Russian employees of the fur company. Several rooms contain cots, beds, and chairs. One room serves as a small carpenter's and tinsmith's shop complete with tools. Another small room is the cooper's shop. One room has a built-in bench alongside the large stone fireplace. There is also a built-in floor-to-ceiling decorated chest. The food storage room has barrels of food and utensils, including a samovar used by the Russians to make tea. There is a kitchen with a large indoor stove and baking oven and a dining room with an icon corner.

The **Kuskov House,** a large two-story building, served as the commandant's house until 1836 when the new commandant's house was built. On the lower floor were a storeroom containing storage barrels, sacks of grain, farm tools, and rope and an armory where weapons and gunpowder were stored. Upstairs were living quarters, which include three bedrooms and a small office with a display of plant specimens, rocks, shells, and bones, and a storage room with cloth, blankets, and lanterns. The walls of this reconstruction are of redwood logs, and both the floors and ceilings are wooden. The windows have large indoor wooden shutters.

In 1820 the Russians planted an orchard near the fort consisting of about one hundred peach, pear, cherry, and apple trees. Fifteen original trees still stand—two Gravenstein and three Bellflower apples, four Russian pears, and six seedling cherries.

A path leads from the fort out on the cliff and down to the beach.

Monterey State Historic Park, Royal Presidio Chapel of Monterey, and Mission San Carlos Borromeo del Rio Carmelo

Restoration and reconstruction of California's second Franciscan mission and second Spanish presidio, 1770–1850; National Register

ADDRESS: Monterey State Historic Park: 20 Custom House Plaza, Monterey, CA 93940; Royal Presidio Chapel: 550 Church St., Monterey, CA 93940; Carmel Mission: 3080 Rio Rd., Carmel, CA 93921
TELEPHONE: MSHP: (408) 649-2836; Presidio: (408) 373-2628; Mission: (408) 624-3600
LOCATION: On California's Monterey Peninsula, south of San Francisco
OPEN: MSHP: daily, 10 A.M. to 5 P.M.; closed Thanksgiving, Christmas, and New Year's Day. Presidio Chapel: daily, 8 A.M. to 6 P.M. Mission: daily, 9:30 A.M to 4:30 P.M.; closed Thanksgiving, Christmas
ADMISSION: MSHP: adults, $3.50; children 6–17, $2; Presidio: free; Mission: $1 donation
MOTELS/HOTELS: Casa Munras, Box 1351, 700 Munras Ave., Monterey 93940, tel. (408) 375-2411 or (800) 222-2558; Hyatt Regency, 1 Old Golf Course Rd., Monterey, tel. (408)

372-1234; Best Western Steinbeck Lodge, 1300 Munras Ave.,
Monterey, tel. (408) 373-3203; Quail Lodge, 8205 Valley
Greens Dr., Carmel 93923, tel. (408) 624-1581 or (800)
538-9516
INNS: Cobblestone Inn, Box 3185, Junipero and 8th St., Car-
mel 93921, tel. (408) 625-5222; Cypress, Box Y, 7th Ave. and
Lincoln St., Carmel 93921, tel. (408) 624-3871; Pine Inn,
Box 250, Junction Monte Verde and Ocean Ave., Carmel
93921, tel. (408) 624-3851; Old Monterey, 500 Martin St.,
Monterey 93940, tel. (408) 375-8284
CAMPING: Pfeiffer–Big Sur State Park, Big Sur 93920, tel.
(408) 667-2315; Andrew Molera State Park, Big Sur 93920,
tel. (408) 667-2315; Bottchers Gap National Forest, Big Sur
93920, tel. (408) 385-5434

History

Juan Rodriquez Cabrillo, a Portuguese navigator who led a
Spanish expedition, was the first European to sight the California coast in 1542. Spanish ships again sailed north in 1602 to
explore the Pacific coast. On this expedition, the goal was to
locate a safe harbor for the Manila galleons sailing from
Acapulco to the Philippines that were being raided by English
pirates. Sebastian Vizcaino and his three ships spent nine
months exploring the California coast. On December 16,
1602, Vizcaino located a harbor which he named "El Puerto
de Monterey" in honor of the viceroy of Mexico.

No Spanish settlements resulted from Vizcaino's discovery
despite his exaggerated description of Monterey Harbor's vir-
tues. Monterey Bay was forgotten until a century and a half
later when the threat of Russian and English expansionism
along the northern Pacific coast compelled Spain to action.

In 1768, Jose de Galvez, visitador general (inspector general) to Mexico appointed by King Charles III of Spain, was
ordered to combat the Russians' advance from the north into
California by fortifying and defending the ports located by

Vizcaino: San Diego and Monterey. Alta California was also to be colonized. To accomplish this, Galvez planned to use the mission system that had proved successful in Baja California and Arizona. These missions had been run by Jesuit priests; but in 1767 the Spanish crown expelled all Jesuits from the missionary field, and Galvez replaced them with Franciscan priests led by Father Junipero Serra.

General Galvez chose Gaspar de Portola, the newly appointed governor of Baja California, to lead the expedition. Two ships, the *San Carlos* and the *San Antonio*, sailed toward San Diego loaded with soldiers and supplies while two other parties went by land. The ships took one hundred ten days to reach San Diego and lost fifty men. The land parties also suffered many losses.

On July 14, 1769, Portola led sixty-four men northward from San Diego toward Monterey. Not recognizing the harbor because of Vizcaino's exaggerated description, Portola's party went beyond it to San Francisco. Then Portola marched his starving, scurvy-ridden group back to San Diego; the trail they blazed would be called *El Camino Real*. Ironically, on the return trip, Portola stopped at Monterey's Point of Pines on December 9, 1769, to erect a cross. A message buried beneath it detailed his frustration at not locating the harbor at Monterey.

When Galvez read Portola's reports and learned of his failure to locate and fortify Monterey, he ordered Portola to return. Portola's land party took only twenty-four days, arriving May 24, 1770, while Father Serra and his sea party arrived about a week later. This time the Monterey Harbor was located, and Father Serra stayed to establish the settlement while Portola sailed back to Mexico. Lt. Pedros Fages was named commandant of Monterey. Monterey's founding settlers included four priests, about thirty soldiers, two artisans, and a half-dozen Christian Indians—not a large contingent to claim northern California for the Spanish and to prevent Russian expansionism.

After dedication ceremonies on June 3, 1770, Father Serra, Father Crespi, and Lieutenant Fages began building the presidio (fort)—El Presidio Royal de Monte Rey—and the mission—San Carlos Borromeo del Rio Carmelo. Father Serra soon found the behavior of the soldiers toward the Indian women morally objectionable since none of the men had brought wives or families. Serra decided to separate the mission and the presidio. Mission Carmel, the second mission established in California, was relocated three miles south of the presidio in December 1771. Although Father Serra would found seven more California missions, the Carmel Mission would serve as his lifelong base.

El Castillo, the Monterey fort, was built of logs and adobe. Originally it protected the harbor for Spain, later for Mexico, and eventually for the United States.

At first, food was a serious problem at Monterey as very little was grown and Mexican supply ships didn't appear on schedule. Fages and his men hunted bear, which kept the colony from starvation. Serra and Fages went to San Diego to beg that the supply ships, which had turned back after encountering violent seas, again proceed north to Monterey. The *San Antonio* sailed to Monterey delivering supplies and ending the famine.

A struggle between the civil and religious authorities at Monterey led Serra to travel to Mexico City in 1773 to present his problems to the new viceroy, Antonio Bucardi. Serra obtained many concessions, including the right of the missionaries to return unsatisfactory mission guards to the presidios. He was also promised that the presidios would be staffed by married soldiers who would be accompanied by their families. Supply lines would be improved, and artisans would be sent to supervise construction of buildings and to train Indians.

As promised, a group of two hundred forty soldiers, wives, and children, along with a large herd of livestock, was led by Don Juan Bautista de Anza from Tubac, Arizona, to Monterey in 1776. Eight babies were born en route and one mother died in childbirth so that two hundred forty-seven people were warmly welcomed to Monterey, along with more than a thousand animals including mules, horses, sheep, and cattle.

Father Serra died at Carmel on August 28, 1784, at the age of seventy. The five-foot-two Franciscan who had founded nine missions in California left a gigantic legacy. His holiness was widely respected and there was much grief at his death. He was buried in the church at Mission San Carlos.

Serra was succeeded as president of the missions by Father Fermin de Lasuen, a scholar and able administrator. By 1786 more than two thousand Indians lived at the mission. Lasuen supervised the building of a new church at the mission that was dedicated in 1797.

In November 1818 two ships entered Monterey Bay commanded by the French privateer Hippolyte de Bouchard. Bouchard demanded supplies and support from Monterey officials to aid in the struggle for independence from Spain. Governor Sola declined. An angered Bouchard met with almost no opposition when he and his men sacked the town, took over El Castillo, set fire to buildings, stole guns, silver, jewelry, and clothing, and then sailed away.

In 1821, Mexico gained its independence from Spain. Governor Sola, the last Spanish governor in California, became the first Mexican governor. He raised the flag of the Mexican Empire over the Custom House on September 26, 1822. Trade restrictions were lifted and land grants were more liberal under Mexican rule. Foreigners still had to report to Monterey, the capital, for permission to stay in California. Since land could only be owned by Mexican citizens, many American traders and sailors who came to Monterey and wanted to stay became naturalized Mexican citizens, converted to Catholicism, and married into Hispanic families.

In 1833 the new Mexican government secularized the Alta California missions, resulting in the end of years of prosperity at the missions. The Indians, who were the intended beneficiaries of secularization, scattered and eventually became servants for the Spanish and Mexican rancheros who were given land grants. After the mission passed out of the padres' hands, the land was sold right up to the walls of the church. Unused mission buildings quickly deteriorated.

Monterey was the capital of Alta California from 1776 until 1849. It was also the port of entry for all foreign shipping on the coast of California under Spanish and Mexican rule. The Custom House served as the government's site for collection of duties.

The town expanded as people constructed homes outside the presidio walls. In 1827 the Mexican government formally authorized Monterey as a pueblo, or town. By 1830 the population had grown to five hundred. Blessed with a mild climate, fertile lands, and a beautiful natural setting, the lifestyle developed by the Spanish rancheros at Monterey was leisurely, romantic, and celebrated with frequent fiestas. The rancheros spent much of their time on horseback and had many Indian servants to do their work.

Despite the idyllic lifestyle enjoyed by the rancheros, not everyone in Alta California was satisfied with the quality of Mexican rule. In 1836 two native-born Californians, Juan Bautista Alvarado, a young customs clerk, and his cousin, Jose Castro, started a revolution against the Mexican governor, Nicholas Gutierrez. After Governor Gutierrez surrendered, the Mexican government acceded to the revolutionaries' demand that military and civic affairs be separated. Alvarado became provisional governor in charge of civil affairs while his uncle, Mariano Vallejo, became the military commander. In 1838, Alvarado accepted the Mexican government's appointment as governor of California.

Dissatisfaction with the Mexican government remained a chronic issue in California. At the same time, both American citizens and the American government became increasingly interested in acquiring California. The Monroe Doctrine expressed America's expansionist mood. Manifest Destiny was the rallying cry. War with Mexico was seen as inevitable.

In 1842 an American naval commander, Thomas Ap Catesby Jones, heard and believed a rumor that the United States had declared war on Mexico. Since Jones had standing orders to seize and hold the ports of California in the event of American war with Mexico, he sailed to Monterey where he and one hundred fifty men occupied the presidio, seizing California's capital without opposition. On October 20, Jones lowered the Mexican flag and raised the American flag. The next day Jones realized his error, restored the Mexican flag, and offered his apologies at Monterey and to the governor at Los Angeles.

The Mexican government was offended by Jones' precipitious action and refused to receive an American agent sent by President Tyler with an offer to purchase California.

The American government's interest in acquiring California included using diplomatic means. Thomas Larkin, a prominent merchant and resident of Monterey, was named U.S. consul and directed to foster annexation and a desire for independence among California's residents. The government assured Larkin that it would support a drive for independence by Californians.

Not everyone was patient enough to wait for dissatisfaction with Mexican rule to move California into the United States' fold. John Fremont was one of those. The American captain led a band of sixty-eight heavily armed men on an ill-defined expedition to California in late 1845. After receiving permission from General Jose Castro to winter in the San Joaquin Valley, Fremont instead encamped near San Jose, where he raised an American flag. The Mexicans were enraged and ordered Fremont out of California. Larkin persuaded Fremont to leave after a few days, and the band moved on to Oregon. There an American marine, Lt. Archibald Gillespie, delivered a message to Fremont that caused him to turn back to California.

On June 14, 1846, about thirty men who had joined Fremont's group invaded Sonoma, captured General Vallejo, and declared California a free and independent republic. Called the Bear Flag Republic because of the flag designed and raised, it was short-lived as word soon came that the United States had declared war on Mexico on May 13, 1846. The Bear Flaggers were incorporated into the United States fighting corps.

When word of the war with Mexico reached California, American ships were already poised along the coast. The *Savannah*, under the command of Commodore John Drake Sloat, was in Monterey Harbor. On July 6, 1846, Commodore Sloat led his men ashore and raised the American flag. The American flag flying over the Monterey Custom House represented the American possession of California. At the end of the Mexican-American War, the Treaty of Guadalupe Hidalgo, signed on February 2, 1848, officially gave California to the United States.

At about the same time as America acquired California, gold was discovered at Sutter's mill near Coloma in January 1848. Not long afterward, a messenger sent by Sutter to Monterey with a request for an American land grant, spread word of the gold find. Monterey, like many other California towns, lost many residents who rushed to the gold fields to make their fortunes. Many sailors who entered Monterey Harbor deserted their ships to be among the first prospectors for gold. One consequence of the gold strike was the sudden increase in California's population. After gold fever abated, many prospectors became permanent residents of California.

After American annexation of California, Mexican and Spanish rancheros were required to legally prove ownership of their properties. Many could not provide adequate documentation, and so their lands were confiscated and wound up in American hands.

No longer a capital city and with large losses of men to the gold fields, Monterey sank into financial disarray. In 1859 to pay off debts, the Monterey city council was forced to sell thirty thousand acres of municipal land. David Jacks purchased it for $1,002.50

After a railroad spur to Monterey from Salinas was added, a huge hotel, the Hotel Del Monte, was built in 1880 on land purchased from Jacks. Monterey became a popular resort town, and one of its attractions was the seventeen-mile drive from the hotel to the ruins of Carmel Mission.

Robert Louis Stevenson visited Monterey in 1879 and did some writing. He also spent time with Fanny Osbourne, his future wife.

Another literary figure associated with Monterey is John Steinbeck from nearby Salinas. From the turn of the century until 1945, Monterey had an extensive sardine canning industry. John Steinbeck's *Cannery Row* immortalized the waterfront business at about the same time as the sardines vanished from Monterey Bay. Since then, Monterey's most important industry has been tourism, and the Cannery Row buildings have become chic shops and restaurants.

Tour

Monterey is another one of California's historic state parks in which its sites are not contiguous. Monterey is a bustling, urban area with residental and tourist traffic and congestion. The Monterey sites cannot be visited quickly and ideally a visit should be spaced over several days. Locating the sites, even with the help of a map, takes some time and involves both walking and driving. One feature which slowed down our touring was the fact that some buildings are not open for touring every day and are only open for guided tours on the hour. In order to see adjacent properties, you must view one site on the hour and then wait until the following hour to see the next house and so on.

Monterey has a designated Walking Path of History which passes by dozens of historic buildings still standing in the town. Many are privately owned. Monterey State Historic Park maintains many of the historic buildings which are interspersed along the streets of the village.

The **Custom House**, 1 Custom House plaza, built in 1827, was established by the Mexican government. It was the only custom house north of Mexico until 1845, and it is the oldest government building still standing on the Pacific coast. Monterey was the chief port of entry for California, and all trading ships were required to declare their cargos and pay import duties at the Custom House. Although it was used until 1867, its importance declined after the gold rush when San Francisco became California's major port of entry. On July 7, 1846, shortly after America had declared war on Mexico, Commodore Sloat of the *Savannah* raised the American flag above the Custom House signifying California's annexation by the United States. This two-story adobe building has an addition to the north end of the building which was completed in 1846. The Custom House was restored by the Native Sons of the Golden West in 1901 and purchased by the state in 1938. It is open daily from 10 A.M. to 4 P.M. The Custom House is listed in the National Register and as a National Historic Landmark.

The **Pacific House**, 8 Custom House Plaza, was built in 1847 by Thomas Larkin, the U.S. consul to Mexico. Originally the U.S. quartermaster used the adobe and stone two-story building as a storehouse. The first floor contains exhibits on California history while the second floor has an exhibit on American Indian artifacts. Open daily from 10 A.M. to 4 P.M.

The **Larkin House**, 464 Calle Principal, was designed and built in 1835 by Thomas Larkin, a Bostonian. The two-story adobe and frame residence was the prototype of the architectural style known as Monterey colonial, a combination of Spanish adobe style with New England frame construction. Larkin was the first and only U.S. consul to Mexico in Monterey (1843–46), during which time the Larkin House was the consulate. Larkin was also a key figure in the American annexation of California. Many Larkin family possessions are among the furnishings of the house. The house is listed in the National Register and as a National Historic Landmark and included in the Historic American Buildings Survey. Closed Tuesday; tours at 10, 11, 1, 2, 3, 4.

Boston Store (Casa del Oro), corner of Scott and Olivier streets, was built in 1845. It was opened in 1849 as the Joseph Boston Store, a general merchandise store. Its Spanish name stems from an unproved rumor that it was used as a gold warehouse. Restored, it now sells replicas of items available in the mid-nineteenth century. Open Wednesday through Sunday from 10 A.M. to 5 P.M.

First Theater, located on the southwest corner of Pacific and Scott streets, was built about 1843. Jack Swan, a sailor, operated a lodging house and bar here. In 1847 it was used as a theater by U.S. military men, the first theater in California. The first production was *Putnam, or the Iron Son of '76,* a stirring military melodrama of the American Revolution. Long since abandoned, the theater was restored in 1937 by the Monterey History and Art Association. It became the home of the Troupers of the Gold Coast. Still performing there today, the Troupers are the oldest active little theater group in the United States. Plays are performed from June through September.

The **Robert Louis Stevenson House,** also known as the Gonzales House, 530 Houston Street, was built in 1835. It was the home of Don Rafael Gonzales, first administrator of customs at Monterey. Sold in 1856 to a Frenchman, Juan Girardin, it was used as a boarding house known as the French Hotel. Robert Louis Stevenson came to Monterey in the fall of 1879 and rented a room at the hotel to be near the woman he loved, Fanny Van de Grift Osbourne. The Scottish writer and the Oakland, California, artist had met three years earlier in France where they had fallen in love. With her two children, Fanny returned to California to obtain a divorce. Fanny and Robert were married in Oakland on May 19, 1880. Several rooms in the house contain Stevenson's portraits, books, manuscripts, and personal belongings. A lovely garden that is open to the public is behind the house. Closed Wednesday. Guided tours at 10, 11, 1, 2, 3, 4.

Casa Soberanes, 336 Pacific, is a two-story adobe house built by Rafael Estrada in 1845. Furnishings reflect a blend of early New England and China trade pieces with modern Mexican folk art. Closed Thursday. Guided tours at 10, 11, 12, 2, 3, 4.

Royal Presidio Chapel, 550 Church Street, is the most important historic building in Monterey. It is the only extant presidio chapel in California and the only building remaining from the presidio at Monterey which was founded in 1770. It was built in 1794 by Father Lasuen, dedicated by him on January 25, 1795, and has been in continuous use ever since.

Manuel Ruiz, the architect who designed Mission Carmel, also designed the chapel, La Capilla Real. Created in the shape of a Latin cross with a front scroll gabled facade and a front corner bell tower, it reflects the influence of Spanish Baroque architecture. The large chapel has a wooden ceiling and a red brick floor, and its walls are painted green and yellow. The ornate church displays the handiwork of Mexican and Indian craftsmen and their naive interpretations of Mexican decorative motifs. The chapel is a parish church with masses daily and Sundays.

In nearby Carmel stands **Mission San Carlos Borromeo del Rio Carmelo,** which had originally been founded on June 3, 1770, at the presidio of Monterey. Father Serra moved the mission three miles away to Carmel in August 1771 after discovering that a mission for Indians and a military outpost of lonely men were not a good combination. The Carmel Mission became the headquarters of the Franciscan priests, Junipero Serra and Fermin Francisco de Lasuen, who established eighteen California missions. Both Serra and Lasuen died and were buried at Carmel.

The first mission buildings built by Serra were of logs. The sandstone church standing today was built by Father Lasuen in

1797. After secularization of the mission in 1834, it quickly fell into disrepair. In 1859 the United States, which had acquired the mission as part of the Gadsden Purchase, returned it to the Catholic Church. In 1884 it was rededicated as a church. Restoration began in the 1920s. In 1960 the Carmel Mission was designated as a basilica, largely because of its association with Father Junipero Serra.

The church's facade and portions of the stone wall are original. The remainder of the structure and all other buildings are reconstructions. The church faces a walled courtyard with gardens of orange poppies, white canna lilies, geraniums, pampas grass, cacti, and palms, along with paved paths and a fountain. There are several other buildings at the mission, some of which are used as museums and are open to the public.

The church itself, considered the most beautiful of the mission churches, has a unique star window on its facade. Careful research has made this among the most authentic mission restorations. Church features include a vaulted ceiling, stuccoed walls, and a side chapel with a wooden ceiling. Decorations include mission-era paintings and original statues of Mary and Jesus dressed in Carmelite habits. Inside the altar rail, stone tablets in the floor mark the tombs of Fathers Serra, Crespi, Lopez, and Lasuen.

Museum exhibits include a sarcophagus by sculptor Jo Mora showing Father Serra in death surrounded by the other three grief-stricken Franciscan padres just mentioned. Looking very much like an Italian opera stage setting is an elaborate Italian navitity scene with many figures; also displayed are the original silver altar candlesticks brought by Serra from Loreto in 1769, a silver monstrance, a painted tabernacle, and decorated altar cloths and vestments. There is also an original music manuscript for the Mass composed by a mission priest.

Rooms furnished as they were in mission days include a kitchen complete with an indoor oven, stoneware, and a lavabo for washing hands and a dining room with a large wooden table. The sala, where visitors were received, is comfortably furnished with a rug, large chairs, and a fireplace. There is also a library with 603 books brought by Father Serra. Serra's room is a small cell with a cot made of boards and a simple writing desk.

The Cooper-Molera Complex, corner of Polk and Munras, consists of several one- and two-story adobe and frame buildings, gardens, and a museum shop. Much of the complex was built by Captain John Rogers Cooper, who was Thomas Larkin's older half-brother. Arriving in Monterey in 1823, Cooper became a major California landholder in addition to being a sea captain and a dealer in hides, tallow, sea otter pelts, and general merchandise. Cooper married Encarnacion Vallejo, sister of General Mariano Vallejo. There is a bookstore and information center in tthe Diaz store portion of the complex and a slide presentation is also shown here. Closed Wednesday; tours of Cooper-Molera adobe at 10, 11, 12, 2, 3, 4; Cooper Store open daily, except Wednesday, 10 A.M. to 5 P.M.

Side Trips

Colton Hall Museum, Pacific Street between Jefferson and Madison, was built as a town hall in 1849. It was the site of the California Constitutional Convention held in 1849. Exhibits relate to the constitutional convention and local history. Free. Open daily from 10 A.M. to 5 P.M., tel. (408) 375-9944.

The Monterey History and Art Association maintains the **Allen Knight Maritime Museum,** 550 Calle Principal. This naval museum displays artifacts from the fishing and whaling days of Monterey. There is also a model of the *Savannah,* Commodore Sloat's flagship when he captured Monterey for the Americans in 1846. Free. Open daily except Monday and national holidays. Hours from June 15 to September 15 are 10

A.M. to 4 P.M. on Tuesday through Friday and 2 to 4 P.M. on Saturday and Sunday. From September 15 to June 15, weekday hours are 1 to 4 P.M.

Seventeen-Mile Drive is a scenic drive along the Pacific coast between Monterey and Carmel. A toll is charged.

San Juan Bautista State Historic Park

Restoration and reconstruction of eighteenth-century Spanish Franciscan mission and pueblo, 1803–50; National Register, National Historic Landmark

ADDRESS: P.O. Box 1110, Second St., Washington and Mariposa Sts., San Juan Bautista, CA 95045
TELEPHONE: (408) 623-4881
LOCATION: 3 miles east of U.S. 101, between Gilroy and Salinas; 33 miles east of Monterey and Carmel
OPEN: Daily, 9:30 A.M. to 4:30 P.M., except Thanksgiving, Christmas, New Year's Day, and Fiesta Day
ADMISSION: Adults, $.50.; children 6–17, $.25
FACILITIES: Gift shop
HOTELS/MOTELS: San Juan Inn, Alameda and S.R. 156, San Juan Bautista 95045, tel. (408) 623-4380
BED AND BREAKFAST: Bed and Breakfast San Juan, 315 The Alameda, San Juan Bautista 95045, tel. (408) 623-4101; Bohn's Bed and Breakfast, 902 Second St., San Juan Bautista 95045, tel. (408) 623-4397
CAMPING: San Luis State Recreation Area, Santa Nella 95322, tel. (209) 816-1196; Sunset State Beach, Watsonville 95076, tel. (408) 724-1266; KOA Campground, 900 Anzar Rd., San Juan Bautista 95045, tel. (408) 623-4263; Mission Farm RV

Park, 400 San Juan-Hollister Rd., San Juan Bautista 95045, tel. (408) 623-4456

History

San Juan Bautista, founded in 1797, was the fifteenth Franciscan mission established in California. Named for St. John the Baptist, this mission was dedicated on St. John's Day, June 24, 1797, by Fathers Fermin de Lasuen, Magin Catala, and Joseph de Martiarena. Father Lasuen was the second president of the Missions, succeeding Father Junipero Serra. Mission sites were usually spaced a day's walk apart. San Juan Bautista was a day's walk from Mission Santa Clara and Mission San Carlos Borromeo at Carmel. The mission system was the primary Spanish method of colonization in the New World. Settlements grew up around each mission. The economy was agrarian, with local Indians doing most of the labor.

In its first year, the structures built at Mission San Juan Bautista included a chapel, missionaries' house, Indian women's house, kitchen, guardhouse, and four soldier's houses. Unknown to Father Lasuen, the mission location he chose was on the edge of the San Andreas Fault. An earthquake in 1800 damaged many buildings. In 1803 a new church with three naves was started; it was completed and blessed in June 1812.

Cattle raising was more successful at San Juan than agriculture. In the best year, 1820, the harvest was 7,420 bushels of grain; yet there were 20,000 head of cattle. Mission income was derived from selling cattle and sheep hides to the captains of the trading vessels at Monterey.

During the mission period in California, 1769–1833, approximately 82,000 Indians were converted to Catholicism by the Franciscan missionaries. At its height, the Indian population at San Juan Bautista was 1,200. Occasionally, missions were attacked by hostile Indians. As early as 1799, and sporadically thereafter, Mission San Juan was attacked by An-saimes, Osos, and Tulare Indians. One of the Franciscan priests who served at the mission from 1808–33 was a scholar and a student of the regional Indian languages. Father de la Cuesta published a book on the subject.

Under Spanish law, the missions were to be secularized—turned into civil pueblos—after ten years, and the property apportioned to the mission Indians. The missionaries opposed this plan and were successful in stalling secularization. Missions became wealthy in terms of land and livestock. During the mission period, few land grants were made to private citizens.

Increased pressure for secularization came after Mexico gained its independence from Spain in 1821. San Juan Bautista was one of ten missions secularized by the Mexican government in 1834. The newly founded Mexican town, or pueblo, was called San Juan de Castro and was administered by Jose Tiburcio Castro and his son, Jose Maria Castro. Only a small number of people remained at the mission. Its quarter million acres were divided into large ranchos which were granted to Mexican officials and military men. The mission orchards were sold.

San Juan Bautista was the site of an incident in the chain of events leading to the eventual acquisition of California by the United States. Captain John C. Fremont, an American ex-plorer, led a band of sixty-eight well-armed men on an ill-defined expedition into California in late 1845. Since Califor-nia was Mexican territory, Fremont and his group were re-quired to request permission from the Mexican general at Monterey, Jose Castro, to remain until spring. Permission was granted on the proviso that the Fremont group return to the San Joaquin Valley and stay away from the coast. Although Fremont agreed, he and his men camped at Mount Gavilan, only one day's march from Monterey. San Juan Bautista is located at the foot of Mt. Gavilan where Fremont encamped and raised an American flag.

Fremont's actions incensed General Castro, who ordered Fremont to leave or his troops would attack the camp. Thomas Larkin, the U.S. consul at Monterey, persuaded Fremont to move on. Fremont's unauthorized flying of the American flag in California was viewed by the Mexicans as a serious American insult and threat. Shortly thereafter, Mexico and the United States would be at war, with possession of California being a major issue.

After the United States acquired California and the gold rush era began, San Juan Bautista became a busy stagecoach stop. The discovery of quicksilver deposits near San Juan Bautista contributed to an influx of people and prosperity in the 1850s and 1860s. However, when the railroad was built, it bypassed the town.

When the gold rush era ended, many former miners who decided to remain in California became squatters on the large ranchos. Later, these Americans acquired title to the lands, and the large Mexican ranchos were divided into small ranches and farms.

The former mission town did not grow or change very much. In 1859 the mission buildings and fifty-five acres were returned to the Catholic Church. In 1934 the State of California acquired the other buildings around the plaza. Restoration began in 1949, financed by the Hearst Foundation.

Tour

The population of the town of San Juan Bautista is about fourteen hundred today. This small town, easily missed by tourists, retains the look of a nineteenth-century Spanish mission town or a Mexican village. Older buildings have been retained, if not restored. The historic park's restored buildings around the plaza are picturesque while some of the town's structures are simply old and dusty looking. It is a sleepy place that is easy to walk in and absorb atmosphere.

The **San Juan Bautista Plaza,** an excellent example of a

nineteenth-century village center with a Spanish-Mexican colonial plaza plan, is the setting for the historic buildings. The plaza was originally used as a parade ground by colonial troops.

The **San Juan Bautista Church,** the second church at the mission, was built in 1803–13 and rebuilt after the 1906 earthquake. It is still owned by the Catholic Church and is a parish church with regular religious services; it is not part of the California State Historic Park.

The church's main altar has a golden reredos with niches containing statues of St. Francis, St. Anthony, St. Michael, St. Christopher, and Jesus against scarlet backgrounds. The painting of the main altar was done by Thomas A. Doak, a sailor from Boston who deserted from the *Albatross*. Ceilings are beamed. After the church was heavily damaged by the 1906 earthquake, concrete buttresses were installed to brace the forty-foot adobe walls.

The convent wing with its shady arcade is all that remains of the quadrangle that enclosed the gardens. Rooms in this wing are furnished as museum rooms. In a former storeroom, there is a gift shop that sells religious articles. The kitchen has an indoor fireplace and oven. The large dining room has a long wooden table. The whitewashed stucco walls are decorated with Spanish designs. Pottery and china are displayed in a large cabinet.

The padres' library has an extensive collection of early books and is furnished with Spanish-style furniture. Another room contains antique priests' vestments and religious articles that include crucifixes, banners, chalices, chairs, candelabra, figures of saints, music books, a barrel organ, and baptismal fonts.

The **Plaza Hotel** was originally a one-story adobe military barracks built in 1813. In 1858 a second story with balconies was added to the building by Angelo Zanetta, who operated it as a hotel. A hotel was needed as the town was a main stagecoach stop between Los Angeles and San Francisco. The hotel dining room, which was noted for its fine food, has wood ceilings and white stucco walls. The barroom is very ornate; it contains a large bar, a billard table, and card tables. The parlor is furnished with Victorian furniture.

The **Plaza stable** was built for the horses of the hotel guests. It now displays nineteenth-century carriages and wagons, including a beer wagon, along with a fully equipped blacksmith shop.

Zanetta built a second two-story building known as the **Plaza Hall.** The adobe building was built of bricks from a previous structure on the site. The first floor was used as the Zanetta family residence and the second floor as a dance hall. The high-ceilinged rooms are furnished with Victorian furniture.

The **Jose Castro House,** built in 1840, is a two-story adobe building with a tiled roof, second-story veranda, two-story rear porch, and a frame two-story side addition. The house has a center stair hall and an interior chimney. It was built as the home of Jose Castro, commander general of Northern California. Outside the house is a small adobe beehive-shaped oven, called a *hornito*, where cooking was done. In 1848, Castro sold the house to Patrick Breen, a survivor of the ill-fated Donner party of 1846.

The **Settler's Cabin,** built around 1850 of redwood logs, has been moved from its location southeast of town to Mariposa Street. There is also a small frame building, the **Old San Juan Jail,** that was built in 1870. There are other adobe buildings dating from the 1850s on Third and Fourth streets.

Behind the mission church is the mission cemetery and a portion of the original **El Camino Real,** California's first road, which connected the missions.

Sonoma State Historic Park

Restoration of Franciscan Mission: San Francisco Solano de Sonoma; Mexican-held Sonoma Presidio; site of Bear Flag Revolt establishing California Republic, 1820–50; National Register, National Historic Landmark

ADDRESS: 20 E. Spain St., Sonoma CA 95476
TELEPHONE: (707) 938-1519
LOCATION: 45 miles north of San Francisco
OPEN: Daily, 10 A.M. to 5 P.M.; closed Thanksgiving, Christmas, and New Year's Day
ADMISSION: Adults, $1; children 6–17, $.50
FACILITIES: Gift shops
RESORTS: Sonoma Mission Inn, P.O. Box 1447, 18140 Sonoma Hwy., Sonoma 95476, tel. (707) 938-9000 or (800) 358-9022
INNS: El Dorado, P.O. Box 463, 405 First St. W., Sonoma 95476, tel. (707) 996-3030; Sonoma Hotel, 110 W. Spain St., at First St., Sonoma 95476, tel. (707) 996-2996
CAMPING: Sugarloaf Ridge State Park, Kenwood 95452, tel. (707) 833-5712; Bothe-Napa Valley State Park, Calistoga 94515, tel. (707) 942-4575

History

The history of Sonoma begins with the Spanish mission era, continues as a secular pueblo under Mexican rule, and plays a significant role in the United States' acquisition of California from Mexico.

California was the last of the Spanish possessions to be colonized. The impetus for the colonization was the threat of Russian expansion north from Alaska toward Mexico. To prevent any Russian claims to California, Spain decided to establish its rights to the area by extending the Spanish mission system from Baja California into Alta California.

California's chain of twenty-one missions began with San Diego de Alcala and continued north to San Francisco Solano, the only mission established under Mexican rule. The mission system was a distinctly Spanish method of colonization. Instead of large numbers of Spanish or Mexican native families migrating to the New World, one or two Spanish priests, along with a few soldiers for protection, would establish a mission. Sites selected for missions were in fertile valleys beside streams. Neighboring Indians would then be induced to settle at the mission. They would be converted to Christianity and taught handicraft skills.

Originally, plans called for the secularization of each mission after ten years. Secularization meant that the missions would be placed under non-church rule and the mission towns would be converted into civic pueblos. At that time, the property and livestock would be divided among the residents of the mission. In practice, secularization usually took much longer, and few Indians received adequate preparation to become successful farmers or ranchers.

The most northerly and the last of the California missions, San Francisco Solano, was founded by Father Jose Altimira in July 1823. Father Altimira, who was a native of Barcelona, was urged by the Mexican governor, Luis Arguello, to establish this mission in the north. A party consisting of Altimira, Francisco Castro, Jose Sanchez, and nineteen others traveled to the mission site. On July 4, 1823, Father Altimira blessed the ground and planted a cross.

Although he had founded San Francisco Solano without permission from his superior, Altimira was appointed its minister. A whitewashed church, 24 by 105 feet long, was built; it was dedicated on Passion Sunday, April 4, 1824. Other buildings soon followed, including the missionaries' house, the granary, and seven houses for the soldiers and their families.

Fruit trees, grape vines, wheat, and barley were planted. Mission Dolores at San Francisco donated sheep, horses, cows, oxen, and farm implements.

By 1825, Father Altimira had made nearly 700 converts. Although the mission originally maintained good relations with the neighboring Indian tribes, Indians sacked and burned the mission in the fall of 1826. Father Altimira barely escaped alive. At its peak in 1830, about 1,000 Indians lived there. Between 1823 and 1834, there were 1,315 baptisms and 278 marriages at Mission Sonoma.

General Mariano G. Vallejo, military commander and director of colonization of the Northern Frontier (La Frontera del Norte), was sent to Sonoma in 1833 by the Mexican government. He secularized Mission San Francisco Solano in 1834, and the church was then used as a parish church by the pueblo's residents. Vallejo, who came to Sonoma from his position as commandant of the presidio at San Francisco, was charged with protecting California, now a Mexican possession, from English, Russian, and American encroahments. In 1836, Vallejo was named commandant general of all Mexican military forces in California.

Sonoma's eight-acre central plaza was laid out by General Vallejo and Captain Richardson. A two-story adobe barracks for Vallejo's Mexican army troops was built on the north side of the plaza. The Mexican flag flew over it.

Also on the plaza was Vallejo's home, La Casa Grande, an imposing, two-story adobe house with second-floor balconies. Other buildings near Vallejo's home housed his relatives and friends. La Casa Grande became the cultural and social center north of San Francisco. Vallejo built another estate a half-mile west of the Sonoma plaza called Lachryma Montis.

Despite Vallejo's impressive presence, the government of California, under both Spain and Mexico, was never very stable. Forts were poorly built and inadequately staffed. Mexican-held California was a fairly vulnerable target for expansionist nations.

The United States had a continuing interest in acquiring California. President James K. Polk, who was elected in 1844, advocated an expansionist policy which included the purchase of California. An emissary sent to Mexico City to purchase California from the Mexican government was unsuccessful.

In 1846, Secretary of State James Buchanan dispatched a message carried by Archibald H. Gillespie to Thomas O. Larkin appointing Larkin the president's confidential agent. Larkin was informed that if a California revolution occurred, the United States would serve as protector. The United States feared that the British were poised to take over California if an opportunity presented itself.

In addition to official U.S. government moves toward the acquisition of California, American private citizens also contributed to wresting it from Mexico. John C. Fremont, an American explorer, led a sixty-eight-man armed party to California in 1845. The ostensible purpose of these scouts was to locate a safe route to the Pacific. The Fremont party arrived at Sutter's Fort in December 1845 and then traveled to Monterey to request permission from the Mexican government to remain until spring 1846. Permission was granted on the condition that Fremont's group return to the Sacramento Valley. Instead, Fremont moved his group to Gavilan Peak, a hill only a day's march from Monterey. An angry General Castro ordered Fremont out of California.

Eventually, Fremont was persuaded to move to Oregon where, in May 1846, Lt. Archibald Gillespie, a courier from Washington, caught up with him. What Gillespie told Fremont is a matter of speculation, but some believe that Fremont was encouraged to stir up American settlers in preparation for a U.S. war against Mexico. Fremont immediately returned to California and established headquarters in the hills fifty miles north of Sonoma. Other disgruntled American settlers soon joined the camp, including a trapper named Ezekiel Merritt.

On June 14 a group of Americans led by Merritt staged a raid on Sonoma, taking General Vallejo and other Mexican officials prisoner. This group declared California to be an independent republic. Referred to as the Bear Flag Revolt, the revolutionaries raised a crudely made flag of unbleached muslin with a red stripe, drawings of a star and a bear, and the words CALIFORNIA REPUBLIC in the Sonoma plaza. The flag was designed by William Todd, a nephew of Mary Todd Lincoln. Vallejo and the other captives were imprisoned in John Sutter's fort, New Helvetia, where they were treated hospitably.

Although they did not participate in the original raid, Fremont and Gillespie soon joined the revolution initiated by Merritt. The Bear Flag Republic was short-lived because in a matter of weeks, word arrived that the United States and Mexico were at war.

American naval ships stationed off the Mexican coast sailed to Monterey in July 1846 and raised the American flag. Troops under Commodore John D. Sloat took possession of California for the United States. In Sonoma, after only three weeks, the Bear Flag was replaced with the American flag, which was raised by Navy Lieutenant Joseph W. Revere, grandson of the American Revolution hero, Paul Revere. The treaty signed at the conclusion of the Mexican-American War acknowledged American possession of California.

The army barracks built by General Vallejo were briefly occupied by American troops in April 1847, abandoned and reoccupied, and finally abandoned in October 1851. A military post was established in 1852 and garrisoned for six years.

In 1881 the buildings and grounds of San Francisco Solano were sold for $3,000. In 1911 the mission property was purchased by the California Landmarks League and given to the state for restoration.

Tour

As with several other California state historic parks, the historic buildings at Sonoma are not located in a contiguous manner on a single piece of property. The state has acquired and restored several historically significant buildings on their original sites for the public to enjoy. However, other buildings—some historical, some modern—that are privately owned are interpersed with the state-owned properties in this living town. Sonoma State Historic Park is not a park in the sense of a single piece of property with well-defined boundaries and distinct entrances and exits. Many of the Sonoma properties face the central plaza, a busy, tourist area which also has shops and restaurants.

Tours are self-guided and include remnants of the San Francisco Solano de Sonoma Mission along with structures from the Mexican provincial headquarters of the Northern Frontier. The **Sonoma Plaza** itself has been declared a National Historic Landmark; it has the appearance of a city park with playgrounds, gardens, and county buildings. The Bear Flag Monument in the plaza marks the spot where, on June 14, 1846, the Bear Flag was raised and California was declared free from Mexican rule. The Bear Flag was replaced by the American flag on July 9.

The oldest building in Sonoma is the **Mission Residence.** Built in 1825 for living quarters, it is a long, low adobe building. The dining room has a large refectory table, and on the walls hang the "Virgil Jorgensen Memorial Collection of California Mission Paintings." A monk's cell is furnished with a simple bed, kneeler, and table.

Adjoining the residence is the only other remaining mission building, the **church,** which was build as a chapel in 1840–43. It has a brick floor and white stuccoed walls. Statues of Mary and Joseph are dressed in ornate cloth robes. There is a large courtyard with a fountain, whose gardens contain beds of lavender and six-foot cacti.

Sonoma Barracks, built by Vallejo in 1836–41, is a large, two-story adobe building with wide balconies overlooking the plaza. Later used as a winery, it was purchased by the state of California in 1958. The barracks is used as a museum with exhibits on the Indians of California, Mission San Francisco de Solano, La Frontera del Norte, secularization of missions, Manifest Destiny, John C. Fremont's California Battalion, the California Republic, and Lachryma Montis. There is a large courtyard.

Next to the barracks is the **Toscano Hotel.** Constructed in 1857 as a retail store, dwelling, and rental library, it soon was converted into a workingman's hotel called the Eureka. Italian immigrants in the 1890s changed the hotel's name. The hotel is decorated as if it were a family home with turn-of-the-century Victorian furniture. A dining room and kitchen are in a separate building.

Although Vallejo's home, La Casa Grande, burned in 1867, a **servants' wing** dating from 1836–40 still stands. This two-story adobe building can only be viewed from the outside.

Portions of the **Blue Wing Inn** are thought to have been built as houses for mission soldiers. A second story was added and other changes were made to the adobe building. Its name derives from its use as a gambling room and saloon in the gold rush days.

A half-mile west of Sonoma plaza lies another part of Sonoma State Historic Park. It is **Lachryma Montis,** Vallejo's large ranchero. Lachryma Montis is Latin for mountain tear, a name given to the mountain spring by local Indians. Vallejo purchased the land in 1850 and he and his wife lived there for more than thirty-five years until his death in 1890 at the age of eighty-two. Buildings date from the early 1850s.

This estate consists of a small complex of beautifully restored buildings surrounded by vineyards. There is a courtyard with lemon and orange trees, rose bushes, and gardens of lilies, oxalis, foxglove, ivy, and white canna. Instead of building a house in the Spanish style, the **Vallejo Main House** is a frame two-story Gothic Revival style that was prefabricated in Boston and shipped to California. Furnishings are Victorian with red plush upholstered pieces in the parlor and a horsehair settee in the general's office. Photographs of the sixteen Vallejo children and many of Vallejo's belongings are displayed in the house.

Other buildings include a **kitchen** for the Vallejo's Chinese cook, who also lived in the three-room building; **El Delirio,** an 1854 small guest and retreat house; the **Hermitage,** a one-room cabin occupied by the youngest son, Napoleon; and a **storehouse** made of brick and timber imported from Europe which serves as a museum and interpretive center. The state acquired the Vallejo home and twenty acres of land in 1933.

Side Trips

Petaluma Adobe State Historic Park contains one of the largest adobe buildings in existence. It was built in 1836 for General Vallejo as the headquarters for his extensive 175,000-acre ranching operation. It is four miles east of Petaluma on Casa Grande Road; tel. (707) 762-4871. Open daily from 10 A.M. to 5 P.M.

Buena Vista Winery was founded in 1857 by Colonel Agaston Haraszthy, a Hungarian nobleman. Tour the stone cellers built in 1856 and the limestone storage caves. Buena Vista is a very important vineyard in the history of winemaking in the well-known Sonoma Valley. Open daily from 10 A.M. to 5 P.M., it is located at 18000 Old Winery Road, Sonoma; tel. (707) 938-1266.

Sutter's Fort State Historic Park

Restoration and reconstruction of the fortified headquarters of an early California private agricultural estate and trading post, 1839–48; National Register, National Historic Landmark

0497894

ADDRESSS: 2701 L St. Sacramento, CA 95816

TELEPHONE: (916) 445-4209

LOCATION: Between 26th and 27th streets, a few blocks east of the state capitol building

OPEN: Daily, 10 A.M. to 5 P.M.; closed Thanksgiving, Christmas, and New Year's Day

ADMISSION: Adults, $1; children, $.50

FACILITIES: Trade Store, period items

HOTELS/MOTELS: Maleville's Coral Reef Lodge, 2700 Fulton Ave., Sacramento 95821, tel. (916) 483-6461; Beverly Garland Hotel, 1780 Tribute Rd., Sacramento 95815, tel. (916) 929-7900 or (800) 824-7800; Clarion, 700 Sixteenth St., Sacramento 95814, tel. (916) 444-8000 or (800) CLARION

INN: The Briggs House, 2209 Capitol Ave., Sacramento 95816, tel. (916) 441-3214

CAMPING: Oak Haven Mobile Home Park, 2150 Auburn Blvd., Sacramento 95821, tel. (916) 922-0814; Stillman RV Park, 6321 Sacramento Blvd., Sacramento 95824, tel. (916) 392-2820; KOA Sacramento Metro, 4851 Lake Rd. W, Sacramento 95691, tel. (916) 371-6771

History

Sutter's Fort was not a military fort. Its founder, Johann (John) Augustus Sutter, was a Swiss-German who, at the age of thirty-one, left his wife, children, and bad debts and immigrated to the United States. From 1834–38 he traveled with fur traders to such exotic places as Fort Vancouver, the Hawaiian Islands, and Sitka, Alaska, after attempting various businesses which had proved unsuccessful.

Sutter arrived in San Francisco in 1839. He soon became a naturalized Mexican citizen so that he could qualify for a land grant from the Mexican government. He received nearly fifty thousand acres located in the rich Sacramento Valley of California, which was a part of Mexico.

For his headquarters and for protection from hostile Indians, Sutter built a fort in 1840. Named New Helvetia, the fort was situated on a knoll at the confluence of the American and Sacramento rivers.

The quadrangular fort was made of adobe walls that were two and a half feet thick and 15 to 18 feet high. It was 330 feet long by 120 to 183 feet wide. Inside the fort was a three-story central building, while storehouses, a distillery, a bakery, granaries, laborers' quarters, and shops for coopers, carpenters, and blacksmiths lined the inside walls.

At Fort New Helvetia, John Sutter finally achieved good fortune. He was a veritable feudal baron of a large and prosperous estate. Sutter's main interest was agriculture. In fact, he is often referred to as the founder of California agriculture because of his pioneering cultivation of crops. Hundreds of laborers, mostly Indians, plowed and irrigated the land and planted and reaped the crops. They also tended huge herds of livestock. In 1841, when the Russians left Fort Ross, Sutter purchased their livestock, equipment, and cannon. By the mid-1840s, he had 12,000 cattle, 2,000 horses and mules, 10,000 sheep, and 1,000 hogs.

Fort New Helvetia was also a trading post, a favorite stopping place for provisions and rest for wagon trains on California's section of the Oregon Trail. Sutter was well known for his hospitality. He offered beds, meals, supplies, comfort, and encouragement to tired travelers. Sutter also maintained harmonious relations with both the fur traders and the Indians. In the 1840s, New Helvetia was the economic, political, and social center of the only settled portion of the interior of California. John Fremont, the explorer and proponent of American annexation of California, was a frequent visitor.

Fort New Helvetia mounted twelve pieces of artillery and was patrolled by sentinels day and night; it was the best and largest fortified fort in California. Since California was a part of Mexico, Sutter's fort flew the Mexican flag. In June 1846, American settlers in California revolted against the Mexican authorities. They declared independence for the state of California, naming it the Bear Flag Republic. Unknown to the revolutionaries, war between the United States and Mexico had begun in May 1846. In July 1847 the U.S. Navy's Pacific Squadron occupied the port of Monterey without resistance. In the same month, California was formally annexed to the United States.

In the Treaty of Guadalupe Hidalgo, signed February 2, 1848, at the conclusion of the war with Mexico, the United States acquired New Mexico and California. Although Sutter's fort had briefly flown the Bear Flag, Sutter soon raised the stars and stripes.

The turmoil created by the Mexican War was soon displaced by the accidental discovery of gold in California. In 1847, Sutter contracted with James Marshall to build a sawmill on the south fork of the American River about fifty miles east of the fort. On January 24, 1848, Marshall noticed some flecks of bright metal in one of the ditches which had been dug for the tailrace. Curious, he gathered some samples and brought them to Sutter at the fort on January 28, 1848. Not sure if it was gold, the two men tested the metal samples using every test they could think of, including some they found by looking in the encyclopedia, before concluding that the metal was really gold. Sutter went to the mill site and found gold all along the river and up tributary ravines and creeks.

Despite the mill workers being pledged to secrecy, tales of the discovery of gold spread like wildfire. Sam Brannan, a Mormon who had a store at Sutter's Fort, fanned the flames when he went to San Francisco announcing the discovery of gold and holding up a vial filled with gold nuggets to convince the skeptics.

Discovery of gold led to Sutter's ruin, not his riches. Hundreds of his farm workers deserted him for the gold camps. Scores of would-be prospectors squatted on Sutter's lands and abused his hospitality. Because of income losses and accumulating debts, Sutter was forced to transfer title to his property to his son in October 1848. In 1849 the fort was sold for $7,000 and Sutter and his family moved to his ranch on the Feather River.

John Sutter Jr. surveyed the land near the fort and offered lots for sale. By November 1849 there were ten thousand residents in what would become the town of Sacramento. The town became the distribution and transportation center for the mines in the Mother Lode country. By 1858 it had become the western terminal of the Pony Express, the Central Overland Mail and Stage Line, and the first transcontinental railroad, the Central Pacific. In 1854, Sacramento became the capital of California.

The fort deteriorated rapidly over the next two deacdes. It was used successively as a gambling casino, hospital, warehouse, residence, and stable. By the mid-1860s, almost all that was left standing at the fort was the central building. In 1890 the Native Sons of the Golden West purchased the property and donated it to the state. California began reconstruction of the fort in 1891. In 1947, Sutter's Fort became a part of the California State Park System, designated as a State Historic Park.

Tour

Sutter's Fort is located in a park-like setting not far from the Capitol area in the modern city of Sacramento. The streets around the fort site are lined with contemporary office buildings, apartment buildings, and residences. The fort appears to be a well-landscaped city park in a moderately sized, clean, but fairly bustling city. One must walk through the wooden gates of the fort to get a sense of the past.

Tours are completely self-guided. Included with your admission is a wand or ear phone which provides a narration at each building.

Sutter's Fort State Historic Park consists of six acres of the original fort site. Most of the fort complex has been reconstructed since only the central building remained intact after decades of neglect. Restoration and reconstruction began in the 1890s, making it one of America's older restorations.

The fort itself is small compared to the important role it holds in California history. Inside the reconstructed adobe fort, the walls are lined with shops and living quarters. Some buildings are adobe colored while others are whitewashed with wooden trim and shutters painted gray. Inside walls are brick and ceilings are wooden.

A **garrison room,** located near the main gate, contains artifacts from Sutter's private Indian army. His army consisted of 225 men; of that number, there were 97 Indian privates, 85 riflemen, 2 black drummers, and several cannoneers.

The **granary** displays foods native to the California Indians, such as acorns, roots, and tubers, along with pottery and utensils.

Sutter developed a self-contained economic unit at the fort. One of the necessary services was provided at the **cooper's shop,** which has a stack of barrels made to store items like fish and liquor, especially the brandy that Sutter produced from native California grapes.

There is a **tanning room** where the beaver, sea otter, and other animal skins were tanned. Saddles and harnesses were also made here.

Cannons are mounted in the two, two-story corner bastions which were used to protect the fort. The **southeastern bastion** was also used as a hospital ward during the cholera epidemic in 1849–50. There is a **jail** in the lower level of the bastion.

The **white settler's room,** where a settler's family would be housed after their overland trek, contains a bed, table, and spinning wheel.

The **weaving room** displays the shuttle looms and spindles which the Spanish trained the Indians to use. The wool used to weave the heavy woolen blankets came from sheep raised at the fort.

A large beehive oven stands outside the **bakery.** Inside are large ovens, a large flour bin, and a pie safe along with many of the utensils needed to supply the fort's residents with bread.

A busy place at the fort was the **trading store** where settlers traded with Sutter. Indians employed by Sutter were paid with tin disks that could be redeemed for merchandise at the store. Available here were salt, tobacco, and iron utensils.

The fort's three-story **central building,** Sutter's headquarters, was erected in 1839. The only original building remaining, it has been restored using many of the original beams. Arms and supplies were stored here. Sutter's private office, or council chamber, contains a desk and bed. In the clerk's office, employees maintained the accounts and records of Sutter's enterprises, including fur trading, the distillery, and payroll. Since Sutter was a magistrate for the Mexican government, he also issued passports. The central building's attic was used as a dormitory where forty-niners could pay $1 a night to sleep on the floor.

A large, high-ceiling building contains the fort's **museum.** There are exhibits on the Donner Party, the founding of Sacramento, beaver trapping, gold mining, the Bear Flag Republic, and Sutter's life.

The **distillery** contains remnants of the still and barrels that Sutter used to make brandy from the native wild grapes which he called Pisco grapes.

The **gristmill** was used to grind wheat and other grains. The **carpenter's shop** exhibits tools and furniture. Popular beaver hats were made at the **hat and boot shop.**

Soldiers slept in the **barrack's room,** which is furnished with beds and furniture with a Mexican decor.

The **blacksmith's shop,** important in any frontier settlement, contains a large forge, bellows, anvil, and a sharpening wheel.

Sutter's bachelor quarters, where Sutter lived before the arrival of his wife and family, contains a bed, chair, and other simple furnishings.

There are also a **gunsmith shop, candle shop, kitchen,** and **corrals.**

A living history program which focuses on events at Sutter's Fort in 1846 is presented on five weekends in March, June, August, October, and November. Costumed docents assist local school children perform daily life activities including cooking, candle making, baking, and carpentry work during our visit. The children, who were also dressed in period costumes, were going to cook their own dinner and sleep overnight in the central building. Britain's Queen Elizabeth and Prince Philip visited Sutter's Fort in March 1983.

Outside the fort but on the same property is located the **State Indian Museum,** 2618 K Street (same phone number and hours as Sutter's Fort). Exhibits on California tribes include dugout canoes, weapons, pottery, and basketry. Admission for adults is $1.00; children 6–17, $.50.

Side Trips

While in Sacramento, spend at least part of a day in the **Old Sacramento Historic District** (National Register, National Historic Landmark). This multiblock area of original Sacramento buildings combines history, museums, shopping, and restaurants in the well-preserved buildings. Bounded by I and L streets, Front Street, and I-5, the historic district is important because this twenty-eight-acre site contains the largest collection of gold-rush-era buildings on the West Coast. The area was the original business district of this port city, transportation center, and state capital. Walking tours are given Saturday and Sunday at 11 A.M. and 1 P.M. The free tours leave from the Central Pacific Depot.

A **Visitors' Center,** Morse Building, 1027-31 Second Street, is open daily from 10 A.M. to 5 P.M., tel. (916) 446-4314.

Stop at the **California State Railroad Museum** at Second and I streets in Old Sacramento. This exceptional, modern museum displays an original Central Pacific train with a Gin

Stanford Engine in a mountain setting. Nearby is a surveyor's tent complete with camping and surveying equipment. Surveying parties moved ahead of the railroad crews and figured out where the railroad track could be laid. The huge interior of this museum is filled with beautifully restored locomotives and railroad cars of various eras. There is even a model railroad exhibit. It is open daily from 10 A.M. to 5 P.M., tel. (916) 445-4209. Admission for adults is $3; children, $1.

Admission to the railroad museum also includes a visit to the reconstructed **Central Pacific Passenger Station,** Front and J streets, the first California terminal for the transcontinental railroad. A six-mile steam train ride is available on summer weekends. Tel (916) 445-4209.

Next to the railroad museum is the railroad museum gift shop, a treasure chest of books and gifts related to railroading. Open daily from 10 A.M. to 5 P.M.

Opened in 1985, the **Sacramento History Center,** 101 I Street, is a reconstruction of the 1854 Sacramento City Hall and Waterworks Building. The museum's modern interior is divided into four galleries focusing on Topomorphology, Community, Agricultural Technology, and the Eleanor McClatchy collection, which emphasizes printing and theater. It is open daily except Thanksgiving, Christmas, and New Year's Day from 10 A.M. to 5 P.M. Admission for adults is $2.50; seniors, $1.50; children 7–17, $1.

Another Sacramento site worth visiting is the restored **State Capitol** and the forty-acre Capital Park. It is open daily from 9 A.M. to 5 P.M. and located at 10th Street between L and N streets; tel. (916) 324-0333. The fifteen-room Victorian **Old Governor's Mansion,** 16th and H streets, is open daily from 10 A.M. to 4 P.M.; tel. (916) 323-3047.

The **Marshall Gold Discovery State Historic Park,** S.R.49, Coloma, seven miles northwest of Placerville, commemorates the mill site where, in 1848, James Marshall first discovered gold in California. The original mill is long gone, but a replica of the mill built by Marshall for John Sutter has been built on the site and is operated on weekends. The Gold Rush History Museum retells the story of Sutter, Marshall, and the gold rush in California. The 173-acre park has preserved an 1847 pioneer cemetery, an 1847 Catholic cemetery, the grave and memorial marker of James Marshall, the Wah Hope store which served the Chinese population, the Thomas House, and ruins of a variety of Coloma buildings. Coloma, which quickly grew up around the site of the gold discovery, was the first white settlement in the foothills of the Sierra Nevada. It is listed in the National Register and is a National Historic Landmark. It is open daily from 10 A.M. to 5 P.M. except Thanksgiving, Christmas, and New Year's Day; tel. (916) 622-3470.

Wells, Fargo & Co., 1858, Columbia State Historic Park, Columbia, California

Wells, Fargo & Co., interior, 1858, Columbia State Historic Park, Columbia, California

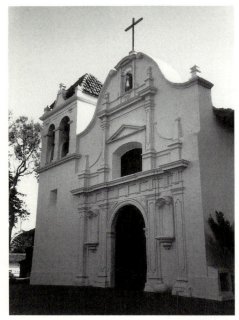

*Royal Presidio
Chapel, 1794,
Monterey, California*

Reconstructed Russian Orthodox chapel, Fort Ross State Historic Park, Jenner, California

Reconstructed Russian Orthodox chapel, Fort Ross State Historic Park, Jenner, California

*San Francisco Solano de Sonoma Mission, 1840, Sonoma State
Historic Park, Sonoma, California*

Central building, Sutter's Headquarters, 1839, Sutter's Fort, Sacramento, California

Reconstructed carpenter's shop, Sutter's Fort, Sacramento, California

Doctor's quarters, 1872, Fort Verde State Historic Park, Camp Verde, Arizona

Montezuma Castle, 12th century, Montezuma Castle National Monument, Camp Verde, Arizona

Mining cars, Pioneer Arizona, Phoenix, Arizona

Reconstructed miner's cabin, Pioneer Arizona, Phoenix, Arizona

Church, San Xavier del Bac Mission, 1797, Tuscon, Arizona

Bashford House, 1877, Sharlot Hall Museum, Prescott, Arizona

Governor's Mansion, 1864, Sharlot Hall Museum, Prescott, Arizona

Church entrance, San Jose de Tumacacori Mission, 1800-1822, Tumacacori National Monument, Tumacacori, Arizona

Interior of room in pueblo, Aztec Ruins National Monument, Aztec, New Mexico

West Ruins, 1106-1124 AD, Aztec Ruins National Monument, Aztec, New Mexico

Frijoles Canyon cave dwelling, Bandelier National Monument, Los Alamos, New Mexico

Interior of room in pueblo, Aztec Ruins National Monument, Aztec, New Mexico

Altar in Salony Cabilla, Old Cienega Village Museum, El Rancho de las Golondrinas, Sante Fe, New Mexico

Reconstructed El Torreon Defensivo, Old Cienega Village Museum, El Rancho de las Golondrinas, Sante Fe, New Mexico

Ruins of San Gregorio de Abo Mission, mid-1600s, Abo, Salinas National Monument, Mountainair, New Mexico

Ruins of Nuestra Senora de la Purisima Concepcion de Curarac Mission, Quarai, 1625, Salinas National Monument, Mountainair, New Mexico

F.H. Stevens House, 1900, Centennial Village, Greeley, Colorado

Georgetown Loop Railway narrow-guage steam train, Georgetown Loop Historic Mining and Railroad Museum, Georgetown, Colorado

Cliff Palace, 1200 AD, Mesa Verde National Park, Colorado

*Hoffman Brothers
Blacksmith Shop, South
Park City Museum,
Fairplay, Colorado*

Old Guardhouse, 1866, Fort Laramie Historic Site, Fort Laramie, Wyoming

Military re-enactment on Parade Ground, Fort Laramie Historic Site, Fort Laramie, Wyoming

PART II

SOUTHWEST

2

ARIZONA

Fort Verde State Historic Park

Restoration of a nineteenth-century United States Army military camp

ADDRESS: P.O. Box 397, Camp Verde AZ 86322
TELEPHONE: (602) 567-3275
LOCATION: 40 miles south of Flagstaff on I-17
OPEN: Daily, 8 A.M. to 5 P.M.
ADMISSION: Adults, $1
FACILITIES: Visitors' Center with museum
HOTELS/MOTELS: Best Western Cottonwood Inn, 993 S. Main St., Cottonwood 86326, tel. (602) 634-5575; Quality Inn–Kings Ranson, P.O. Box 180, Sedona 86336, tel. (602) 282-7151; Orchards at L'Auberge, 300 N. U.S. 89A, Sedona 86336, tel. (602) 282-7131 or (800) 272-6776.
CAMPING: Beaver Creek, tel. (602) 567-4501, and Clear Creek, tel. (602) 567-4501, Campgrounds, Coconino National For-

est, Camp Verde; Yavapai-Apache RV Park, I-17 and Middle
Verde Rd., P.O. Box 1687, Camp Verde 86322, tel. (602)
567-3109

History

Until the 1850s, the only inhabitants of the Verde Valley
were Indians. Although a few Spanish explorers passed
through the valley in the late sixteenth and early seventeenth
centuries, it was in the nineteenth century that the region was
penetrated by mountain men, trappers, and explorers.

Real growth in the Euro-American population in the Verde
Valley occurred after Arizona became a territory in 1863 and
nearby Prescott became the capital. The growing population
produced a market for food. The Verde became an important
agricultural region because it had fertile land, a reliable water
supply, and a long growing season.

After a small group of men led by James Parrish determined
that the Verde would make a good farming area, a settlement
was begun in early 1865 by nine men. They traveled from
Prescott bringing six wagonloads of supplies. Because of the
threat of Indian attacks, their first task was to build a 60-by-40-
foot stone fort in a Sinagua Indian ruin near the confluence of
the Verde River and Clear Creek. Then they planted crops and
dug irrigation ditches.

A few months later the new settlement, which had grown to
seventeen men, three women, and three children, suffered an
Indian attack. Although no lives were lost, much of the crops
and livestock was taken. Because of their dangerous situation,
the community requested protection from the military.

United States Army protection was not that easy to obtain
since troops were still engaged in the Civil War in the East.
However, in August 1865, seventeen privates and one sergeant
from the First Cavalry, New Mexico Volunteers, arrived. Because of the scarcity of horses, they came on foot and without

equipment as their wagon had been burned during an attack en route.

Though this uninspiring garrison originally set up camp at Clear Creek, they moved three miles upriver in December. The post they established at the confluence of Beaver Creek and Verde was named Camp Lincoln. Military population ebbed and flowed. One hundred twenty-three men from the First Arizona Volunteer Infantry were assigned to Camp Lincoln. However, since pay was poor, food wasn't good or plentiful, and supplies were inadequate, most men did not reenlist and the garrison dropped to a handful by late summer.

Attacks on the settlers by Yavapai and Apache Indians continued. The first regular army troops, thirty-nine men from the Fourteenth Infantry, arrived in September 1866. A second infantry company arrived in April 1867. The infantry was not that successful against its highly mobile enemy. Relief came in August 1870 when three companies of the Third Cavalry arrived. Camp Lincoln had been renamed Camp Verde in November 1868.

Since Camp Verde was not large enough to accommodate the new arrivals, a new camp was begun across the river. When building was completed in the spring of 1872, the entire camp was moved to the new site and the old post was abandoned. Fort Verde State Historic Park is located at this later site, and its buildings date from the early 1870s.

As the American frontier moved westward, a pattern emerged of white settlers dislocating Indians from their homelands. Conflicts ensued and the military was enlisted to fight, subjugate, and move Indians onto reservations. The pattern repeated itself in the Southwest, where the Apache Indians and the army continued to battle.

In 1871 the government formulated an Apache policy. Money was appropriated by Congress to move the Apaches of Arizona and New Mexico to reservations. Vincent Colyer of the Board of Indian Commissioners was assigned the task of peacefully enforcing that policy.

At the same time, General George Crook, who had a great deal of experience fighting Indian wars in the Northwest, was placed in command of the Department of Arizona. Crook was anxious to confront the Apaches militarily. However, he delayed because a second peace mission headed by General O. O. Howard was begun. Its task was to formalize the locations of the reservations which would be protected by military posts. A reservation for the Tonto Apaches was located near Camp Verde.

General Crook sent out word that all Indians away from the reservations would be regarded as hostile. Using Apache scouts and traveling in mule pack trains, Crook's men tracked these hostiles in the mountains and canyons of the Tonto Basin. Crook's strategy included starving the Indians into submission by hunting them during the winter. The Indians would have to keep on the move and would not be able to get to their stored winter food supplies. The policy was effective. Crook's campaign began in November 1872; in April 1873, emaciated Yavapai Indians surrendered to General Crook at Camp Verde.

Crook organized some of the former hostiles into an army unit: Company B, Apache Indian Scouts. In the succeeding years, this Camp Verde company engaged in many campaigns against Tonto Apaches who were still at large. Hostilities in the area gradually ended.

Although it was a violation of a treaty with the Indians, in 1875 the Indian Office decided to close the Verde reservation and move its residents to the San Carlos reservation. Economy of administration was cited as the reason, but as with previous resettlements, the whites' hunger for land was the underlying cause. The fifteen hundred Yavapai from the Verde reservation marched one hundred eighty miles to San Carlos.

The removal of the Indians greatly diminished the need for Camp Verde. By the time the post was renamed Fort Verde in April 1879, it had almost ceased operations. The post was officially abandoned in July 1881 only to resume operations four months later. An incident involving the arrest of an Indian medicine man increased tension in the area again. Little activity occurred at the fort, which was abandoned by the army a decade later.

In 1895, fort lands were opened to homesteading. Fort buildings were sold at public auction in 1899. Most were then torn down for materials. Only four of the original twenty-two major buildings remain at Fort Verde. Local citizens began a museum in the administration building in 1956 and donated the buildings to the state in 1970.

Tour

Fort Verde was never a fort as such. It didn't have a wall around it nor was it ever attacked. It served as a base for military actions against Apache Indians in the surrounding area.

At Fort Verde, there were originally over twenty buildings which were constructed by the troops in the early 1870s. Buildings were laid out in a quadrangle surrounding a parade ground and consisted of living quarters, storehouses, offices, and service buildings. There were corrals for the cavalry horses.

Fort Verde State Historic Park consists of a ten-acre site with three officers' quarters, the administration building, and a portion of the parade ground.

Start your self-guided tour at the **Administration Building.** This building, which was used for offices, contains restored offices and museum exhibits. Used from 1871–91, the outer adobe walls were formed by casting massive adobe units in a temporary wooden form. This technique, which was called "pice," was simpler and faster than making adobe bricks. Plain offices had adobe walls, wide plank floors, and fireplaces. Simple furnishings include several desks and chairs, an Indian rug, and a flag.

Museum exhibits recall the history of the fort. One exhibit

focuses on the conflicting needs of the various residents, which included Indians, settlers, military, and miners.

Subjects of other exhibits are: soldiers and officers in Indian wars; telegraph systems connecting Arizona military posts; post chaplains; medical practice at the fort; sutler's store; garrison life; munitions; military uniforms; and Apache scouts.

Next stop on the tour is the **Commanding Officer's Quarters,** a two-story frame building with a gambrel roof and a wide porch. It was on the front porch of this building that Chalipun, the Tonto Apache chief, and three hundred of his people officially surrendered to General George Crook in 1873.

On the first floor of the house is a living room which has an organ and both a fireplace and an iron stove. The living room and dining room are furnished in Victorian style and were used for the entertaining that fell to the post's highest ranking officer. A master bedroom and a kitchen are also on the first floor. Upstairs is the children's room furnished with an iron bed, toys, and a sewing machine in addition to a room for the enlisted man called a striker, who performed household duties. The striker's room is furnished with a brass bed and Eastlake furniture.

The **Bachelor Officers' Quarters** is a one-story adobe building of pice construction. It has a shake roof and a wraparound porch. Furnishings are basic necessities: army cots, wash stands, trunks, tables, and chairs. The dining room, which was used as a common lounge, has a table with playing cards and bottles. The communal kitchen was also the striker's quarters and has his army cot.

Every permanent military post had a medical doctor. Fort Verde had a hospital which was used for quarantines and recuperation. The doctor's office and surgery were in the doctor's home. The **Doctor's Quarters** has an operating room complete with operating table, surgical tools, and a desk. The living quarters consist of a parlor, bedroom, and kitchen. Many frontier physicians were also natural scientists, which explains a collection of animal specimens displayed in the living room.

Jerome State Historic Park

Restoration of a mansion of a copper mining executive in mining ghost town; National Register, National Historic Landmark

ADDRESS: P.O. Box D, Jerome AZ 86331
TELEPHONE: (602) 634-5381
LOCATION: Between Prescott and Flagstaff; 8 miles west of Cottonwood on U.S. 89A
OPEN: Daily, 8 A.M. to 5 P.M.
ADMISSION: Adults $1
FACILITIES: Picnic area
HOTELS/MOTELS: See Tuzigoot National Monument, Fort Verde State Historic Park, and Montezuma Castle National Monument.
CAMPING: See sites listed above.

History

Jerome was a copper mining town that was founded a century ago. Perched on a mountainside overlooking the Verde Valley, Jerome's population has fluctuated from a high of fifteen thousand in the 1920s to a low of one hundred twenty in the 1950s.

Copper was discovered in the Mingus Mountain one thousand years ago by Indians, who used the ore for decoration and painting pottery. Fittingly, it was an Indian, Al Sieber, an Apache scout for General George Crook, who staked the first claim in present-day Jerome in 1876. Other claims soon followed.

One of the difficulties of profitable copper mining is economical transportation of the ore. This problem was greatly lessened when the railroad reached Arizona in 1882. The United Verde Copper Company was formed the same year. Since substantial capital was needed to buy equipment and transport the ore, backing came from New York financiers James A. MacDonald and Eugene Jerome, for whom the town was named. Mr. Jerome, a cousin of Winston Churchill's mother, Jennie Jerome, agreed to invest in the copper mining project only on the condition that the town be named after him.

The United Verde set up two water-jacket blast furnaces fueled by New Mexico coal. Copper, as well as small amounts of gold and silver, were obtained. However in 1884, when the price of copper plunged, the mine was forced to close.

In 1885, William A. Clark, who was impressed by a United Verde copper ore exhibit at the New Orleans Exposition, decided to invest heavily in the United Verde Company. As copper prices rose, the now-profitable United Verde Company built a narrow-gauge railroad called the United Verde and Pacific Railroad. It connected Jerome to the Sante Fe spur between Ash Fork and Prescott and greatly simplified ore transportation.

The town of Jerome grew as the mines prospered. Wood and canvas shacks appeared overnight. Three times in the years 1897–99 Jerome was devastated by fire. Yet when the town of Jerome incorporated in 1899, it was the fifth largest city in the Arizona Territory.

Another mine, called the Little Daisy, was started in 1900. Ten years later it was purchased by James S. Douglas. The Little Daisy was the site of an exceptionally rich ore find. Because it was under six hundred feet of lava and limestone, open-pit mining was required to remove the copper. That necessitated moving the smelting operation down to Clarkdale, located on the floor of the Verde Valley. Open-pit mining began in 1929. Jerome was then a town of fifteen thousand people with almost twenty-five hundred of them employed by the mines.

When the bottom fell out of the copper market during the stock market crash of 1929, copper mining declined and ceased entirely in 1932. Jerome's population dropped by two-thirds.

Mining in Jerome was not finished yet. In 1935 the Phelps-Dodge Corporation bought the United Verde Company for over $20 million. World War II created a sudden need for copper, which was used in war materiels, shells, ships, and communication equipment. The tremendous war production depleted the ore, and by 1950 mining operations ceased again. Lack of employment forced the town's population down to little more than one hundred.

The Douglas family mansion was given to the Arizona state park system in 1962. It was dedicated as Jerome State Historic Park in 1965. In 1967 the town of Jerome was designated a National Historic Landmark. Present-day Jerome has about five hundred residents.

Tour

Jerome State Historic Park is small, consisting only of the Douglas Mansion and its grounds, which overlook the Little Daisy mine. The town of Jerome, which is not a part of the state historic park, lies directly across the valley from the Douglas Mansion.

Many of Jerome's larger buildings are no longer standing. Most of the remaining buildings are strung along Main Street, and some are occupied by gift shops, art galleries, and restaurants. This picturesque old mining town located on the east slope of Mingus Mountain is unique because of its steep streets and its mountain setting. It attracts many daytime visitors, making it a very lively ghost town.

The **Douglas Mansion** was built by "Rawhide Jimmy" Douglas in 1916 at a cost of $150,000. The 8,000-square-foot house is constructed of adobe brick that was made on the site. Floors are of poured concrete. It occupies a hilltop position with views of the Little Daisy mine and the town of Jerome.

Douglas used the large house as a hotel for visiting mining officials and investors as well as a home for his family. There is a wine cellar, billiard room, and servants' quarters.

Now used as a visitors' center and museum, a slide show on the history of Jerome and its mining business is shown here. Exhibits include photographs of the Douglas family and copper mining in Jerome, mine lighting, and the United Verde and Pacific Railroad. There is also a diorama of the town and mines.

The Douglas Mineral Gallery displays many large mineral samples. One room is used as an assay office. The unfurnished living room has French doors on two sides which provide panoramic views of the town and the surrounding area from this hilltop location. Upstairs, some of the spacious, well-decorated bedrooms and bathrooms have been restored.

Outside exhibits include the carriage house containing the Douglas carriages and wagons, ore cars, and milling machinery.

In the town of Jerome, there is a **mine museum,** operated by the Jerome Historical Society, located on Main and Jerome streets. It is housed in an 1898 brick building that was originally the Fashion Saloon. During Prohibition, the saloon was turned into a drugstore.

Most of Jerome's original buildings are now privately owned and may only be viewed from the outside. They include the United Verde Hospital, the Clubhouse Hospital, the surgeon's mansion, Christ Episcopal Church, the United Verde apartment building, the gutted remains of the Little Daisy Hotel, and the Bartlett Hotel.

Montezuma Castle
National Monument

Archaeological ruins of a twelfth-century Hohokam-Sinagua
Indian cliff dwelling; National Register

ADDRESS: P.O. Box 219, Camp Verde, AZ 86322
TELEPHONE: (602) 567-3322
LOCATION: 40 miles south of Flagstaff on I-17; Montezuma
Well is 11 miles northeast of the Castle on I-17
OPEN: Daily, 7 A.M. to 7 P.M. in summer, and 8 A.M. to 5 P.M.
in winter
ADMISSION: $3 per car
FACILITIES: Visitors' Center with bookstore and exhibits, picnic
area, handicapped accessible; additional site at Montezuma
Well located 11 miles north
MOTELS/HOTELS: Best Western Cottonwood Inn, 993 S. Main,
Cottonwood 86326, tel. (602) 634-5575; Bell Rock Inn, 6246
S.R. 179, Sedona 86336, tel. (602) 282-4161; Best Western
Arroyo Roble, P.O. Box NN, 400 N. U.S. 89A, Sedona
86336, tel. (602) 282-4001
RESORTS: Los Abrigados, 160 Portal Lane, Sedona 86336, tel.
(602) 282-1777 or (800) 521-3131; Poco Diablo, Box 1709,
Sedona 86336, tel. (602) 282-7333 or (800) 528-4275
INNS: L'Auberge de Sedona, P.O. Box B, 301 Little Lane,
Sedona 86336, tel. (602) 282-1661 or 800-331-2820
CAMPING: Coconino National Forest: campgrounds at Bonito,
tel. (602) 527-7042; Ashurst Lake, tel. (602) 527-7474; Forked
Pine, tel. (602) 527-7474; and Pinegrove, tel. (602) 527-7474

History

Montezuma Castle National Monument is located in the
Verde River basin in central Arizona. The Verde Valley was a

desirable farming and living area because it featured a steady water supply, arable bottomland, and a variety of wild food, plants, berries, fish, and game. Raw materials for building, tool manufacture, and ceramics were also available.

The Verde Valley lay between the desert dwellers to the south and plateau people to the north. Both of these groups occupied the valley at different periods. Hohokam farmers occupied the valley by A.D. 700. Many Hohokam resided near Montezuma Well, a large limestone sink partly filled with water from a constantly flowing spring. This was the water source the Indian farmers used to irrigate their fields.

Another Indian tribe of farmers, the Sinagua, lived near the San Francisco Peaks north of the Verde Valley. When a volcanic eruption buried their fields and houses in 1065, the Sinagua discovered that the layer of volcanic ash now covering their fields greatly improved their farmland. Productivity was so high that other farmers were attracted to the area.

Early in the twelfth century, overpopulation of the Sinagua lands drove small bands of these Indians south into the Verde Valley, where they joined the Hohokam. Some blending of the two cultures gradually occurred. The Sinagua farmers, who had traditionally relied on rain to water their crops, learned from the Hohokam how to irrigate fields. Although they had formerly lived in pit houses, the Sinagua adopted the Hohokam above-ground, pueblo-style houses like those at Montezuma Castle.

Construction of the first pueblo rooms in the limestone cave overlooking Beaver Creek occurred in the early twelfth century. When less than a century later, drought sent large numbers of Sinagua to their relatives in the Verde Valley, more rooms were added. By 1300 the cliff dwelling was occupied by about fifty people. It was the center of a large Sinagua community that occupied the valley below.

The cliff dwelling was occupied between 1100 and 1400. It was designed as a fort as well as a home. Its position high in the cliff made access to it severely limited. Just why the site was abandoned is not known. Some theories are that droughts in adjoining areas caused the valley to become overcrowded, the farmland was exhausted, natural resources were depleted, and there were often attacks by enemies. Verde Valley occupants are believed to have moved south to Hohokan villages in the Gila Valley.

Montezuma Castle was the name given by early white settlers to the five-story Indian cliff dwelling. These settlers erroneously believed that the Aztec ruler or his people had migrated through the area.

In 1892, Cosmos Mindeleff of the Bureau of American Ethnology, did the initial archeological survey of the valley, including Montezuma Castle. To stop disintegration or collapse of the cliff dwelling, the Arizona Antiquarium Association repaired some of its walls between 1896 and 1900.

In 1906 President Theodore Roosevelt proclaimed Montezuma Castle a national monument. The National Park Service repaired and stabilized the ruins in the 1930s, although 90 percent of this ancient ruin is still original construction.

Tour

A sense of surprise and awe accompany your first glimpse of 800-year-old **Montezuma Castle**. A five-story building, a small skyscraper, is perched on the ledge of a 100-foot-high-cliff. And the castle is blended so well into its cliff setting that it would be easy to miss. Primitive Indians with simple tools not only designed and constructed this multistory structure but had to haul their building materials 100 feet up a sheer cliff.

A self-guiding, one-third-mile loop trail begins at the Visitors' Center and leads to the base of the limestone cliff in which the castle is located. The cliff house can only be viewed from the path, as entry to the fragile ruins is prohibited.

Montezuma Castle, a fourteenth-century Indian structure, is considered one of the Southwest's best-preserved archaeological sites. The castle is a five-story, twenty-room cliff house built in a shallow limestone cave a hundred feet above the floor of Beaver Creek Canyon. Sheltered under a deep overhang in the cliff, castle walls are made of rough, chunked limestone blocks laid together with pulverized-clay mortar and plastered with mud. Roofs are of large sycamore timbers overlaid by poles, sticks, grass, and several inches of mud. The outer walls sit close to the edge of the high ledge and are curved to conform to the arc of the surrounding cave.

The inaccessible placement of the building was for security reasons. The cliff house was a fortress as well as a dwelling, and access to it was restricted to two paths. One path led from the valley floor and required the use of ladders. The other path ran along the side of the cliff. Both paths joined before entering the pueblo. At the junction of the two paths is a small, smoke-blackened room that was undoubtedly a sentry post.

Doorways in the castle are very small. They were designed to conserve energy and keep out hostile intruders as visitors were forced to enter head first.

Cooking was probably done outside except in cold weather. Since there are no smoke holes in the rooms, they would have been dark and smoky.

From the path can also be seen the ruins called Castle "A" at the base of the cliff. Castle "A" was a six-story, forty-five-room structure of which only ruins remain. The path returns to the Visitors' Center along Beaver Creek.

The museum at the Visitors' Center has exhibits on Indians in Arizona; the Sinagua's exit from Verde Valley; Indian handicrafts including baskets, jewelry, textiles, and pottery; occupations such as hunting, farming, and mining; and construction methods.

A second part of Montezuma Castle National Monument is **Montezuma Well**, which is located eleven miles north of the castle. The well is a 470-foot-deep water source in limestone that pumps 1.5 million gallons of water a day into Beaver Creek. Two hundred feet in diameter, it looks like a small, spring-fed lake placed in a deep round cavity on top of a hill. The water is icy cold. Although edible plants grow in the well, there are no fish because of a high carbon dioxide content.

The well supplied the water that the Indian farmers used to irrigate their fields. Hohokan settled near the well in the eighth century. They dug ditches from the well to irrigate an estimated sixty-acre garden. Some small cliff dwellings and a larger pueblo complex are located near the well.

A self-guided trail leads from the parking lot. Montezuma Well is open during the same hours as Montezuma Castle. No additional admission fee is charged.

Side Trips

The **Yavapai-Apache Visitor Center**, housed in a modern-istic stucco building, provides tourists with information about points of interest within the Verde Valley area. The National Park Service operates an information desk and maintains the museum's exhibits and slide programs. There is an arts and crafts shop which sells Indian crafts. Open seven days a week, the center is located just off I-17 at Middle Verde Road.

Sunset Crater National Monument preserves a volcanic cinder cone with summit crater formed just before the twelfth century. This is the volcano that erupted in the Sinagua territory and that eventually caused the Sinagua to move south to the Verde Valley. The upper slopes of the crater are colored as if by the glow of sunset. It is open all year; the address is Tuba Star Route, Flagstaff, AZ 86001; tel. (602) 774-7000. The monument is located 15 miles north of Flagstaff on U.S. 89 and then 2 miles east on Sunset.

Wupatki National Monument contains numerous ruins of pueblo dwellings. The eruption of Sunset Crater laid a cover-ing of fine cinder ash on the fields, which fostered good crop production. This area was farmed extensively by several pre-historic Indian groups including the Sinagua, who converged here and shared their cultures for one hundred fifty years.

Open all year. The address is Tuba Star Route, Flagstaff, AZ
86001; tel. (602) 774-7000. It is located 30 miles north of
Flagstaff on U.S. 89.

Pioneer Arizona

Recreation of a frontier Arizona town from the territory period of the mid-nineteenth century to statehood in 1912

ADDRESS: P.O.Box 1677, Black Canyon Stage, Phoenix, AZ
85029
TELEPHONE: (602) 993-0212
LOCATION: 25 miles north of Phoenix, Pioneer Road exit, I-17;
12 miles north of Bell Road.
OPEN: Wednesday-Sunday, 9 A.M. to 5 P.M.
ADMISSION: Adults $3; senior citizens, $2; students 13–college,
$2; children 5–12 $1; group rates available.
FACILITIES: Gift shop, restaurant and bar, craft demonstrations
HOTELS/MOTELS: Best Western Bell, 17211 N. Black Canyon
Hwy., Phoenix 85023, tel. (602) 993-8300; Rodeway Inn Met-
rocenter, 10402 N. Black Canyon Hwy., Phoenix 85051, tel.
(602) 943-2371; Crescent, 2620 W. Dunlap Ave., Phoenix
85021, tel. (602) 943-8200 or (800) 423-4126.
CAMPING: Dirty Shirt Campground, Carefree Hwy., Phoenix,
tel. (602) 272-8871; McDowell Mountain Reg. Pk. Campground, McDowell Mountain Rd., Fountain Hills, tel. (602)
837-0173; Desert Shadows, 19203 N. 29th Ave., Phoenix
85027, tel. (602) 869-8178

History

Pioneer Arizona, an outdoor living history museum designated as a 1976 Bicentennial project, recreates the pioneer
history of Arizona, the last state in the continental United

States to be admitted to the Union. Incorporated by interested Arizona citizens in 1956 as a public, nonprofit educational corporation, it receives no tax support and is funded through admission and membership fees and contributions.

Pioneer Arizona is "dedicated to the preservation of the material goods and spiritual values of an era in American history that is fast becoming a fading memory." Visitors can recapture the history of Arizona from a territory in the mid-nineteenth century to statehood in 1912.

The buildings, many of which were moved from other locations to Pioneer Arizona, are located on a 550-acre desert site that was once part of the Lockett ranch, owned by an early Arizona ranching family.

The very location of Pioneer Arizona helps the visitor recapture the atmosphere of frontier Arizona in territorial days. With volcanic foothills on the horizon, Pioneer Arizona is also a scenic nature area. Large saguaro cacti, desert plants, and flowers complete the scene as do signs warning visitors to watch out for rattlesnakes.

Tour

The **Opera House** is a reconstruction of the first Goldwater Brothers store built in Prescott in 1877. When the Goldwaters vacated the store in 1879, the first floor was converted into an opera house and the second floor into a Masonic Hall. Of special interest is the ornate lobby which is outfitted in Victorian style. Shows are often presented on weekends.

The **lumberyard** depicts a late nineteenth century lumber storage facility. Sawn lumber, building materials, and other construction items of the 1880s and 1890s are displayed. The lumberyard was an important facility in southern Arizona where trees were scarce and most construction was of adobe or brick. Miners, seeking to build cabins, used such a resource.

The **carpenter shop** is modeled on an 1880 shop in Prescott. Of special interest is the pressed tin ceiling. On display are a variety of period saws, such as circular and two-men saws, as well as drills, planes, and spindle-makers.

The **John Marion Sears House,** a one-story Victorian structure, was moved to the site from Phoenix where it had been built in the 1890s by Sears, a wealthy cattleman. The house, of total wood frame construction, was an exception to the adobe and brick buildings that were common to the Southwest. Furnished in Victorian style, the interior of the house contains a living room with red velvet wallpaper and an unusual flatiron stove. The kitchen has a cast-iron Acne stove, dry sink, and table. The children's bedroom contains a bed and a collection of dolls and miniature doll furniture. In the dining room are a marble-top buffet, a large circular table, and a display of chinaware. A docent is present in the house to provide information and answer questions.

The **tin** and **weaving shops** are a reconstruction of shops in Prescott owned by Charles Fredericks. The shops feature displays of weaving equipment, looms, spinning wheels, and tinsmithing equipment.

There is an operating forge in the **blacksmith shop,** where a blacksmith demonstrates his trade. The shop is a reconstruction of the Middleton and Pascoe Blacksmith Shop which was located in Globe in the 1870s.

A primitive trail leads to the **miner's cabin,** a reconstruction of an original which was located in Clifton. The interior is very basic and contains a bed, table, and chairs.

The **stage stop** is especially interesting because it depicts a style of shelter that was unique to the Southwest. A reconstruction of a stop on the Phoenix-Wickenburg route, it was of wattle and daub construction and made of cacti ribs, mud, and straw which were allowed to dry in the hot desert sun. The major support is a large tree trunk. The wattle and daub method of construction was also used by Indians living in the Southwest. Unless constantly repaired, such buildings deteriorate and return to earth.

The **church,** a white wooden frame structure, is a reconstruction of St. Paul's Methodist Episcopal Church built in Globe in 1879. Its plain interior contains a wooden pulpit, organ, flags, dark wooden pews, and six chandeliers. Such churches were important places of worship and social gatherings on the Arizona frontier. Today, it is a nondenominational chapel used for weddings and holiday services.

The **school,** moved to its site in 1966, served as a one-room country school from 1890 until the 1920s. A log structure, its interior evokes America's frontier educational past. There is a large teacher's desk and rows of students' desks—some of which were designed to seat two students. Behind the teacher's desk is a large slate blackboard. On the wall is a map of territorial Arizona. Adjacent to the school is a **teacherage,** which was the residence of the teacher. Although simply furnished with a bed, table, stove, chair, and stand, it afforded the frontier teacher some privacy. Such a teacherage was an advantage over the frontier practice of "boarding" the teacher with students' families.

The **ranch complex,** containing a ranch house, spring house, root cellar, barn, and poultry house, recreates an Arizona ranch of the 1870s. The ranch house, an original 1870 building from Gordon Canyon made of logs chinked with wattle, is a homesteader's dwelling of the type common to northern and eastern Arizona. A fireplace was used for heat and cooking. It is simply furnished with bed, chairs, and table. The stone springhouse was used for cooling food, and the root cellar for storing food. There is a log barn. The corral has several horses.

The **Flying V Cabin,** moved to its site from the Young area, is a very primitive building with a dirt floor and furnished with a cot and bench. Of interest are the rifle ports, cut into the walls, which were used to defend the occupants against attack. Nearby is the **Ashurst Cabin,** the boyhood home of Arizona's first U.S. senator, Henry Ashurst (1912–41).

The **Northern Arizona Cabin,** a large building made from ponderosa pines, moved in 1967 to its present site from Newman Canyon, near Flagstaff, is very different from the central and southern Arizona structures. Its spacious interior contains an iron stove, large wooden table and chairs, and other furnishings. It has a full loft, which was used as a children's bedroom. A costumed docent performs household tasks, describes the cabin, and answers questions. In contrast to the durable pine northern cabin, the nearby **Southern Cabin,** reconstructed from 1858 woodcuts, is a more primitive wattle and daub building.

A street of shops and offices, such as the **Pioneer Print Shop, Valley Bank, Gila County Sheriff's Office, wagonmaker's shop,** and **bandstand,** recreates small town territorial Arizona. In the Pioneer Print Shop is a vertical model platin press, a hand-set, hand-fed press, which is operated by a docent.

The Valley Bank, which represents an 1884 bank from Phoenix, contains tellers' cages, manager's desk, and a large Victor safe block vault.

The Gila County Sheriff's Office, of 1881 vintage, houses a prisoners' cell enclosed by iron bars and containing six cots, the sheriff's large pigeon-hole desk and chairs, files labeled "horse thieves," "con men," and "cattle thieves," and leg and hand irons.

The wagonmaker's shop, a reconstruction of a Yuma shop of the late nineteenth century, contains equipment used to build and repair wagons.

San Xavier del Bac Mission

Restoration of Spanish colonial Indian mission; National Register, National Historic Landmark, HABS

ADDRESS: S.R. 11, Box 645, Tucson AZ 85746
TELEPHONE: (602) 294-2624

LOCATION: On San Xavier Indian Reservation, 9 miles south of Tucson; take I-19 to Valencia Rd. West exit to Mission Rd., left to San Xavier Rd.

OPEN: Daily, 9 A.M. to 6 P.M.; Masses daily at 8 A.M., 11 A.M., 12:30 P.M.

ADMISSION: Free

FACILITIES: Gift shop

HOTELS/MOTELS: Best Western Inn at the airport, 7060 S. Tucson Blvd., Tucson 85706, tel. (602) 746-0271; Skytel Motor Inn—Airport, 2803 E. Valencia, Tucson 85706, tel. (602) 294-2500 or (800) 624-3286

RESORTS: Westward Look, 245 E. Ina Rd., Tucson 85704, tel. (602) 297-1151 or (800) 722-2500; Tucson National Resort and Spa, 2727 W. Club Dr., Tucson 85741, tel. (602) 297-2271 or (800) 528-4856; White Stallion Guest Ranch, 9251 W. Twin Peaks Rd., Tucson 85743, tel. (602) 297-0252

CAMPING: Coronado National Forest: General Hitchcock, Rose Canyon, Spencer Canyon, and Peppersauce Campgrounds, Tucson, tel. (602) 629-5101; Palms Trailer Court, 1421 E. Benson, Tucson 85714, tel. (602) 294-8831

History

San Xavier del Bac Mission, founded by Father Eusebio Kino in 1700, was the northernmost of the twenty-four Spanish missions in the Pimeria Alta, a vast expanse of desert lying in the northern part of Sonora, Mexico, and the southern section of Arizona. Kino, a Jesuit missionary, was invited by the Piman-speaking Sobaipuri Indians to visit their farming village at Bac.

Kino first visited Bac in September 1692. Although Europeans had traveled through Arizona as early as 1536, no white settlements had developed by the time Kino visited one hundred fifty years later. This area of present-day Arizona was still the frontier of New Spain.

In 1692, Bac was a rancheria of about eight hundred Sobaipuri Indians living in a river valley named Rio de Santa Maria by Kino. Bac means a watering place in an otherwise dry river—a place in a streambed where water re-emerges from its underground floor. Water, a highly prized commodity in this desert region, permitted the Indians to farm and irrigate their fields.

The Indians professed their wish to become Christians. Kino visited the Indian village at Bac in the succeeding years and brought cattle, sheep, goats, and mares.

When Kino returned to Bac in October 1699, he was accompanied by Reverend Father Visitor Antonio Leal. Father Leal was impressed with the fertile, irrigated fields and the fine grazing lands. He promised the Indians that they would soon have a resident priest at Bac.

The mission was founded by Kino in April 1700, two miles from its present site. Kino laid the foundation of the church and named it San Xavier del Bac. Although Kino, who was at Mission Dolores, requested reassignment to San Xavier del Bac Mission, it was not to be.

Simultaneously with the founding of the mission, Kino established that California was not an island as had been thought and thus could be reached by an overland route. Proof took the form of blue abalone shells which Kino had acquired in Pimeria Alta. Through questioning the Indians near Bac, Kino was able to prove that these shells came only from the Pacific Ocean and had been traded by Indians who had carried them overland. Finding the overland route to California would occupy most of Kino's remaining years.

Father Francisco Gonzalvo became San Xavier's first resident priest in 1701. When Gonzalvo died in 1702, Father Agustin de Campos from Mission San Ignacio serviced both missions. A severe shortage of priests resulted in the frequent lack of a resident missionary at San Xavier.

In November 1751, northern Piman-speaking Indians revolted against the Spanish government. At Mission San

Xavier, Father Franz Bauer was able to escape unharmed, but the church built by Kino was destroyed.

In 1756 after peace had been restored, Father Alonso Espinosa became the resident missionary. He built a church and a house and enlarged the herd of cattle to a thousand head. Frequent Apache raids, however, drove many mission Indians away. Apaches also stole most of the mission's cattle and all of its horses.

When all Jesuit priests were expelled from Spanish lands in 1767, the Jesuit era at Bac ended and the Franciscan era began. Franciscan friars, Juan Bautista Velderrain and Juan Bautista Llorenz, built the mission's present church, which is generally considered to be the finest example of mission architecture in the country. Construction began in 1783 and lasted until 1797. Apparently the Espinosa church had been destroyed or severely damaged by this time; no traces of the church remain today.

In 1821, Mexico gained its independence from Spain, and financial support of the missions ended. The last Franciscan of this era, Father Rafael Diaz, left San Xavier in 1828. Mission buildings began to decline. Mexico secularized the missions in 1841, and the mission churches became parish churches. At San Xavier, mission Indians moved some of the church furnishings into their homes for safekeeping.

A provision of the 1848 Treaty of Guadalupe Hidalgo, signed at the end of the Mexican-American War, was that all of Arizona north of the Gila River would become United States property. The Gadsden Purchase of 1854 added land south of the Gila River and established the current boundary between Arizona and Mexico. Mission San Xavier del Bac now belonged to the United States.

The Catholic Church placed all of the Arizona territory, including the mission at Bac, in the Santa Fe Diocese. After surveying the mission property, the church's roof was repaired. Extensive restoration and repair work were applied to mission buildings in 1906 by Bishop Henry Granjon of Tucson. He also erected additional buildings.

In 1913 the Franciscan order resumed responsibility for the mission and its clerical staff. Still the administrators today, the Franciscans operate schools and serve the religious needs of the eleven thousand Papago Indians who live on San Xavier Reservation and are descendents of the original mission Indians.

Tour

Mission San Xavier del Bac, considered one of the most beautifully preserved Spanish missions in the Southwest, is situated in the center of a Papago Indian reservation along the banks of the Santa Cruz River. The beauty of the gleaming white-domed church is in stark contrast to its desert setting.

The tour is self-guided. The mission includes the church, the cemetery, mortuary chapel, the original living quarters and workrooms, and a more recent monastery section and classrooms.

The church, the main feature of this historical site, is constructed of burned brick covered with lime plaster. It is separated from the plaza by an enclosed quadrangle known as the atrium. The wall has the stations of the cross set in it.

From here, view the facade of the church. The linear symmetry of the two white towers contrasts with the curving, ornately decorated reddish center piece. This centerpiece consists of two stories and a gable supported by ten narrow pilasters decorated with statues of saints placed in niches, grapevine arabesques, and the Franciscan coat-of-arms. The tower to the right was never finished during the original construction.

San Xavier has been acclaimed by some to be the finest example of mission architecture in the United States. Mission architecture is defined as the Spanish Colonial style of Mexico modified by the availability of local material, labor, and artistic aptitute. While the labor was undoubtedly done by local Indians, guild members from Spain were brought as artisans. The church is a blend of Moorish, Byzantine, and late Mexico Renaissance styles both in construction techniques and in decoration.

The use of brick throughout and the pendentives as supports for the dome and vaults are Byzantine in origin, while the high arches and flat vaults are Moorish. Decoratively, the abundance of arabesque (ornamentation consisting of a fantastic interlacing pattern of flowers, foliage, fruit, people, and animals) is Moorish, whereas the simulated patterned marble, the gold leaf, and the frescoes are Byzantine.

The floor plan of the church is in the form of a Latin cross. The main aisle is separated from the sanctuary by the cross aisle, which has side chapels at either end. Above the crossing of the main aisle and the cross aisle is the dome, which is fifty-two feet high and is supported by arches and pendentives. Walls are three feet thick except at the base of the towers, where they are six feet wide.

The church walls and ceilings are ornately decorated. The main altar background is divided into three tiers supported by eight columns. Built entirely of burned brick, it is covered with gilded and plaster embellishments. Above the main altar is a statue of St. Francis Xavier clothed in satin and velvet. Other statues above the main altar include Mary, St. Peter, and St. Paul. The Franciscan symbol, a knotted cord, is one of the plaster decorations. It begins at the right side of the main altar, goes around the church, and ends at the left side.

The mesquite doors between the sacristy and the sanctuary are the original doors. Burned into the wooden doors are a name, *Pedro Bojorquez*, and a date, Ano 1797. Debate goes on as to whether this was the name of the builder/architect or some other workman. Two semicircular railings of mesquite enclose the sanctuary. Suspended from the pilasters flanking the sanctuary are identical life-sized angels.

There are two heavily decorated side chapels. The Chapel

of the Suffering Savior has a reclining statue of St. Francis Xavier lying in a sepulcher. It is a place of pilgrimage, and many faithful leave pictures or small items on the statue. Opposite this chapel is the ornate Chapel of the Sorrowful Mother.

A taped historical lecture is played every twenty minutes in the church.

The small white **mortuary chapel** was used for the dead who were awaiting burial. The small structure with its three-bell gable has two missionary priests from Tumacacori buried in the floor. Father Carrillo, who died in 1795, and Father Gutierrez, who died in 1821, were interred at San Xavier in 1935. The chapel stands in the old cemetery, which no longer has any grave markers.

The mission grounds have an interior garden with a fountain and many cacti, flowers, and palm trees.

The ceiling of the wing that was built in 1810 is made from the original mesquite beams and saguaro catcus ribs of the church built by the Jesuit missionary, Father Espinosa.

Side Trips

Tubac Presidio State Historic Park preserves the remains of the presidio which was built to protect the mission after the 1751 Indian rebellion. Low mounds mark the outline of the foundation of the oldest Spanish military outpost in Arizona. The park has exhibits in the interpretive center and an underground view of the old fort's remains. The town that grew up around the fort is the oldest town in Arizona established by Europeans. It is located 20 miles north of Nogales off I-19 and U.S. 89 and open daily. Admission is $1 for adults. Tel. (602) 398-2252.

Titan Missile Museum displays a deactivated Titan II missile. A one-hour guided tour includes a visit to the missile silo. It is located in Green Valley, approximately 20 miles south of Tucson via I-19; take exit 69, Duval Mine Rd., then proceed west past La Canada and turn right and follow signs. Open daily, November–April; Wednesday through Sunday, May through October. Admission for adults is $4; seniors and military, $3; children 10–17, $2. Tel. (602) 791-2929.

Sharlot Hall Museum

Restoration of Arizona's territorial capitol; National Register

ADDRESS: 415 W. Gurley St., Prescott, AZ 86301
TELEPHONE: (602) 445-3122
LOCATION: Near downtown Prescott
OPEN: Tuesday–Saturday from 9 A.M. to 5 P.M., Sunday from 1–5 P.M., April through October; Tuesday–Saturday from 10 A.M. to 4 P.M., Sunday from 1–5 P.M., November through March; closed Monday except for national holidays
ADMISSION: Free; donations requested
FACILITIES: Gift shop, museum, library, archives
HOTELS/MOTELS: Hotel Vendome, 230 S. Cortez St., Prescott 86303, tel. (602) 776-0900; Hassayampa Hotel, 122 E. Gurley St., Prescott 86301, tel. (602) 778-9434; Comfort Inn, 1290 White Spar Rd., Prescott 86301, tel. (602) 778-5770; Best Western Prescottonian Motel, 1317 E. Gurley St., Prescott 86301, tel. (602) 445-3096.
INNS: Prescott Pines Inn, 901 White Spar Rd. (U.S. 89S), Prescott 86303, tel. (602) 445-7270
CAMPING: Prescott National Forest: Hilltop, Indian Creek, Lower Wolf Creek, Lynx Lake, Upper Wolf Creek, White Spar, and Granite Basin Campgrounds, Prescott, tel. (602) 445-7253; Willow Lake Camping Resort, S.R. 10, Heritage Park Rd., Prescott 86301, tel. (602) 445-6311; Point of Rocks Campground, S.R. 5., Box 636, U.S. 89N, tel. (602) 445-9018

History

Sharlot Hall Museum, combining an indoor and outdoor museum village, is a restoration of Arizona's territorial capitol and other buildings of that period. It is named for Sharlot Mabridth Hall (1870–1943), a historian and poet who devoted her life to the preservation of Arizona's history.

Miss Hall came to the Arizona Territory from Kansas with her parents at the age of twelve. Arizona, with its mountains and deserts, made a dramatic impact on the young woman. Intrigued with her new home, she began to collect historic artifacts and write the territory's history. From 1908–11 she served as the territorial historian. In 1928 she located her historical collection in the Old Governor's Mansion. After her death in 1943, the historical society developed the extensive museum complex which bears her name. Sharlot Hall was elected in 1981 to the Arizona Women's Hall of Fame.

Because of Sharlot Hall's dedication, visitors can experience Arizona's territorial history. While the museum complex depicts Arizona's history from prehistoric times to World War II, the emphasis is on the territorial years from 1863 to statehood in 1912.

The Arizona Territory was created by an act signed by President Abraham Lincoln in 1863. In 1864 the federally appointed officials of the territory, Governor John N. Goodwin, Secretary of State Richard McCormick, and Henry Fleury, the governor's secretary, selected the site which is now Prescott as the location of the first territorial capital. Governor Goodwin served from 1863–66 and was succeeded by Richard C. McCormick, who served from 1866–69. McCormick was also a pioneer journalist who published the *Arizona Journal Miner.*

Construction of the governor's mansion, a large log structure, which began in July 1864 was completed in September. Although large, the term "mansion" was an exaggeration. The governor's residence was mansionlike only in comparison to the crude shacks and lean-tos that formed the town. The territorial capital was located in Prescott until 1867, when it was moved to Tucson. The capital was returned to Prescott in 1877, but the old log mansion was no longer used as the governor's residence. In 1889, Phoenix became Arizona's permanent capital. From 1876 until its purchase by the state of Arizona in 1917, the Old Governor's Mansion had a variety of owners and uses. In 1929, Sharlot Hall began restoring the building and moved her collection of Arizona artifacts and historical memorabilia into it.

Tour

The **Old Governor's Mansion,** a hewn log structure, is divided into six large rooms: the West Room; Room II—the Dining Room; Room III—the Bachelors' Quarters; Room IV—the Governor's Office; Room V—the Bride's Room; and Room VI—the McCormicks' Bedroom.

The **West Room,** which memorializes Sharlot Hall, contains some of her possessions. Furnished in mission style, the room contains a desk, recliner, rocker, and bookshelf. A display case contains jewelry belonging to Miss Hall. There is also a collection of photographs of Sharlot Hall and excerpts from her writing.

Room II, the Dining Room, contains a large ponderosa pine log dining table and benches. The drop-leaf table, lamp, and pie safe are period pieces. On display are tinware, black glass items, and a silver water pitcher. The dining room served all the residents of the mansion as well as visitors who came to conduct territorial business.

Room III, the Bachelors' Quarters, was occupied by unmarried army officers and territorial officials. It contains a display of late nineteenth century U.S. Army equipment used by troops garrisoned in the western territories. The right bunk area has a mannequin dressed as an infantry captain. The bunk is covered by an army blanket and a haversack, and a coat hangs from the wall. Other items on display are a double-barreled muzzle-loading Maynard carbine, powder and shot flasks, an officer's sword, and a Colt revolver.

The corner bunk area depicts the dress and artifacts of a civilian. Displayed in this area are a buffalo robe, Missouri rifle, shotgun, lantern, and a Remington revolver. The left bunk area has an antelope hide, a folding lap desk, and an army-issue blue folding military table.

Room IV, the Governor's Office, was used by the Arizona territorial governors. The items on display include a safe made by Tilton, Trillman and McFarland, Richard McCormick's law library, a letterpress, and furniture from the First Territorial Legislature.

On display in **Room V,** called **A Few Nice Things to Cheer a Bride,** are the dress and furnishings of Margaret McCormick, wife of Governor Richard McCormick. A mannequin wears a dress with a hoop skirt and a Zouave-style jacket. Among the furnishings are an 1840s Empire sewing table, a walnut rococo-revival settee, a horsehair chair, a tilt-top table, and a handmade pine rocker. The large picture is of President Lincoln and his cabinet.

Room VI, the McCormicks' bedroom, contains an 1870s bed, a chest, handcrafted rocker, trunk, and other period pieces.

The **Museum Center** houses administrative offices, archives and research collections and library, a community program and exhibition hall, conservation laboratory, and workshops. While the exhibits change, the theme generally is of western art and history. A recent exhibition was the work of the sculptor Solon H. Borglum.

Constructed of native stones and pine logs, the **Sharlot Hall Building,** the museum's primary exhibition center, was built by the Civil Works Administration in 1934. The main hall features an exhibit of "Life in Old Yavapai, 1864–1920," which depicts Prescott's history through artifacts and photographs. Noteworthy features are the exhibits on the territorial government, the clash of Indian and white cultures, and the career of General George Crook, who was military commander of the Arizona Territory from 1871–75 and 1882–86. Other displays feature recreation and entertainment, cowboys and cattle ranching, the Arizona Rough Riders in the Spanish American War of 1898, and Arizonans in World War I.

The **Hartzell Room** contains displays on prehistoric and historic southwestern Indian cultures. Among the exhibits in this room are displays of artifacts of the four major Indian cultures in the region: Anasazi, Mogollon, Hohokam, and Patayan. There are baskets, pottery, shell and beadwork, and arrowhead exhibits of the Hopi, Hualapai, and Havasupai tribes.

The **John C. Fremont House** built in 1875 was the home of Arizona's fifth territorial governor, who served from 1878–81. Fremont had a varied career as a western explorer and politician. Called the "Pathfinder" because of his many expeditions into the uncharted western territories, he was the unsuccessful nominee for US president of the new Republican Party in 1856. The Fremont house was decorated and furnished according to the descriptions left by Mrs. Fremont.

The **Bashford House** is a mid-Victorian two-story frame house. The first floor contains a well-stocked gift store. The second floor has a bedroom and sitting room with period appointments.

Other buildings are **Fort Misery,** a simple cabin furnished with a cot, pie safe, stove, and bench, and a **blacksmith shop** containing an anvil, forge, and period tools. The **ranch house** contains an exhibit of saddles, branding irons, spurs, and other artifacts. The **schoolhouse,** a replica of a one-room elementary school, contains a teacher's desk, students' desks, and slates.

The grounds are well landscaped and planted with poppies, columbine, and irises. There is a herb garden near the Old Governor's Mansion and a large Memorial Rose Garden. On the museum grounds are an iron turbine windmill and a Porter locomotive.

Side Trips

The **Phippen Museum of Western Art,** P.O. Box 1642, Prescott, AZ 86302, tel. (602) 7789-1385, is named for George Phippen, founder and first president of the Cowboy Artists of America. It features exhibits of western artists and is open May 15–September 15, Wednesday through Monday, 10 A.M. to 4 P.M.; Sunday, 1–4 P.M. From September 16–May 14, it is open Wednesday through Monday, 1–4 P.M.; Sunday, 1–4 P.M. Closed on Tuesday.

The area around Prescott also has a number of scenic drives in the Prescott National Forest.

Tumacacori National Monument

Ruins of a Spanish mission church of the early 1800s; National Register

ADDRESS: Box 67, Tumacacori, AZ 85640
TELEPHONE: (602) 398-2341
LOCATION: On I-19, 45 miles south of Tucson; 18 miles north of Nogales and the Mexican border
OPEN: Daily, 8 A.M. to 5 P.M.
ADMISSION: $3 per car
FACILITIES: Picnic area, Visitors' Center with book and gift shop
HOTELS/MOTELS: Rio Rico Resort, Box 1515, Camino a la Posada, Rio Rico 85621, tel. (602) 281-1901; Best Western Nogales InnSuites, I-19 at Mariposa Road exit, Nogales

85621, tel. (602) 281-2242; Americana, 850 Grand Ave.,
Nogales 85621, tel. (602) 287-7211 or (800) 231-8070
CAMPING: Coronado National Forest: White Rock and Bog
Springs Campgrounds, Nogales 85621, tel. (602) 281-2296;
Mi Casa RV Trailer Park, 3420 Tucson Hwy., Nogales 85621,
tel. (602) 281-1150

History

Tumacacori National Monument consists of the stabilized
ruins of the San Jose de Tumacacori Mission, a Spanish
frontier mission established by Father Kino in the 1690s
among the Pima Indians. Eusebio Kino, born in the northern
Italian village of Segno, was a Jesuit missionary assigned by
Spain to work in its northern mission territory, Pimeria Alta.
This territory now lies in southwestern Arizona and the northwestern part of Sonora, Mexico. It was occupied by the Pimas
Altos Indians, who were farmers.

Jesuits had been establishing missions in New Spain for half
a century before Kino arrived in 1687. Ordinarily the Jesuits
chose a permanent Indian village for a mission site, and new
missions were usually within a reasonable walking distance of
established missions.

Missionaries brought not only Christianity to the Indians
but also seeds, plants, agricultural knowledge, and herds of
cattle. Because Indian villages became more prosperous under
the mission system, Indians sometimes requested the padres to
establish a mission at their village. That is what happened at
Tumacacori.

The Pima Indians from Tumacacori, a village on the east
bank of the Santa Cruz River, invited Father Kino to their
village. Kino came to the village in 1691, said Mass, and
named the site San Cayetano de Tumacacori. In the succeeding years, missionaries visited regularly. They encouraged
farming and cattle raising. Tumacacori was a visita, or small
missionary outpost, of Los Angeles de Guevavi Mission,

twelve miles upriver, which had a resident missionary. Although Kino built a church at Tumacacori, no traces of it remain.

After the Pima rebellion of 1751, the village was moved to the present mission site and renamed San Jose de Tumacacori. A presidio was founded at Tubac, which was three miles north.

A major mission complex was built by Kino's successor, Father Johann Gazhofer. After the Jesuits were expelled from New Spain by the Spanish crown in 1767, they were replaced by Franciscan priests. The Franciscans decided to abandon the mission at Guevavi in 1773 and center their activities at Tumacacori.

The church that remains at Tumacacori was built by Father Narciso Gutierrez, a Spanish Franciscan, who lived at the mission from 1794 until 1820. Begun around 1800, it was the last in a series of churches built at the mission. Although the bell tower of the church was never fully completed, the church was dedicated in 1822. Services were held there until its abandonment in 1848.

In 1821, Mexico achieved independence from Spain, and the Mexican government did not continue financial support of the missions as Spain had. Mexico ordered the missions to secularize, with only the church itself remaining in the hands of the clergy while the other property including land was dispersed. Mission San Jose de Tumacacori was secularized in the 1840s, and the church was abandoned. In 1844, Mexico sold the mission lands to a private citizen. Some of the statues and other religious artifacts were brought to San Xavier del Bac Mission.

After the roof rotted and caved in, the church fell into disrepair. Other adobe structures at the mission disintegrated. Begun in 1691, the mission community had lasted until 1848.

The ten-acre Tumacacori mission site was declared a national monument in 1908 and is administered by the National Park Service. In 1921 a roof was placed on the church to prevent further damage. The church has not been restored, but the remaining portions of the church are being preserved.

Tour

Enter the **Visitors' Center** to begin your self-guided walking tour. Your first glance of the **church** through an arched window is dramatic. Despite the fact that the church has not been restored, the building is unexpectedly beautiful and awe inspiring in its desert setting.

The church's facade is pretty much intact, even with its unfinished bell tower. The entry arch was painted and grooved to make it resemble a European stone arch.

The massive thickness of the church's walls is what prevented the total disintegration of the adobe walls. The church has a long and narrow nave with two small wings jutting out of one side, the baptistry at the entrance end, and the sacristry at the altar end. The unfinished bell tower of burnt brick is positioned above the baptistry, and a bell is hung in each of the four arches.

The original ceiling of ponderosa pine, hauled twenty-five miles from the Santa Rita Mountains, collapsed over a century ago. The roofless church then suffered much damage from the elements. When the roof was reconstructed in the 1920s as the first step in preserving the remains of the church, it was again built of ponderosa pine beams from the Santa Rita Mountains.

On each side of the church stand two side altars, and above the altars are niches in which statues of saints once stood. Remnants of holy water fonts remain at each side of the entrance as do oval depressions in the walls for the stations of the cross. The choir loft, which was just inside the church entrance, is gone; but adobe piers on each side of the nave mark the place where an arch supported the near end of the loft. The loft entry is visible high up in the wall as is the groove in which the loft floor fitted.

The church has not been redecorated so that only traces remain of the original vivid colors used to decorate both the interior and exterior of the church. Above the main altar in the sanctuary, some of the flowered designs can still be seen. In the domed sanctuary, a large niche remains above the main altar where a statue of St. Joseph (San Jose), patron saint of Tumacacori, once stood. There were never any seats or pews in the church.

The baptistry has nine-foot-thick walls, which were needed to support the bell tower above it. There was a water font where new converts were baptized. A now-closed stairway led up to the choir loft.

The walls are made of adobe brick covered with lime plaster. Window placement in the domed sanctuary is such that light was focused on the main altar where Mass was celebrated. Despite the condition of the church, it is an architectural gem, a holy place, and a marvel when encountered in the desert.

In back of the church is the walled **cemetery,** or *Campo Santo,* and a **mortuary chapel.** This chapel, which was never completed, is a small, circular adobe building with an arched doorway where burial vigils and preparation for burial occurred. After abandonment of the mission, the cemetery was used for a corral by cattlemen. The cattle leveled the ground, obscuring the graves. Also grave robbers vandalized the graves looking for buried treasure. Early in the twentieth century, people began using the graveyard again, and the graves you'll see date from that period.

After viewing the church and cemetery, walk the marked trail where archeological excavations have uncovered other mission buildings. The foundation of an earlier Jesuit church has been uncovered. A limekiln where plaster was prepared is also visible. The limestone was brought from the Santa Rita Mountains.

Originally the mission held kitchens, workshops, slaughterhouses, granaries, classrooms, and guest rooms. Protected by a roof are the foundations of a series of rooms including a *sala*, or main living room for priests, and an arcade room.

The **mission garden** contains herbs such as castilian rose, rosemary, and oregano. There is a small stone fountain and a pond. Trees include the pomegranate, desert honeysuckle, and monks' peppertree. Several varieties of cactus also grow in the garden.

The **mission museum** contains a diorama of the mission during the 1820s. It is very helpful in visualizing the grounds as they had been. There is a fourteen-minute film shown in the museum which gives the history of the mission.

Exhibits in the museum include one on the mission frontier in 1776 and a display of Indian artifacts like baskets and other items found at the missions. Other exhibits are on Father Kino, construction materials and methods used at the mission, lists of Franciscan and Jesuit priests who served at Tumacacori, and a diorama showing the interior decoration of the church.

Most impressive of the exhibits are the statues of saints which originally stood in the church. When the church was abandoned, loyal Indians carried the statues to the San Xavier del Bac Mission for safekeeping. Returned to Tumacacori are statues of St. Francis Assisi, St. Anthony de Padua, St. Cajetan, St. Bonaventure, and St. Peter Alcantara.

Tuzigoot National Monument

Archeological ruins of a twelfth century Sinaguan Indian pueblo village; National Register

ADDRESS: P.O. Box 68, Clarkdale, AZ 86324
TELEPHONE: (602)634-5564
LOCATION: 51 miles southwest of Flagstaff; 2 miles northwest of Cottonwood on U.S. 89A, then 1 mile north on Broadway
OPEN: Daily, from 7 A.M. to 7 P.M. in summer and 8 A.M. to 5 P.M. in winter
ADMISSION: $3 per car
FACILITIES: Visitors' Center with museum
HOTELS/MOTELS: Best Western Cottonwood Inn, 993 S. Main St., at S.R. 899 and 279, Cottonwood 86326, tel. (602)634-5575
CAMPING: Dead Horse Ranch State Park, P.O. Box 144, Cottonwood 86326, tel. (602)634-5283 (For additional lodging and camping information, see listings under Montezuma Castle National Monument.)

History

Tuzigoot National Monument preserves a twelfth century Sinaguan Indian village. It is located in the Verde Valley twenty-five miles northwest of Montezuma Castle National Monument, a twelfth-century Sinaguan Indian cliff dwelling. They share the same history.

Both areas were settled around A.D. 700 by Hohokam Indians, who farmed the land using water from Montezuma Well to irrigate their fields. The Sinagua, who were also farmers, lived north of the Verde Valley in the Flagstaff region. This region, dominated by the San Francisco Peaks, experienced a huge volcanic explosion in 1065. A volcanic cone, now called Sunset Crater, resulted.

Another result of the volcanic eruption was that an even layer of volcanic cinder and ash covered eight hundred square miles around Flagstaff. The covering acted as a moisture-conserving mulch that provided nutrients to the underlying soil. When the Sinagua resumed farming after the volcano subsided, they found that the land was far more productive than it had been. Sinaguan farmers, who had eked out a marginal existence, became more prosperous.

The news of fertile soil attracted many neighboring Indian tribes to the Sinaguan territory. Eventually this led to overpopulation and depletion of natural resources. Small bands of Sinagua decided to move south to less-crowded Hohokan territory in the Verde Valley. Some went to Montezuma Castle, some to Walnut Canyon, some to Wupatki, and some to Tuzigoot.

Several Sinagua villages were established in the rolling hill country of the upper Verde River Valley. The pueblo at Tuzigoot stands on top of a limestone and sandstone ridge just above the flood plain on the north side of the Verde Valley. Tuzigoot is an Apache word for crooked water and was so named because of a nearby crescent-shaped lake.

The pueblo at Tuzigoot grew to more than ninety rooms housing four hundred people. Originally the twelfth-century village was small. The village was expanded when drought in the Flagstaff area drove large numbers of Sinagua south to existing Sinagua settlements in the Verde Valley. Tuzigoot expanded to accommodate the new settlers. Residents relied not only on farming but also on hunting and gathering for their food.

By 1400, Tuzigoot had been abandoned. Historians and archeologists have not been able to prove why the Sinagua left their homes but theorize that overpopulation, drought, or hostile enemies could have been the causes. It also is not clear where the people went, although some say they joined the Hopi who lived northeast of the valley.

Tuzigoot was excavated by University of Arizona archeologists in 1933–34. Floors and masonry walls were preserved and some rooms were restored. Official monument status was granted in 1939.

Tour

Tuzigoot Monument is a stabilized, partially restored, pueblo-style twelfth-to fourteenth-century Sinagua village built on a 125-foot hill overlooking the Verde River. The tour is self-guided. Paths take you all around and through the excavated ruins. You are able to get close to the ruins and take a good look.

Walls at Tuzigoot, which were 24 to 30 inches thick, were made from limestone blocks and river stones laid together with mud mortar. There were few exterior doorways. Dwellings were entered by means of hatchlike openings in the roofs, reached by wooden ladders from the ground floor. Rooms averaged 12 by 18 feet with ceiling heights of 5 feet 6 inches. There were fireplaces and storage pits in the floor.

The ruins are more extensive than they first appear. It is easy to visualize where rooms were added during expansion periods. The ruins consist of low walls showing the outline of the structures. There are no roofs except for one room which has been rebuilt and can be entered. The room has a raised platform, and it is believed that it may have been a kiva—a room used for religious ceremonies.

The **Visitor's Center museum** has displays of Sinagua culture. There is also a model of Tuzigoot as it must have looked when occupied. The ceiling of the museum recreates the type of roofs used in the pueblo.

A tool exhibit shows stone axes, bone tools, and mortars and pestles. Also exhibited are arrowheads, pottery, baskets, textiles, religious objects, and agricultural crops.

Side Trips

See the side trips listed under Montezuma Castle National Monument.

3

NEW MEXICO

Aztec Ruins National Monument

Ruins of a twelfth-century Anasazi Indian pueblo; National Register

ADDRESS: PO Box 640, Aztec, NM 87410-0640
TELEPHONE: (505) 334-6714
LOCATION: In the northwest corner of New Mexico; northwest of the city of Aztec, near the junction of U.S. 550 and S.R. 44
OPEN: Daily, 8 A.M. to 5 P.M.; closed Christmas and New Year's Day
ADMISSION: $1 per person or $3 per car; children under 16 and seniors, free
FACILITIES: Visitors' Center with museum; picnic area
HOTELS/MOTELS: Enchantment Lodge, U.S. 550, Aztec 87410, tel. (505) 334-6143; Holiday Inn, 600 E. Broadway, Farmington 87401, tel. (505) 327-9811; The Inn, 700 Scott Ave., Farmington 87401, tel. (505) 327-5221; La Quinta, 675

Scott Ave., Farmington 87401, tel. (505) 327-4706
CAMPING: Navajo Lake Campsites: Cottonwood, Simms Mesa,
Pine River, Navajo Lake State Park, P.O. Box 6429, Navajo
Dam 87419, tel. (505) 632-2278; KOA Campground, 1900 E.
Blanco Blvd., Bloomfield 87413, tel. (505) 632-8339; River
Grove Trailer Park, 801 E. Broadway, Farmington 87401, tel.
(505) 327-0974

History

Aztec Ruins contains the remains of a large pueblo town
occupied by Anasazi Indians from A.D. 1100 to 1300. The
name "Aztec" is a misnomer. In the mid-nineteenth century,
the ruins were mistakenly attributed to the Aztec Indians of
Mexico by American settlers in the Animas Valley.

Aztec Ruins is significant in that it was occupied successively by Anasazi from Chaco Canyon and from Mesa
Verde. Located midway between these major Anasazi settlements, Aztec combines characteristics of their distinctive
cultures. The Chacoan culture was more advanced, especially
in its architectural design and building techniques, than the
Mesa Verdean culture.

The Anasazi community at Aztec Ruins was originally one
of the "outliers" or satellites of the Chaco Canyon community, a central town which consisted of about 4,000 people
who engaged in farming and hunting. Chaco became the
economic center of the region with strong ties to dozens of
smaller settlements in a 100-mile radius that had a combined
population of about 20,000. By using aerial photography and
remote sensing, archeologists have discovered a system of
roads connecting the outliers with Chaco. One of these roads
extends 65 miles from Aztec to the canyon center.

Building at Aztec began about A.D. 1110, and the original
builders are believed to have come from Chaco Canyon. The
rectangular pueblo had almost 500 rooms including 29 kivas

and one great kiva, was three stories high, and surrounded a central plaza. Between 400 and 700 people lived there.

The location of the new pueblo was selected because of its proximity to the Animas River, which provided water for irrigating fields. Like other Anasazi, the residents of Aztec were farmers who raised corn, squash, and beans.

The Chacoan occupation of Aztec lasted one hundred years until about A.D. 1200 at which time the site was abandoned. Little is known about the reasons for abandonment or where the people went. However, at about the same time the people in the larger communities at Chaco Canyon and Mesa Verde were leaving their homes. Depletion of natural resources, drought and overpopulation are believed to be related to the departures.

Aztec was unoccupied for 25 years until A.D. 1225 when it was reoccupied by Mesa Verdeans who had lived 40 miles northwest. The new residents remodeled the town and built several new dwellings. Their masonry techniques were not of the same high quality as the Chacoan work. The Mesa Verdeans remained until sometime between A.D. 1276 and 1300 at which time the settlement was permanently abandoned.

The earliest recorded reference to the ruins appears in notes of the Spanish explorers Escalante and Dominguez in 1776. In 1859, John S. Newberry, a geologist, visited and recorded his impressions of Aztec Ruins. Lewis H. Morgan, a distinguished anthropologist, visited the ruins in 1878 and made a detailed ground plan of the structures.

The major excavation was conducted from 1915 to 1922 by Earl H. Morris, an archeologist under the sponsorship of the American Museum of Natural History. Morris excavated the West Ruin and restored the Great Kiva.

On January 23, 1923, Aztec Ruins National Monument was established. The Hubbard Site, a small ruin, was excavated in 1953 by National Park Service archeologists. It revealed a distinctive tri-wall structure.

Tour

Aztec Ruins is a rather small, compact archeological site tucked away in the town of Aztec. It features a **Visitors' Center,** the excavated **West Ruins** only a short walk away, the **Hubbard Tri-Wall Site,** and its crowning jewel, the restored **Great Kiva.** Several other ruins have not been excavated.

Begin your tour at the **Visitors' Center.** The museum contains exhibits on Anasazi agriculture, pottery, cooking, weaving, basket making and religion. Items displayed in the museum were found during excavation. A film on the site is shown here.

A self-guided tour of the **West Ruins** provides the rare opportunity to actually enter the pueblo; its walls have been stabilized by the National Park Service. Once inside the rooms, you get a sense of the size of the living areas, the interconnectedness of the communal structure, and the use of rooms for separate functions such as food preparation, sleeping, storage and religious practices. In some rooms, the original wooden timbers, used for roof supports, are visible.

The pueblo was constructed of sandstone blocks quarried about a mile away. Stones were removed with hammers and wedges, then shaped and dressed with pecking stones. Notice the different styles of masonry. The Chaco style alternates bands of large and small stones giving a decorative appearance. The Mesa Verde style uses stones which are all the same size.

Windows provided ventilation and light to the outer ground floor rooms, which were entered by roof hatches. North walls were high while south walls were low to take advantage of solar heat. Doorways were small and had high sills to cut down on drafts and conserve heat.

The pueblo was pre-planned as evidenced by the thicker bottom walls constructed to bear the weight of several stories. Ceilings were of widely spaced heavy pine beams set into solid masonry walls providing support for the next story. Cottonwood poles overlaid the pine beams and supported a layer of split juniper and juniper bark which was the base for a six to eight-inch layer of clay which formed the floor for the upper story. Each suite of rooms had a small firepit for heating and cooking. Since there were no chimneys, smoke and soot collected on the roof beams resulting in blackened ceilings. Rooms with light-colored ceilings were probably unheated storage rooms.

In the West Ruins, there are several small kivas which are underground, circular chambers used for religious ceremonies. All of the Anasazi sites have kivas which follow the same design. Entry into the chamber was through a roof hatch which also served as an escape hole for smoke from a central fire pit. Air was circulated by means of a ventilator shaft. A bench ran along the walls. Several columns along the wall were used to support log roofs. Kivas also had a *sipapu*, a passage way to the spirit world.

The only fully restored **Great Kiva** is at Aztec Ruins. The structure was excavated by Earl Morris in 1921 and reconstructed by him in 1934. Great kivas were public buildings which were used by a large community for religious ceremonies. They may also have served economic and social functions.

Aztec's restored great kiva has an interior diameter of just over 48 feet. Although the kiva is below ground, there are a series of 15 roofed surface rooms, each with an exterior doorway leading to the courtyard. Small ladders set into the walls lead to the perimeter chambers.

The kiva is encircled by a bench. It also has four massive pillars of alternating masonry and horizontal poles which rested on 375-pound stone discs. The pillars held up ceiling beams which in turn supported a roof whose weight has been estimated at 95 tons.

In addition to the central firepit, there are two large floor vaults. Their purpose is not known, but it is speculated that they were used in magic rites or as foot drums or sweat baths.

Today, recorded music plays in the great kiva. The interior

is painted a dark red. It is a very large, high-ceilinged, impressive building.

The **Hubbard Site** is a smaller kiva that was excavated in 1953. Archeologists found a ruin, 64 feet across, which consisted of three concentric circular walls. The spaces between the outer two rings were partitioned into a series of small rooms, eight in the inner ring and fourteen in the outer. The central circular space was a kiva. This is one of only ten tri-wall structures known to exist in the Southwest. Fascinating to archeologists, their meaning and uses have not yet been determined. Although the kiva was excavated, it has now been backfilled.

Side Trips

Salmon Ruins, another outlier from Chaco Canyon, was occupied from 1088 to 1130 by Chacoans and was later occupied by people from Mesa Verde. A portion of a 250-room pueblo has been excavated.

Also of interest is the **San Juan County Archeological Research Center and Library.** Open from 9 A.M. to 5 P.M. daily, it is located on U.S. 64 between Bloomfield and Farmington. Tel. (505) 632-2013.

Bandelier National Monument

Ruins of fifteenth-century Anasazi Indian cliff dwellings and pueblo; National Register

ADDRESS: Los Alamos, NM 87544
TELEPHONE: (505) 672-3861
LOCATION: 46 miles west of Santa Fe on S.R. 4

OPEN: Daily, 8 A.M. to 7 P.M., Memorial Day to Labor Day; 8
A.M. to 5 P.M., Labor Day to Memorial Day; closed Christmas
ADMISSION: $5 per car
FACILITIES: Visitors' Center with museum exhibits and slide
program; curio shop and snack bar; picnic area; campgrounds;
hiking trails; 33,000 acres, of which 23,000 are wilderness
HOTELS/MOTELS: Hilltop House Hotel, Trinity and Central,
Los Alamos 87545, tel. (505) 662-2441; Los Alamos Inn, 2201
Trinity Dr., Los Alamos 87545, tel. (505) 662-7211; White
Rock Motor Lodge, S.R. 4 at White Rock Shopping Center,
White Rock, tel. (505) 672-3838; La Posada de Santa Fe, 330
E. Palace Ave., Santa Fe 87501, tel. (505) 983-6351; La
Fonda, 100 E. San Francisco St., Santa Fe 87501, tel. (505)
982-5511
GUEST RANCHES: Bishop's Lodge, P.O. Box 2367, Bishop's
Lodge Rd., Santa Fe 87504, tel. (505) 983-6377; Rancho
Encantado, S.R. 4, Box 57C, U.S. 285, Tesuque exit, tel.
(505) 982-3537
CAMPING: Juniper Family Campground, Bandelier National
Monument, Los Alamos 87544, tel. (505) 672-3861; Pon-
derosa Group Campground (advance reservations required),
Bandelier National Monument, Los Alamos 87544, tel. (505)
672-3861

History

Bandelier National Monument is located on the Pajarito
Plateau, a long topographical shelf built up from volcanic ash
and lava deposited more than a million years ago. Erosion by
wind and water transformed the plateau into a network of deep
canyons and narrow upland mesas. Fertile volcanic soil attracted prehistoric Indians to the plateau.

Although the Pajarito Plateau was visited by seminomadic
hunters and food gatherers, there is little evidence that the area
had a permanent population until about A.D. 1200 when
Anasazi from the Four Corners area began to settle there. The

Four Corners refers to the area where the present-day states of New Mexico, Arizona, Colorado, and Utah meet.

The settlers were an agricultural people who were attracted by the canyon's permanent stream, El Rito de los Frijoles, as well as the fertile volcanic soil. The farmers raised corn, beans, and squash both on the bottomlands and, primarily, on the mesa tops. They also used water control and soil retention techniques that included irrigation canals, terraces, and gardens divided into small grids. Irrigation was needed to supplement rainfall in the arid region.

Bandelier's first residents built hundreds of small dwellings near their small farms. As the population increased, the Pajariton Anasazi began to establish large villages in the canyons or at the base of the cliffs. Although the soft volcanic deposits did not provide good building material for stonemasons, the cliffs contained many cavities that could easily be quarried. Structures with walls of irregular-shaped building blocks set in large amounts of mud mortar were built against the bases of cliffs.

Some large pueblos were also built in the canyon bottoms or on mesa tops. Construction of the large pueblos took place from the late 1300s until the mid-1400s. Many of these pueblo communities numbered from 100 to 200 rooms; a few may have reached 500 rooms or more. A typical pueblo was several stories high and was built around a central plaza.

In the 1500s the Pajariton Anasazi began to migrate from the area, moving closer to the Rio Grande. By 1550 the Anasazi pueblos were completely abandoned. Their descendents can be found today in the pueblos of San Ildefonso, Santa Clara, and Cochiti.

Our knowledge of the Pajariton Anasazi was advanced by the research of the pioneering archeologist, scholar, and novelist Adolph F. Bandelier, 1840–1914. In the 1880s, Bandelier, for whom the park is named, explored the area. In 1907, Dr. Edgar L. Hewett, first director of the School of American Research and the Museum of New Mexico, began excavating

Frijoles Canyon. He conducted summer field camps for arch-eology students over the next few years. In 1916, Congress designated forty-two square miles of the plateau as a national park to preserve its rich archeological heritage.

Tour

A variety of large, masonry pueblos along with exceptional cliff and cave dwellings can be viewed by visitors to scenic Frijoles Canyon. The shaded, tree-lined stream that winds through the valley framed by stately, reddish cliffs forms a compellingly beautiful landscape. The starkly attractive south-western landscape along with the many ancient Anasazi ruins justifiably attracts hundreds of thousands of visitors each year. Fascinating history in an incredible natural setting is an un-beatable combination for the history buff and nature lover.

Begin your tour at the **Visitors' Center.** Museum exhibits interpret the occupation of this general area from about A.D. 1200 to modern pueblo times. Pottery and stone tools pro-duced between 1200 and 1500 and found during excavation are exhibited. There are models of a cave dwelling, a masonry room, and a 1915 pueblo room. The art of Helmut Naumer is exhibited. A slide show is also shown.

Numerous excavated and stabilized archeological sites can be seen from the Ruins Trail, a one-mile loop from the Visitors' Center. A two-mile round-trip trail leads to the Cere-monial Cave. There are also several longer trails to other ruins for the visitor with more time.

Tyuonyi Ruin is an oval-shaped, four-story, 400-room pueblo built around a central plaza. Completely enclosed except for a narrow entryway, it was once a thriving Anasazi community of about 100 persons. The ground floor, which had more than 300 cell-like rooms made of blocks of volcanic tuff, is all that remains of the communal house. Rooms were used for cooking, sleeping, working, and storage. There are three kivas set in the plaza of this canyon-bottom pueblo. Tree-ring dating shows construction of Tyuonyi began over 600 years ago. Continue to the upper portion of the trail to get a panoramic perspective on Tyuonyi.

At the same time that some Indians were occupying Tyuonyi, others were making their homes in caves. Many caves occurred naturally in the volcanic rock, and stone tools were often used to enlarge them. The National Park Service has provided sturdy wooden ladders so you can climb into a few caves. The Anasazi probably entered these caves by using hand and toe holds carved into the rock. Notice the cool interiors even on hot, sunny days. The cave dwellings are located along the south-facing canyon wall. In the summer the fronts of the dwellings receive the sun's heat while the inner portions stay cool. Due to the sun's low orientation in the winter, the south side is much warmer than the north-facing wall.

The reconstructed **Talus House** is built on talus, the rock debris at the base of the cliff. Many dwellings like this lined the Frijoles Canyon wall. Since they were built of mud, wood, and rock and had mud walls and floors, they deteriorated easily and needed frequent repairs.

The extensive ruin known as **Long House** was a con-dominium-style community that extended for 800 feet along the southward-facing canyon wall. Originally two or three stories high, Long House was attached to the cliff face itself. Floor and ceiling beams of the rear rooms rested in holes cut into the tuff. Additional interior rooms were created by cutting doorways in the rear soft volcanic tuff walls to expand into room-shaped caves. Long House is partially excavated.

Above the top row of viga (ceiling beam) sockets, are **pet-roglyps,** designs of people, birds, and other animals carved into the rock.

Take the lovely half-mile walk to the site of **Ceremonial Cave.** The climb to the cave is steep and includes climbing four ladders. Because Bandelier is already at a height of 7,000 feet, persons with a fear of heights or any health problems should think carefully before attempting the 140-foot climb. Ceremonial Cave is a shallow overhang in the tuff cliff which was once the home of some Anasazi. Explore the well-preserved kiva and several other rooms. The view of Frijoles Canyon from Ceremonial Cave is breathtaking.

Tsankawi Ruin, an unexcavated, 350-room pueblo located on the eastern edge of Pajarito Plateau, may have been home to 200 residents. Access to the Tsankawi Ruin, a detached portion of Bandelier National Monument, is from a roadside pullout on S.R. 4. The round-trip trail is two miles long and requires some strenuous climbing.

Side Trips

The nearby city of **Los Alamos** was once a closed town hidden in the mountains where American government scientists worked on the top-secret Manhattan Project which culminated in the first atom bomb explosion at Hiroshima, Japan, in 1945. Los Alamos is no longer a closed city. The **Bradbury Science Museum** offers a glimpse into the history of that wartime project and also features exhibits reflecting the advanced science and technology of Los Alamos National Laboratory today. It is open from 9 A.M. to 5 P.M., Tuesday-Friday, and from 1-5 P.M., Saturday-Monday.

Chaco Culture National Historical Park

Ruins of Anasazi Indian pueblos which date from A.D. 900–1180; National Register

ADDRESS: Star Route 4, Box 6500, Bloomfield, NM 87413
TELEPHONE: (505) 988-6727,(505) 988-6716

LOCATION: In northwestern New Mexico; from the north, exit S.R. 44 at Nageezi and follow San Juan County road 7800 for 11 miles to S.R. 57; Visitors' Center is 15 miles ahead. From the south, turn north onto S.R. 57 from I-40 at Thoreau and go 44 miles on the paved road. Two miles north of Crownpoint, S.R. 57 turns east; follow S.R. 57 to a marked turnoff and proceed north 20 miles on unpaved road; call park about road conditions during bad weather

OPEN: Daily, 8 A.M. to 6 P.M. in summer, and 8 A.M. to 5 P.M. in winter

ADMISSION: $3 per car or $1 per person arriving other than by car

FACILITIES: Visitors' Center with museum, campgrounds, interpretative trails

HOTELS/MOTELS: Regal 8 Inn, 510 Scott Ave., Farmington 87401, tel. (505) 327-0242; Best Western—The Inn, 700 Scott Ave. at Bloomfield Hwy., Farmington 87401, tel (505) 327-5221; Holiday Inn, Box 689, 600 E. Broadway, (U.S. 64) at Scott Ave., Farmington 87401, tel. (505) 327-9811

CAMPING: Chaco Culture National Historical Park, Star Route 4, Box 6500, Bloomfield 87413, tel (505) 988-6727 or (505) 988-6716

History

Chaco Canyon is twenty miles long, three hundred feet deep, and about three-quarters of a mile wide. Bordered on the north and south by long mesa cliffs, the canyon is set in a desert landscape which includes gray sand, wild grass, a few clinging shrubs, and piles of sandstone and shale, all constantly whipped by the wind. The climate includes long winters, short growing seasons, and marginal rainfall.

In this arid, inhospitable environment once lived thousands of people in an integrated system of cooperating towns and villages which extended up to a hundred miles in all directions. These people are known for their outstanding architectural and construction methods and their engineering skills in harnessing and distributing runoff waters for irrigating farmland. They produced and assembled goods for local consumption and for trading. The Anasazi of Chaco Canyon reached a complexity of community life, social organization, and cultural heights unsurpassed by their contemporaries.

As early as A.D. 500 there were people occupying Chaco Canyon. These early residents are referred to as Anasazi, which is a Navajo Indian word meaning "ancient strangers" or "ancient enemies." Anasazi settled throughout what is now called the Four Corners area where the states of Arizona, New Mexico, Utah, and Colorado meet. Archeologists have identified the remains of nearly two thousand prehistoric dwellings in the Chaco Canyon area, making it the largest Anasazi community in the Southwest.

Anthropologists have defined and labeled six stages of Anasazi historical development, three of which apply to the Anasazi who lived in Chaco Canyon. They are A.D. 450 to 750, Modified Basketmaker; A.D. 750 to 1100, Developmental Pueblo; and A.D. 1100 to 1300, Great or Classic Pueblo.

The Anasazi who came to Chaco Canyon around A.D. 500 were in a period of transition from itinerant seed gatherers and hunters to a more sedentary, agricultural lifestyle. Their first permanent homes were pit houses, which were partially dug into the ground with above-ground walls. Roofs were made of mud-covered poles and brush. Pit house sites have been located by archeologists at Chaco Canyon. During this Modified Basketmaker time period, the Anasazi grew beans and corn, made pottery and baskets, and developed the bow and arrow as a hunting tool.

During the Developmental Pueblo stage, there were increases in population due in part to agriculture, which produced a more reliable food source. Housing developed from pit houses to communal structures consisting of flat-roofed clusters of small rectangular rooms. Walls were initially made of rock, mud, and vertical poles, a form of construction called "jacal." Later, horizontal masonry was put on top of standing slab foundations; eventually all masonry was horizontal. More and more rooms were strung together and stacked up to form pueblos, which were the beginnings of towns.

Kivas also appeared during the Developmental Pueblo period. Consisting of circular, semi-subterranean rooms, which seemed to be an adaption of the earlier pit houses, kivas were used for religious purposes. Other changes included making black on white pottery and the introduction of cotton textiles. Mothers began carrying their babies in hard-backed cradles instead of the former soft-backed carriers. The result was that babies developed flattened skulls. For some time, archeologists mistakedly believed that a new race of people who had flattened skulls had moved into the area.

During the period of Anasazi occupation of Chaco Canyon, the environment was similar to what it is today: dry, treeless, without a perennial stream, and subject to annual variations in precipitation. Due to population increases and their dependence on agriculture, the Anasazi adapted their farming methods in the harsh environment to increase productivity. Anasazi farmers engineered water control systems to collect the runoff from rain and spring melt for farming. Dams or diversion walls were designed to catch the runoff. Ditches or canals consisting of earth and stone dikes diverted the water up canyon to slow it down. The ditches ended in gates through which the water was distributed into fields.

During the Great or Classic Pueblo period at Chaco Canyon, the Anasazi reached their cultural height. The population of the canyon doubled between 1025 and 1075. People who had previously lived in small, scattered pueblos of ten to thirty rooms began building great houses of three to five stories. The Indians were able to build multistoried, communal dwellings because of a new masonry technique which featured walls with rubble cores and outer surfaces of shaped stones.

Pueblo Bonito, the largest single prehistoric Indian building in the Southwest, is estimated to have contained 800 rooms, be five stories high, contain great kivas, have courtyards, and house a population of 1,000. Built between 1030 and 1079, it is an example of Chacoan advances in masonry. Bonito is also the archetype of the height of Chaocan architecture and construction. Similar pueblos are called "Bonito Phase" structures.

There were 13 large towns in the canyon with an estimated 4,000 residents. Another 20,000 people lived in related towns, known as "outliers," which exhibited Chacoan influence. These towns were located as much as 90 miles to the north, south, and west and were connected to the main settlement by a major network of prehistoric roads. Recent archeological work reveals that there may have been visual lines of communication connecting the Chaco system also.

During the Classic Pueblo period, craftsmen produced an array of high-quality pottery, baskets, and ornaments, some of which were used for trading as Chaco Canyon had become a trading center. Great quantities of turquoise were found in Pueblo Bonito although the nearest turquoise mine was 115 miles southeast. Some items found have been traced to as far away as Mexico.

Archeoastronomers have examined solstice markers and other astronomical features of Chaco Canyon since there are indications that the Anasazi regulated their lives by the sun, moon, and stars.

Despite the cultural heights achieved by the Anasazi, the Chaco phenomenon suffered a rapid decline. By A.D. 1200 the large apartment houses of Chaco Canyon had been vacated. Reasons for the abandonment of Chaco Canyon given by archeologists include drought, overpopulation, infertile fields, overconsumption of natural resources, and breakdown of organized agricultural, commercial, social, and religious patterns. Although it is not certain, it is believed that the Anasazi went south and southeast. Their leaving was gradual, and they probably were dispersed over a wide area.

Chaco Canyon was periodically reoccupied. In the 1600s, the Navajos were in the Chaco area, living in hogans. Pueblo joined the Navajo around 1700.

Chaco Canyon has been the site of many archeological expeditions. It is one of the most thoroughly studied prehistoric Indian sites in the Southwest. The first substantive report on Chaco's ruins was in 1849 by James H. Simpson, a US Army officer who was pursuing Navajo. Simpson described and named seven of the larger ruins. He had drawings and measurements made of them.

In May 1877 the US Geological and Geographical Survey of the Territories sent a field party led by William H. Jackson. Jackson mapped, sketched, reconnoitered, and took notes on Chaco Canyon's ruins.

Richard Wetherill, who had discovered the Mesa Verde Indian sites, brought the Hyde Exploring Expedition to Chaco Canyon in 1896. After four years of excavations, 190 rooms and many kivas had been cleared. Ten thousand pieces of pottery, 5,000 stone implements, 1,000 bone and wooden objects, a small number of copper bells, and a large quantity of turquoise had been recovered and shipped to the American Museum of Natural History. Wetherill filed a homestead claim on land in Chaco Canyon and stayed on after the excavation to operate a trading post. In 1910, Wetherill was shot to death by a Navajo and buried in the canyon.

A presidential proclamation of March 11, 1907, included Chaco Canyon National Monument among a group of eighteen areas reserved during Theodore Roosevelt's tenure.

In 1921 the National Geographic Society began a seven-year archeological study. In 1929 the Smithsonian Institution conducted a study. The University of New Mexico got involved in the 1930s and 1940s, and in 1971 the National Park Service in cooperation with the University of New Mexico launched still another study using infrared aerial photography.

On December 19, 1980, the US Congress enlarged the

monument and changed its name to Chaco Culture National Historical Park.

Tour

Chaco Canyon National Historical Park is a little like Cinderella—a beauty that is treated like a poor stepchild. There is much to see and much to appreciate at Chaco Canyon, but getting there can be a problem. The two roads that lead to the park are both unpaved dirt roads with many deep ruts. They are impassable when wet and should not be attempted in that condition. Call the rangers for road information. There are no restaurants, gasoline stations, lodging or medical facilities in the park; the nearest town is sixty miles away. Our hope is that the National Park Service can find a way to pave the roads leading to this park.

Once you get to Chaco Canyon, there is a modern **Visitors' Center** which has a museum displaying many artifacts found during excavations. Of particular interest is an extensive exhibit on the development of Chacoan masonry. Films are shown in the auditorium. Roads in the park are paved, and most ruins are easily accessible from a six-mile loop road.

Begin your tour at **Una Vida Pueblo,** which is accessible by a short trail which begins at the Visitors' Center parking lot. Una Vida Pueblo was a carefully planned building which was constructed and occupied over a 250-year period beginning in A.D. 850. Built on a natural mound, it is one of the oldest of the pueblo-style buildings in Chaco Canyon.

Una Vida is an L-shaped, two- to three-story structure which has a large walled plaza. There were from 150 to 200 rooms. Receding rooflines created a terraced effect, with single-story rooms fronting the plaza then stepping back to a second story around the back wall. Several of the room blocks rose to three stories.

A depression in the east end of the plaza indicates the site of a great kiva which has not been excavated. Navajos who later occupied this area built an oven, a corral, and a hogan here. View the petroglyphs on a canyon wall above Una Vida.

The stabilized ruins of **Pueblo Bonito** are mind-boggling. This ancient pueblo, which covers a three-acre site, is enormous. Its size, the endless number of rooms, the kivas, and courtyards in this remote and barren canyon make you wonder where you are. Forget about going to Greece or Rome until you've explored these fascinating American Indian archeological sites.

Pueblo Bonito is the most famous Chacoan pueblo because of both its size and its advanced masonry techniques. Constructed between A.D. 1030 and 1079, its thick walls had an inner core of rough, unshaped random stones laid in mud mortar. Both inner and outer walls were veneered with carefully fitted sandstone quarried from the cliff behind the pueblo. Walls are thicker at the bottom so that they could support four or five stories, an indication that the structure was preplanned. Round holes in walls are for ceiling beams.

Excavations by the Hyde Exploring Expedition in 1896 and the National Geographic Society in 1921 have exposed 800 rooms and 33 kivas. Pueblo Bonito was built on the site of an existing southeast-facing pueblo built between 919 and 936. The eastern end of the old pueblo was leveled to make way for new rooms, and many of the older rooms were filled with trash. Burials were also discovered in these rooms.

A large rock, called Threatening Rock, which threatened to fall on Bonito even during its occupation, fell on the pueblo in January 1941 and destroyed a whole section of the building.

You may enter some rooms of the pueblo and see original ceilings and original ponderosa pine vigas from which wood samples were removed. Tree-ring dating indicates the trees were cut around 1078. Note the corner windows in a couple of rooms. On the morning of the winter solstice in December, the rays of the rising sun shine through the windows, striking the opposite corner of the room behind it. The plazas are divided by a single row of rooms which were community centers for grinding corn into meal.

Near Pueblo Bonito is **Chetro Ketl,** another large pueblo built between 1038 and 1054. Like most of the Chacoan buildings, there were subsequent additions to this preplanned, 500-room, five-story structure.

As is true of most National Park Service archeological sites, not all of Chetro Ketl has been excavated. Current archeological policy is to leave sites or partial sites for future generations of archeological study. Even the most careful excavations are destructive to the original site, and it is hoped that noninvasive methods will be developed.

Chetro Ketl has a southerly orientation. It is built behind an enclosed plaza fronted by a line of one-story rooms. Some well-preserved rooms have their original mud plaster and flooring as well as original wooden beams.

The long front wall facing the plaza was originally built as a row of masonry columns which probably held horizontal timbers to support a roof over an open cloister-like porch. Pillars and colonades are features of prehistoric architecture in central Mexico but were previously unknown in the American Southwest.

Another large Chacoan structure is **Pueblo del Arroyo,** which was constructed during the building boom that occurred between 1025 and 1075. A Bonito Phase structure, it was a D-shaped terraced house with a four-story section at the rear that stepped down to one-story rooms facing the plaza. It had 280 rooms and more than 20 kivas.

Del Arroyo differs from Bonito in that it faces east rather than south, is set out in the open floodplain away from the cliffs, and is built not only of dark brown sandstone but also of a lighter colored, blocky stone taken from another part of the cliff.

Pueblo del Arroyo takes its name from the abandoned

streambed on its left, which was the main channel of Chaco
Wash. The pueblo's three- to four-story south wall built close
to the old arroyo began to settle shortly after construction. A
series of masonry buttresses, roughly four feet long and five
feet high, were placed at the base of the wall. Settlers who
came to Chaco from Mesa Verde extended the buttresses and
added an outer wall to build a two-story annex with eight or
more ground-floor rooms. Note the contrast between the Chacoan fine veneer and the cruder Mesa Verde masonry work.

Another unique feature of Pueblo del Arroyo is the tri-wall
structure that abuts its rear wall. It consists of two concentric
bands of rooms encircling a central area and is one of ten
similar complexes known in the Southwest. The function of
tri-wall structures is not known, but most enclose a kiva.

Casa Rinconada, built about 1100, is one of the largest
great kivas in the Southwest. Because it is not close to any
village, this kiva may have been a center of some sort for the
whole community.

Near Casa Rinconada are the **Hosta Butte Phase Sites,**
which are small villages seldom more than one story high.
Rooms seem to have been added as needed rather than preplanned, and the masonry is thin and crude. Though very
simple in comparison to the Bonito Phase pueblos, they are
contemporaneous.

Kin Klesto is an example of McElmo Phase construction.
Built by people new to the canyon, they were planned, multi-
storied apartments. Rooms were grouped in solid rectangles
with enclosed kivas and no plazas. McElmo Phase masonry is
similar to the Mesa Verde style; it is cored but thinner than
Bonito masonry. Sandstone used came from a different stra-
tum than was used in Bonito Phase structures and required
more shaping. Blocks were chunkier, less angular, and more
uniform in size. Other McElmo Phase sites in Chaco Canyon
are **Casa Chiquita, New Alto,** and **Tsin Kletzin.** Two prehistoric stairways are also visible in the park.

Old Cienega Village Museum, El Rancho de las Golondrinas

Restoration of seventeenth- and eighteenth-century Spanish Colonial ranches and recreated New Mexico village

ADDRESS: S.R. 14, Box 214, Santa Fe, NM 87505

TELEPHONE: (505) 471-2261

LOCATION: 15 miles south of Santa Fe; from Santa Fe, take Cerrillos Rd. south, turn right on Frontage Rd. toward Santa Fe Downs Racetrack; from Albuquerque, take I-25N to La Cienega exit 271

OPEN: First Sunday of July, August, and September from 10 A.M. to 4 P.M. for self-guided tours; Spring Festival held the first weekend in June from 9 A.M. to 4 P.M. and Fall Festival held the first weekend in October from 9 A.M. to 4 P.M.; guided tours are given at 10 A.M. on Wednesday and Saturday from June through August by reservation only; from April 1 to October 31, weekday group tours by reservation only

ADMISSION: Self-guided tours: adults, $2; children 13–18, $1, children 5–12, $.50. Festival admission: adults, $5; children 13–18, $2; children 5–12, $1. Guided tours: adults, $2; children 13–18, $1; children 5–12, $.50

FACILITIES: Guided tours, festival weekends

HOTEL/MOTELS: El Dorado Hotel, 309 W. San Francisco St., Santa Fe 87501, tel. (505) 988-4455; Best Western High Mesa Inn, 3347 Cerrillos Rd., Santa Fe 87501, tel. (505) 473-2800; Best Western Inn at Loretto, 211 Old Santa Fe Trail, Santa Fe 87501, tel. (505) 988-5531; La Fonda Hotel, 100 E. San Francisco St., P.O. Box 1209, Santa Fe 87501, tel. (505) 982-5511

RESORTS: Bishop's Lodge, P.O. Box 2367, Bishop's Lodge Rd.,
Santa Fe 87504, tel. (505) 983-6377; La Posada de Santa Fe,
330 E. Palace Ave., Sante Fe 87501, tel. (505) 983-6351 or
(800) 727-5276

History

Old Cienega Village Museum at El Rancho de las Golondrinas is named for the swallows that nest in the eaves of its
buildings. It was a stopping off place, or *paraje*, where travelers, merchants, soldiers, and priests rested on their long
1,500-mile journey on the El Camino Real, the Royal Road,
that began in Mexico City, went through the state of
Chihuahua, and ended in Sante Fe.

Old Cienega, a living history outdoor museum, interprets
the era of Spanish colonial settlement and culture in the
southwest, especially in New Mexico. The present state of
New Mexico was part of the large Spanish empire in North
America known as New Spain.

The Spanish heritage in New Mexico began with Francisco
Vasquez de Coronado who in 1540 explored the region while
searching in vain for the legendary but mythical cities of
Cibola, which were alleged to possess gold and great wealth.
The *conquistadores*—the explorers, soldiers, and adven-
turers—who established Spain's claims in the New World
brought with them the Spanish language and culture and the
Roman Catholic religion. Don Juan de Onate established the
first Spanish colony in New Mexico in 1598. In 1610, Don
Pedro Peralta founded Santa Fe, the colony's capital.

With the soldiers and colonists who established New Spain
in the New World also came missionary priests, at first Jesuits
and then Franciscans, who brought Catholicism to the Indians
living in the area. The treatment of the Indians varied at the
hands of the Spanish. Some Indians were enslaved and regarded as property of those who owned the large estates, or
encomiendas. While the Franciscan priests protected the In-

dians, especially the Pueblo Indians from exploitation, the priests often became unpopular for their concerted attempts to suppress the kachinas religious practices and to destroy the kivas where the Indians practiced their ancient rituals. In 1680 the Pueblo Indians revolted and temporarily forced the Spanish to withdraw from New Mexico. The year 1692 saw Spanish soldiers, commanded by Don Diego de Vargas, reconquering the territory and establishing Spanish rule.

Spain's rule ended when Mexico revolted and won its independence in 1821. New Mexico now passed under the jurisdiction of Mexico. Mexican rule of New Mexico was to be short-lived, however. The famous Sante Fe Trail, the rough 780-mile route that began in Independence, Missouri, and ended in Sante Fe, brought American traders and settlers into New Mexico. Spanish culture and American culture met in Sante Fe, the old colonial capital with its governor's palace and cathedral, which in 1830 boasted a population of 3,000. A brisk trade developed in Sante Fe as goods were exchanged between Mexicans and Americans.

In 1846, war broke out between the United States and Mexico over disputed territory in Texas and the Southwest. During the war, the US Army of the West, commanded by General Stephen Watts Kearny, captured Sante Fe and proclaimed New Mexico's annexation to the United States. The Treaty of Guadalupe Hidalgo, ending the conflict between the United States and Mexico, ceded New Mexico and California to the United States for $15 million. New Mexico, now a part of an expanding United States, was organized as a territory in 1850 and became a state in 1912.

At Old Cienega Village Museum, the time traveler can experience the presence of Spanish culture in the New World. Here the Spanish cultural heritage finds historical expression in the buildings, crafts, and art objects preserved in the museum village.

At Old Cienega's El Rancho de las Golondrinas, the story of New Mexico as a Spanish colony is told through the life of the

Baca family who once owned the ranch. El Rancho de las Golondrinas began as one of the estates, or *haciendas*, granted or sold to certain prominent settlers by the king of Spain. In 1710, Miguel Vaga y Coco purchased the ranch from the king of Spain. The property passed into the Baca family when Vaga's daughters married that family's sons. The Baca ranch became famous for the shelter and hospitality that it provided to travelers who made it their last encampment or stopover before proceeding to Santa Fe, which was a day's horseback ride away.

In 1932 the ranch property was acquired by the Curtin family. Y.A. Paloheimo Sr., a Finnish immigrant to the United States, married Leonora Curtin in 1946. While visiting the ranch, Paloheimo was impressed with its cultural and historical significance. Paloheimo, who was familiar with the use of museum villages to preserve important cultural sites in his native Scandinavia, decided to begin the restoration of its buildings, which were showing signs of deterioration. Existing ranch buildings were either restored or rebuilt on their original foundations. Additional buildings were moved to the site from other locations to recreate the various aspects of Spanish colonial culture in New Mexico. Paloheimo's efforts at historic preservation and restoration have led to today's 205-acre open-air museum, operated by the nonprofit Rancho de las Golondrinas Charitable Trust, which seeks to preserve and interpret the culture of colonial Spanish New Mexico.

Tour

The tour of **El Rancho de las Golondrinas** includes two major sites that together provide an excellent perspective on the Spanish cultural heritage in New Mexico—the hacienda or ranch buildings that were the Baca family home and the buildings that were brought to the site and were situated in various locations on the ranch property.

The main hacienda buildings were constructed as a walled

complex of solidly constructed adobe structures. Entry to the complex is by way of two doors, a smaller door for persons and a larger one for animals and wagons. Passing through the doors, you enter the world of Spanish colonial America and find yourself in a small plaza, or *placita*, in which are trees, a well, and *hornos*, adobe ovens, used for baking bread. The design of these ovens came to Spain from the Moors of North Africa and southern Spain. The Spanish brought the horno to the Southwest, where it was used by the Spanish colonists and adopted by the Indians. Surrounding the plaza is the complex of rooms arranged in a rectangular-shaped adobe structure. The roofs generally consist of vigas (large wooden beams) with latias (peeled wooden sticks) placed between the larger beams.

The first room in the complex is the **salon y capilla,** or chapel, an important place of worship for the Baca family, who were devout Catholics as were most of the Spanish settlers in New Mexico. The altar, covered by a hand-embroidered altar cloth, is decorated as it would have been for the important religious feast day of Corpus Christi. The altar features an antique reliquary, handmade wooden crosses, carved wooden statues of saints, called *santos*, and candlesticks. The floor is made of wooden planks, and there is a ceiling of log beams. Also of interest are the wooden chandeliers, called *oronias*, because of their spider-like shape. Since the number of priests in colonial New Mexico was few, the families on the ranches conducted their own religious services while awaiting a visit from a priest.

La sala de fundadores is the dining room that was used by the family and guests. It is furnished with antique dining room period pieces.

La cocina, the kitchen, is typical of those located on Spanish haciendas in colonial New Mexico during the 1600s and 1700s. In the corner of the kitchen is the fireplace used to cook food. Of interest are the clay pots used to store food and the local herbs hung from the ceiling to dry. An important feature in the kitchens of the Spanish colonists and in the dwellings of

the Indians as well was the stone *metate*, on which corn, a
dietary staple, was ground by hand with a *mano*. Also in the
kitchen is a handmade *cuna*, or baby's cradle. There is a bed,
really a shelf over the fireplace, called a shepherd's bed, since
weak baby lambs were sometimes brought indoors at night to
sleep above the warm fire.

The **cuarto de recibo** was a receiving room used to greet and
entertain guests at the ranch. Its whitewashed walls are trimmed with yellow and red. Of interest are the large wooden
chest, or *caja de madera*, and the large wooden chair, or
silleta.

The **torreon defensivo,** or defense tower, was built upon
order of the king of Spain. In the fortified lookout tower, a
sentinel would survey the landscape watching for bands of
hostile Indians, often Apaches, who raided both the haciendas
of the Spanish settlers and the homes of the Pueblo Indians.
Upon sighting suspicious intruders on the horizon, the sentinel would sound the alarm by blowing a ram's horn. Those
working outside would return to the safety of the thick hacienda walls. The men trained in arms would enter the tower,
which was stocked with guns, swords, crossbows, and lances.

Also in the series of rooms that composed the hacienda
complex were those used for special purposes, such as the
carding room where wool was combed and prepared for weaving, the weaving room outfitted with looms, and the *dispensa*,
a communal storage room for food that was reserved for times
of scarcity.

Adjacent to the old ranch buildings is the newer **Casa e
Manuel de Baca,** built by Manuel de Baca in 1812. A two-
room adobe dwelling, it resembles the later Mexican-style
house more than the earlier fortress-like buildings of the colonial ranch. Its five-foot-thick walls were designed for insula-
tion and to keep out domestic animals rather than raiding
Apaches. It is furnished with comfortable furniture and some
religious objects.

The ranch area also contains workshops that made and

repaired equipment needed for farming and herding. The **carreteria,** or wagon shop, repaired carts, wagons, and carriages. **El molino viejo** was an old mill brought to the site from the mountain town of Talpa. **La herreria apodaca,** or blacksmith shop, an important part of ranch life, features an adobe forge and bellows of leather and wood.

After visiting the Baca ranch buildings, the next part of the walking tour leads to the buildings that have been brought to La Cienega from other locations and restored. Among the buildings are:

The 1820s **Shepherd's Cabin** was moved to the site from southern California. It is a simple log cabin with a plaster interior and hard-packed dirt floor. The cabin was lived in by shepherds who were tending flocks. Among the artifacts in the cabin are burro boxes used to carry supplies, shears, and tools related to sheep herding.

The **Sierra Village** has been reconstructed in the style of a New Mexico mountain village of the 1850s. The **Casa Mora,** an example of a house owned by a prosperous family, is a large structure with a wooden plank roof. It has an extensive porch covered by a portal. The interior is furnished with period pieces such as the *rinconera,* or painted wooden corner cupboard, tables, chairs, beds, and other items.

Adjacent to the Casa Mora is the **casa de la abuelita,** or grandmother's house. Its location near the main house meant that the family could watch out for the grandparents, provide them with food, care for them when they were ill, but still allow them the privacy of their own house. The house is simply but comfortably furnished. The *camalta,* or high bed, was for the grandmother while a smaller bed and a *silleta de nina,* or child's chair, was available when one of the grandchildren stayed overnight. The house has an iron *estufa,* or stove, which by the mid-1800s had replaced the fireplace. There is a pantry with flour and grain bins.

The **casita primitiva,** or primitive house, was also known as the honeymooners' cottage since it was the sort of very simple dwelling where a young married couple began housekeeping. The exterior is of logs with an adobe veneer. The interior walls are plastered, and the floor is hard-packed swept dirt. The house is simply furnished with handmade furniture.

In the Sierra Village are a barn, chicken coop, a corral, and several out-structures.

El molino grande de Sapello, the largest of several mills at Las Golondrinas, was moved to the site from the village of Sapello in the Las Vegas area. The mill was owned by the Leger family, a French family. The mill's waterwheel and working parts were made in Buffalo, New York, and were shipped to New Mexico. A series of flumes and aquaducts carried water from springs in the hills to turn the wheel. The water was then diverted into a picturesque millpond. The mill, which operates during festivals and special events, is capable of milling 1,000 pounds of corn meal per day.

Near the mill is the **Madrid House,** a small house that was used in several motion pictures shot at La Cienega. The house was used in the 20th Century Fox film *Butch Cassidy and the Sun Dance Kid,* filmed in 1978.

An unusual building is the **Morada de la Conquistadora,** which is a reproduction of the Morada los Hermanos de Nuestro Padre Jesus Nazareno. The morada is dedicated to Nuestra Senora del Roasario, La Conquistadora. A *morada* is a chapel used by the *Penitentes,* a religious fraternity that developed in the period when priests were scarce in New Mexico and Catholic lay people conducted their religious services in the absence of the clergy. The Penitentes performed charitable works and also developed their own religious rituals which emphasized mortification and penance. For example, during Holy Week, some of the Penitentes practiced self-flagellation, a practice which was not sanctioned by the Roman Catholic Church. The famous Archbishop Lamy, the subject of Willa Cather's novel *Death Comes for the Archbishop,* opposed these rituals. Today, the Penitentes continue to exist in New Mexico and maintain chapels such as the one at La Cienega.

The chapel and altar have a number of antique religious objects. There is a large figure of Christ with movable arms, a carved wooden statue of St. Anthony that dates from 1720, and a statue of St. Francis of Assisi that dates from 1690. Also of interest are several crucifixes, one of which has a figure of Christ with a ministering angel. Another cross is trimmed with a silvered hammer, pliers, and nails.

The one-room country schoolhouse is a school of turn-of-the century New Mexico. It contains a teacher's desk, pupils' desks, collections of books, and other educational items. At times classes are conducted in the building for the groups of school children who come to La Cienega on field trips.

Side Trips

Sante Fe is a traveler's mecca with many shops, restaurants, historical sites, and museums.

The **Museum of New Mexico** consists of five separate museums in five different locations in Sante Fe. The museums are open daily from 10 A.M. to 5 P.M.; they are closed on Mondays during January and February. The admission for adults is $3; children from 6–16, $1.25; and children under 6 are free. A two-day pass is $5 for adults and $2.50 for children. The five museums are: the **Laboratory of Anthropology,** 708 Camino Lejo, tel. (505) 827-8941; the **Museum of Fine Arts,** 107 West Palace Ave., tel. (505) 827-4452, which features Southwestern photography, painting, and sculpture; the **Museum of Indian Arts and Cultures,** 710 Camino Lejo; the **Museum of International Folk Art,** 706 Camino Lejo, tel. (505) 827-8350; and the **Palace of the Governor's Museum** on the Santa Fe Plaza, tel (505) 827-6483.

Salinas National Monument

Ruins of ninth- to seventeenth-century Indian pueblos and seventeenth-century Spanish missionary churches at three separate locations; National Register

ADDRESS: P.O. Box 496, Mountainair, NM 87036-0496
TELEPHONE: (505) 847-2585
LOCATION: Park headquarters is in Mountainair, at the historic Shaffer Hotel, one block south of junction of U.S. 60 and S.R. 14. Abo Ruins are 9 miles west of Mountainair on U.S. 60 and one-half mile north on S.R. 513; Gran Quivira Ruins are 26 miles south of Mountainair on S.R. 14; Quarai Ruins are 8 miles north of Mountainair on S.R. 14 and 1 mile west.
OPEN: Daily, 8 A.M. to 5 P.M.
ADMISSION: At Gran Quivira and Quarai: $3 per carload, $1 per person for those not arriving by car
FACILITIES: Visitors' Center with orientation exhibits, media presentation, and picnic area at park headquarters in Shaffer Hotel at Mountainair; privately owned restaurant in Shaffer Hotel. At Abo ruins: picnic area; at Quarai: Visitors' Center with museum, picnic area; at Gran Quivira: Visitors' Center with museum, film, and picnic area.
HOTELS/MOTELS: Trails End Motel and Campground, U.S. 60E., Box 156, Mountainair 87036, tel. (505) 847-2544; Best Western Golden Manor, 507 N. California St. (U.S. 60, U.S. 85, I-25 Business), Socorro 87801, tel. (505) 835-0230; San Miguel, 916 California NE (U.S. 60, U.S. 85, I-25 Business), Socorro 87801, tel. (505) 835-0211
CAMPING: Manzano Mountains State Park, P.O. Box 224, Mountainair 87036, tel. (505) 847-2820; Trails End Motel and Campground, Box 156, U.S. 60E, Mountainair 87036, tel. (505) 847-2544; Red Canyon Campground, Cibola National Forest, Torreon, tel. (505) 847-2990

History

Talk about interesting! Salinas National Monument combines ruins of two disparate cultures—ancient Indian pueblos and Spanish colonial missions—at three separate historic sites.

The Indians were, of course, there first, About A.D. 800, Mogollon people from the south moved into the Salinas Valley. Salinas is a Spanish word meaning saline or salt lagoons; naming the valley Salinas indicates the importance of the nearby salt flats.

The Indians in Salinas Valley lived in small pit house villages near natural springs. About A.D. 1000, Anasazi began settling in the valley. A century later the Mogollons and Anasazi groups had blended culturally. About that time, eleven large pueblo towns were built in the Salinas Valley. A marginal farming area, Pueblo farmers grew corn and beans, hunted for buffalo, antelope, and deer, and traded pottery, corn, cotton, salt, and pinon nuts for buffalo meat and hides from the Plains Indians.

The first contact between Salinas Pueblo Indians and Europeans came in 1598. Spanish expeditions from Mexico into what is the American Southwest were searching for legendary cities of gold and riches. Although the Coronado expedition of 1540 found no gold in the inhospitable land, hope lingered on. Juan de Onate, sanctioned by the Spanish crown and leading a powerful force, led a colonizing expedition to New Mexico in 1598. Abo, Quarai, and Gran Quivira, the three sites that comprise Salinas National Monument, were inspected by Onate, then the governor of New Mexico.

This first contact between the Spanish and the Indians was friendly. By 1600, interaction between the natives and Spanish authorities was no longer friendly. Onate had urged many Indians to take oaths of allegiance to the Spanish crown. Not realizing its implications, the Indians agreed. When Onate's agent demanded tributes of blankets and provisions, the Indians refused, which led to bloodshed.

In addition to acquiring a larger empire, the Spanish wanted to bring the Christian religion to the Indians. Franciscan friars who had accompanied Onate brought their evangelical work to the Indian pueblos. In the second decade of the seventeenth century, twenty priests were serving thirty thousand Indian converts in forty small churches in the upper Rio Grande area. The missionaries prohibited Indian religions and ceremonies and destroyed ceremonial paraphernalia and buildings. Secretly, native religious rites were practiced by some Christian Indians.

Only the apparent success of the mission effort kept the Spanish in New Mexico, for the venture proved unrewarding otherwise. Civilian and military personnel numbered only a few hundred, yet Spanish clergy and civil authorities vied for control of the Indians, who were the source of their food, clothing, and labor. Indian labor and products such as food, cotton, woolen cloth, deer and buffalo skins, firewood, clothes, and salt were demanded by government officials. *Encomenderos*, who had been granted land near pueblos, expected labor for their ranches and a portion of the food produced by Indians living on their granted lands.

Intense missionary activities in the Salinas Province began in the early 1600s. Franciscan friars directed the building of missions at Abo, Quarai, and Gran Quivira. The Indians provided the labor. They cut timbers, quarried rock, made abode brick, carried water, and erected the buildings. Missions were self-supporting units. Indian parishioners helped prepare and tend gardens, maintain buildings and grounds, and tend livestock.

Before Spanish occupation, the Salinas Pueblos had friendly trading relationships with Apache Indians. Angered by the Spanish militia and the practice of trading of Apache slaves by the ranchers, the Apaches attacked the missions, stealing food and killing warriors. Small military garrisons were unable to fight off attacks from marauding Apaches, who were now mobilized by their acquisition of the horse. Apaches attacked the Spanish and Christian Indians alike.

From 1666–70 there was a severe drought in the Salinas Valley which sharply curtailed food production. By the late 1670s, every village and mission in the Salinas country was deserted and remained so for the next two hundred years. The Indians probably joined Rio Grande River pueblos and the Spanish returned to Santa Fe. The Apache menace was finally ended in the latter part of the 1800s and homesteaders began coming into the valley.

Salinas National Monument was established in 1980 when President Carter signed a bill abolishing Gran Quivira National Monument, a National Park Service area since 1909. Gran Quivira was combined administratively with the New Mexico state monuments of Abo and Quarai. Park headquarters were located in the historic Shaffer Hotel in Mountainair.

Tour

The three units of Salinas National Monument are the Abo, the Gran Quivira and the Quarai. The Abo Unit consists of unexcavated Indian pueblos and the excavated ruins of the San Gregorio de Abo Mission. In the Gran Quivira Unit, which contains the ruins of two seventeenth century Franciscan missions, five kivas, three-hundred rooms in two of the Indian pueblos, and one of the missions have been excavated. The Quarai Unit has unexcavated Indian pueblos and the excavated Nuestra Senora de la Concepcion Mission.

Gran Quivira is a 610-acre site. Begin your self-guided tour by watching the slide show in the Visitors' Center. The museum has exhibits of pottery, arrowheads, and tools discovered at the site.

An easy one-half mile trail leads to the two churches and the pueblo ruins. Read the signs posted on the trail carefully and take a guidebook. Because both Indian and Spanish construction used limestone quarried locally as building materials and because you are looking at ruins or partial structures, help is required to distinguish Indian sites from Spanish ones. Buildings have not been rebuilt, but they have been stabilized.

Gran Quivira, which was known as Pueblo de las Humanas, was the largest pueblo in the Salinas Province with a population of three thousand. Excavation here has been done by the Museum of New Mexico and the School of American Research under the direction of Edgar Hewett from 1923–25. Excavation was carried out by the National Park Service in the early 1950s. These exquisite ruins are reminiscent of Greek archeological sites.

Surrounded by native small and broad leaf yuccas, the **Mission of San Buenaventura** was built under the direction of Fray Diego de Santander beginning in 1659. The impressive cross-shaped church was one hundred forty feet long with walls five and six feet thick. The large church contained a baptistry, a choir loft, main and side altars, and a sacristy.

The church was only part of the mission complex. Attached to the church is the *convento*, the home and offices of the priests. At the entrance to the convento was the porter's lodge where people waited to see the priests. A large convento room was the dining hall. Smaller rooms with corner fireplaces were used as the priests' quarters while other rooms served as food storage rooms and a kitchen. Also a part of the mission were the corrals for sheep, goats, and oxen, stables, work areas, and a plaza.

Mound 7 is the name given to the Indian dwelling which, during excavation, was found to contain three superimposed structures dating from the 1300s to the mid-1500s. The Early Phase structure was a single-story, circular houseblock with five or six concentric circles containing up to two hundred nine rooms. It was arranged around a small plaza with one kiva. In the Middle Phase, a small linear block of rooms and three kivas, used from approximately 1400 to the early 1500s, was attached to the original complex. The rectangular, one-story, F-shaped building with two hundred rooms and five kivas represents the Late Phase, built between 1550 and 1670.

The kivas of Mound 7 appear to have been deliberately destroyed in the 1600s. It was at that time that missionaries tried to stamp out the Indians' native religion. A portion of the Indian houseblock was adapted by Fray Francisco Letrado as a convento. He widened the doors and windows in eight rooms and added eight larger exterior rooms.

The **Chapel of San Isidro** was the first Christian church in Pueblo de Las Humanas and was built in 1629 by Fray Letrado, the first resident priest. The church consisted of a simple parallelogram composed of a long nave and the chancel. The walled area in front of the church is the *campo santo*, or graveyard, for the burial of Christian Indians.

Fray Letrado left for the Zuni Pueblo after two years. Pueblo de Las Humanas did not have a resident priest again until 1659 and was ministered to by the priests from Abo Pueblo until then. The Chapel of San Isidro was in ruins by 1659.

House A is typical of Pueblo architecture from the 1550s to the 1670s. It appears to have been built on an earlier house. Walls are two stones wide with no central core. Rooms and doorways are small. The section of the house toward the plaza has two rows of rooms while the other half of the house has smaller rooms with no particular pattern.

The **Quarai Unit** of Salinas National Monument is a 15-acre site containing an excavated church and convento and unexcavated Indian ruins. Quarai had a population of from 400 to 600 Indians who were farmers and traders in the 1600s when the Spanish arrived.

La Purisima Concepción de Cuarac Mission was built in 1630 by Fray Estevan de Perea. Its red sandstone walls are 40 feet high and stand on foundations that are seven feet deep and six feet wide. The cross-shaped church is 100 feet long, with a 27-foot-wide nave and a 50-foot-wide transept. There were two side altars in addition to the raised main altar, a choir loft, a baptistry, and a sacristy.

Even in ruins, this Spanish missionary church is beautiful, awe inspiring, and almost unbelievable in this southwestern desert landscape. It was about this church that the writer Charles F. Lummis, who visited Quarai in the late 1800s, wrote in *Land of Poco Tiempo:* "An edifice in ruins . . . but so tall, so solemn, so dominant of that strange lonely landscape. . . . On the Rhine it would be a superlative; in the wilderness of the Manzano it is a miracle."

The passageway between the church and the convento was called the *ambulatorio*. This covered walkway led to the convento rooms. The *porteria* was an entry and waiting room where people waited to see the priests. The convento opened to a private patio which contains, astonishingly enough, a kiva believed to have been built while the mission was in use. Other convento rooms included sleeping quarters, kitchen and refectory, and storage rooms. Three of the priests who served Quarai were provincial heads of the Inquisition, and a few rooms were set aside for conducting investigations.

The missionary complex was contained within a wall built for protection. During Apache attacks, people and livestock would go inside the wall.

Excavations were conducted at Quarai in 1913 and 1920 by the School of American Archeology and by the School of American Research in the 1930s. The Museum of New Mexico stabilized the buildings.

The **Abo Unit** of Salinas National Monument contains unexcavated Indian pueblos and stabilized Spanish mission ruins. There was an Indian village here for five-hundred years before the arrival of the Spanish.

Mission San Gregorio de Abo was built in the mid-1600s under the supervision of Fray Francisco de Acevedo. It combines medieval European design with Indian construction materials and techniques. Walls are made of sandstone rock and mud mortar. The rather thin walls are supported by two exterior buttresses and a bell tower on the west side and by convento walls on the east side.

The roof was supported by vigas, heavy roof timbers, which were crossed with small poles of aspen wood and then covered with a foot of heavily packed earth. The roof over the chancel, where the altars were located, was eight feet higher than the nave roof. A clerestory at the transept crossing allowed brilliant daylight to flood the chancel. Interior walls were plastered and then painted by the natives under the supervision of the priests.

Also a part of the mission is the convento, a large rectangular block of rooms containing offices and quarters for the priests and their staff.

PART III

WEST

4

COLORADO

Bent's Old Fort National Historic Site

Reconstruction of the Bent, St. Vrain and Company fortified fur trading post, the largest commercial site on the Santa Fe Trail during the 1830s and 40s; National Register

ADDRESS: 35110 S.R. 194E, La Junta, CO 81050-9523
TELEPHONE: (719) 384-2596
LOCATION: 8 miles east of La Junta and 15 miles west of Las Animas on S.R. 194
OPEN: Daily, 8 A.M. to 6 P.M., Memorial Day through Labor Day; 8 A.M. to 4:30 P.M., September through May; closed major holidays
ADMISSION: $1 per person or $3 per car
FACILITIES: Audio-visual program; gift and book shop; living history programs, handicapped accessible
HOTELS/MOTELS: Best Western Bent's Fort Inn, U.S. 50E, Las Animas 81054, tel. (719) 456-0011; Best Western Stagecoach

Motor Inn, Box 826, 905 W. 3rd St., La Junta 81050, tel.
(719) 384-5476
CAMPING: KOA Bent's Fort, 2668 U.S. 50W., La Junta, CO
81050, tel. (719) 384-9580; Fowler Auto Camp, U.S. 50E,
P.O. Box 83, Folwer 81039, tel. (303) 263-4287; Lake Hasty
Recreational Area, John Martin Reservoir, Hasty, tel. (303)
336-3476

History

When the American frontier did not extend much beyond
the Mississippi and Missouri Rivers, among the few Americans who ventured further west were the trappers and the
traders. In addition to the Indians who occupied this vast
territory, the Spanish who had conquered Mexico had moved
north into what is now the state of New Mexico.

The earliest Spanish expeditions north of Mexico in the late
sixteenth century were unsuccessful attempts to locate the
fabled seven cities of gold. Spain's motivation for establishing a
permanent settlement in northern New Mexico in 1598 was to
locate the Strait of Anin, a sea passage that was believed to
exist from the Pacific to the Atlantic Ocean.

The Spaniards' belief that the strait existed was based on the
quick retreat of Sir Francis Drake after he raided Spanish ships
off the Pacific coast of South America. Although Drake followed the conventional route, the Spanish thought he took a
quick sea route back to the Atlantic Ocean. Their determina-
tion to find that sea route, along with a conviction that gold
could be found and a desire to save the souls of the Indians, led
to the decision to start the settlement.

An expedition led by Juan de Onate and 400 men, 130 of
whom were accompanied by their wives and children, left
Mexico in 1598. Onate first established the religious center,
Santo Domingo Pueblo, and then continued further north to
found the first political capital and European settlement deep
in America's interior on July 11, 1598.

Called San Juan de los Caballeras, the Spanish settlement was at the confluence of the Rio Grande and the Chama River in a wide, fertile valley surrounded by the Sangre de Cristo Mountains to the east and the rugged lava cliffs and Jemez Mountains to the west. Dissatisfaction with Onate's leadership and the inability of the settlement to flourish due to poor land led to Onate's removal.

In 1608, Pedro de Peralta, Onate's replacement, was ordered to move the provincial capital of the kingdom of New Mexico to a militarily defensible location with good grazing land and an abundant water supply. Peralta moved the capital to a higher location near the Santa Fe River and the site of an abandoned Pueblo village. Occupied in 1610, the capital was named Villa de Santa Fe and eventually was called Santa Fe.

Relations between the Spanish and the local Indians were bad, and in 1680 the Pueblo Indians took over the city. In 1693 the Spanish reclaimed the city, and in the early 1700s, many more settlers arrived from Mexico. One of the major problems facing the residents of Santa Fe was Indian attacks; but by 1786, Juan Bautista de Anza, the governor of New Mexico, had either defeated or made peace with the Co-manche, Apache, and Hopi Indians. Peace made trade with the East possible. Pedro Vial, a French explorer hired by Spain, blazed a trail from Santa Fe to St. Louis that would lead to the development of the Santa Fe Trail.

By 1820, American traders were taking the trail southwest-ward to Santa Fe. The trail ran for 780 miles from Independence, Missouri, to Santa Fe. Hunters and traders came to Spanish-held Santa Fe because of the new, profitable markets for eastern goods. However, the Spaniards in Santa Fe did not want American competition for trade, and many of the Americans who showed up there around 1810 were imprisoned.

Spanish control of Mexico ended in 1821, and the new Mexican government was more tolerant of American traders. In 1821, William Becknell brought the first major trade car-avan west over the Santa Fe Trail. He was followed by hundreds of other caravans as the Santa Fe Trail became a well-worn route with well-known landmarks. One of the trail landmarks was Bent's Fort.

Located on the north bank of the Arkansas River, about twelve miles west of the mouth of the Purgatoire River in present-day southeastern Colorado, the fur trading post was established in 1833 by Charles and William Bent and Ceran St. Vrain, traders from St. Louis.

In 1830, Charles Bent and Ceran St. Vrain, both of whom traded in Santa Fe, formed a partnership. They decided to open an office in Santa Fe where they could store their goods. They based that decision on the fact that Missouri merchandise was becoming plentiful in Santa Fe but money was scarce. Traders from Missouri were forced to take whatever price they could get so that they could return home. By storing their merchandise, Bent and St. Vrain could wait to sell when prices improved.

Their plan called for Charles Bent to make buying trips to Missouri while St. Vrain stayed in Sante Fe to sell the goods. The plan worked well, and they opened a store on the south side of the main plaza opposite the Palace of the Governors and a store in Taos, another trading center seventy miles north.

William Bent, Charles' brother, joined the successful business. William had been trading with the Indians, with whom he had exceptionally good relations, from a trading camp near present-day Pueblo, Colorado. By 1831, William Bent convinced his partners that there was money to be made in the Indian trade along the Arkansas River, then the international boundary between the United States and Mexico. The partners agreed to build a large trading post on the Arkansas River.

Named Bent's Fort, the 180-by-135-foot fortress with 15-foot-high and 2-foot-thick walls was built of large adobe bricks. Adobe was selected as the building material because trees were scarce on the plains and because it was fireproof. At the southeast and northwest corners of the fort were two bastions. Over the main gate on the east side was a watchtower room with windows on all four sides. On top of the watch-tower was a belfry, which was used by the guard to sound the alarm. In the heart of Indian country, the trading post was as well fortified as any military post.

From their location on the Santa Fe Trail, the Bent brothers and St. Vrain conducted a lucrative trade with Indians for buffalo skins. Each spring, a pack train loaded with thousands of buffalo skins, purchased from the Indians for approximately 25 cents worth of trade goods per skin, traveled the Santa Fe Trail east to Missouri. The demand for buffalo skins in the East brought prices of $5 to $6 apiece. Cattle and horses acquired by trading with the Indians were also sold there.

After laying in a large quantity of trade goods and supplies, the caravan returned to Bent's Fort. The round-trip between Bent's Fort and Missouri took about five months, and during those months very few people were at the fort. During the winter, there was a large population. All the employees were there except those traders, teamsters, and laborers who were away trading in Indian camps.

Bent, St. Vrain and Company pretty much had a monoply on the Indian trade from the South Platte southward to what is now the Texas panhandle by the early 1840s. It was the largest and strongest merchandising and fur trading firm in the Southwest during the mid-nineteenth century.

However, major changes occurred in the West around 1846. The United States declared war on the Republic of Mexico that year. Bent's Fort was designated as the American army's base for the invasion of New Mexico. In July, General Stephen Watts Kearny arrived with a force of 1,650 dragoons and Missouri volunteers. After Kearny's army left in August, government wagon trains congregated at the fort in ever-increasing numbers. Their cattle overgrazed nearby pastures and their soldiers occupied the rooms. In 1846 the United States Government choose the fort as the headquarters for the Upper Platte and Arkansas Indian Agency.

In addition to the soldiers, many other whites were heading west over the Great Plains to find gold, seek adventure, or become settlers. The influx of whites threatened the survival of the Plains Indians, who retaliated by attacking whites. Although the Bents and St. Vrain had maintained good relationships with the Indians, they were caught in the middle of the Indian wars.

When the war with Mexico had ended, the United States had expanded to include Texas, Oregon, California, and New Mexico. Charles Bent was appointed governor of the Territory of New Mexico; he was killed at Taos during an Indian revolt in 1847. Bent's death, plus a sharp decline in business because of white-Indian hostilities, brought about the end of the fur trading firm. St. Vrain sold his interest in the fort to William Bent and left for New Mexico.

In 1849, cholera brought by emigrants spread through the Plains Indian tribes, ending whatever business Bent's Fort still did with them. William Bent left Bent's Fort with his family and employees on August 21, 1848, after setting fire to the fort, thus putting an end to the seventeen-year giant commercial empire.

Despite the fire, William Bent did not completely destroy the fort. The solidly built complex was renovated and in 1861 was used as a stage stop on the express route between Kansas City and Santa Fe. After railroads displaced the stage, the fort was used as cattle corrals. Eventually the fort did collapse and disintegrate.

The National Park Service declared Bent's Old Fort a National Historic Site in 1963 and completed comprehensive archeological excavations.

Tour

Bent's Old Fort has been reconstructed by the National Park Service to its appearance in 1845–46. Both archeological research and written records of visitors to the fort provided an accurate picture of the fur trading post erected by Bent, St. Vrain and Company. The reconstructed fort has been built on its original foundation. Furnishings are a combination of antiques of the period and reproductions. Guides in period costumes give demonstrations and answer questions.

The reconstructed fort, like the original, is a 180-by-135-foot rectangular adobe fortress with 15-foot-high walls. After walking through the main gate with its heavy wooden doors, you enter a 100-by-80-foot plaza surrounded by a series of buildings. Because of its isolated position on the plains, the fort was a completely self-sufficient unit with living quarters, business facilities, and all necessary services.

The **trade room** and **council room** were at the center of the fur trading business. Representatives of the Indian tribes met with the trader in the council room to negotiate deals in which the Indian hunters' buffalo robes, beaver pelts, and horses were exchanged for factory-made items from Missouri. The trade room was a store which contained a variety of those items, along with supplies which would be purchased by trappers and traders passing along the Santa Fe Trail.

The largest room in the fort is the **dining room** in which traders, trappers, hunters, and all employees ate their simple meals. When a special guest, like John C. Fremont, arrived, a more elaborate meal was prepared to celebrate the occasion. Next to the dining room is the **cook's room** where Black Charlotte, the fort cook, and her husband, Dick Green, lived. The Greens had been Bent family slaves in Missouri.

Cooking was done in the **kitchen** with its simple fireplace; cookware and supplies were stored in the adjoining **pantry**. There was also an adobe oven outside where bread was baked.

William Bent's Quarters consisted of two rooms: an office and a bedroom. Bent's office had an Eastern-style fireplace.

Between sixty and one hundred persons were employed at the fort including carpenters, coopers, wheelwrights, gunsmiths, and blacksmiths. The **blacksmith** and **carpenter shops** were always busy making and repairing items for the fort and for the travelers on the Santa Fe Trail who stopped at the fort.

The **Laborers' Quarters** housed the Mexican workers from Santa Fe and Taos who were hired to build and maintain the fort. Their wives often performed cooking, cleaning, and gardening chores.

The **Trappers' Quarters** were accommodations for the salaried trappers employed by the company and those free trappers who came to the fort to trade their furs and stay for a while.

The **Military Quarters** are restored to 1846 when General Kearny's Army of the West rested here before fighting in the war with Mexico. Some of the soldiers who were ill with dysentery and scurvy when they arrived were left behind to recuperate when the army moved out.

All travelers who stopped were welcome and could stay as long as they liked. There were a number of small, simply furnished rooms that were set aside for visitors. **Susan Magoffin's Quarters** bears the name of a nineteen-year-old woman who stopped at the fort in 1846 for ten days. Susan was traveling to Santa Fe with her husband and lost a baby while at the fort. To make her more comfortable, her own furnishings were brought from the wagon and used to furnish her room during her convalescence. Susan kept a diary of her trip which provided a record of her experience at Bent's Fort.

A billiard table was carried by wagon hundreds of miles from Missouri for the fort's **billiard room**. Winters were long at the fort, and people were always looking for entertainment; billiards was one of the most popular games. Tobacco, drinking, gambling, and hunting were all ways the residents passed their time. Dances were also held occasionally.

Each year the company sent a wagon train to Missouri laden with the furs it had acquired. The **warehouses** were used to store all the items acquired from the trappers and all the trade goods brought from Missouri when the wagon train returned to the fort.

Two **bastions** located at opposite corners of the fort had weapons stored in them. One bastion also was used to store agricultural and tack equipment.

A large stock of animals was kept at the fort. Wagons leaving the fort were pulled by a team of oxen. Horses were acquired by trade with the Indians and brought to Missouri to sell. On the south side of the fort is a large **corral** where these animals were kept. For security, even the attached corral had eight-foot-high walls. The corral gate leading to the outside was constructed of metal plate.

Centennial Village

Recreation of a Colorado high plains planned community, 1869–1920

ADDRESS: 14th Ave. and A St, Greeley, CO 80631

TELEPHONE: (303) 353-6123

LOCATION: 50 miles west of Denver; 50 miles east of Rocky Mountain National Park

OPEN: Memorial Day to Labor Day, Monday through Friday from 10 A.M. to 6 P.M., Saturday, Sunday, and holidays from 1–6 P.M.; mid-April to Memorial Day and Labor Day to mid-October, Tuesday through Saturday from 10 A.M. to 3 P.M.

ADMISSION: Free

FACILITIES: Visitors' Center; guided tours; picnic tables; Selma's Store, gift shop featuring handcrafted items; summer school for grades 2–6; adjacent to Island Grove Park; partially handicapped accessible.

HOTELS/MOTELS: Holiday Inn, 609 Eighth Ave. Greeley 80631, tel. (303) 356-3000; Travelodge, 721 Thirteenth St., Greeley 80631, tel. (303) 353-3216; Inn Towne Motel, 1803 Ninth St., Greeley 80631, tel. (303) 353-0447; Heritage Motor Inn, U.S. 85, Evans 80620, tel: (303) 339-5900

CAMPING: Gateway Campground, 501 E. 27th Street, Greeley 80631, tel. (303) 353-6476; Kamper Kountry, 11505 N. C5, Wellington 80549; Byrd Lake State Recreation Area, Loveland, tel (303) 669-1739

History

Centennial Village was created in 1976, the nation's Bicentennial and Colorado's centennial year; hence, the name. The village was built to show the growth and development of Greeley and Weld County from the 1860s to the 1920s.

Originally called Union Colony, the town was founded in 1870 by Nathan C. Meeker, an agricultural editor employed by Horace Greeley. Meeker later named the town for Greeley.

Horace Greeley, the influential editor and founder of the *New York Tribune* and unsuccessful presidential candidate in 1872, was an advocate of western expansion. Greeley is the person who said the oft-quoted, "Go west, young man." Both Greeley and Meeker were also interested in the utopian communities of their day—Brooke Farm transcendentalists, the Mormons, the Campbellites, and especially the Fourierites.

With Greeley's encouragement, Meeker decided to form a cooperative agricultural community in the West. He placed an advertisement in the *New York Tribune* entitled "The Call" in which temperate men were invited to subscribe at a cost of $155 apiece. They would then receive a town lot and 160 acres of bottom land. Although conditions for joining the community were stringent, thousands of people responded.

Since economic conditions in the East during the post-Civil War years were not good, many people were ready to start a new life. Four hundred fifty people were selected for the community. They had to be religious, abstain from liquor, be educated, have agricultural, business, or crafts skills, and have enough money to buy their land. Three-quarters of the people who migrated to Colorado, almost all of whom came from the original thirteen colonies, stayed.

Meeker purchased a 12,000-acre site located in the high plains between the Cache la Poudre and the South Platte Rivers. Before the soil could be cultivated, it had to be irrigated. Canals were dug from the Cache at higher elevations to accomplish this purpose. Crops were planted; churches and schools were built. The town had to be completely fenced at a cost of $20,000 after the first crop was eaten by cattle. In 1889 a State Normal School was founded.

Meeker, who was the leader of the group, started a newspaper on money borrowed from Greeley. After Greeley died in 1872, the loan was called but Meeker was unable to pay. To help pay off his debt, Meeker obtained a position in 1878 as Indian agent at the White River Agency, where Ute Indians lived. Meeker tried to force the Utes, who raised horses, to become farmers. Resistance by the Utes led to the Meeker Massacre on September 29, 1879. The Indians attacked the agency, burned its buildings, killed Meeker and nine of his employees, and kidnapped Meeker's wife, daughter, and another woman. Twenty-three days later, the women were released and returned to their homes in Greeley.

Greeley was not a typical western town. It was preplanned and organized. Residents were carefully selected and were equally divided between farmers, craftsmen, and businessmen who moved from New York and other established communities in the East. It was a community of families, with an emphasis on education. Even Indians were not a problem as they had already moved to the mountains.

Centennial Village is owned and operated by the city of Greeley.

Tour

Start your tour at the **Union Pacific Depot,** which serves as the Reception Center. Tours are conducted by guides who provide an introduction before leaving the depot. Most of the buildings on the five-and-one-half-acre site are original and have been moved to the site from Greeley or nearby towns.

The depot itself was built in 1910 at Burns, Wyoming. If this Union Pacific depot looks similar to other small depots in the West, it is because it is one of many tract-plan depots. Pre-cut materials were shipped via rail, unloaded, and assembled on the site according to construction plans which accompanied the materials. The depot has a waiting room, a ticket and telegraph office, freight room, and living quarters for the station agent.

Because Centennial Village's goal is to trace the history of Weld County, it is appropriate that its first stop is an **Indian teepee.** Arapaho and Cheyenne Indians inhabited the high plains before the white men migrated westward seeking land and gold. Teepees were used by migratory Indians who followed the buffalo herds, but the large numbers of travelers and their animals heading west ruined the Indians' hunting and grazing lands. The Indians were eventually moved to reservations. Teepees consisted of fifteen to twenty poles supporting a cover of about a dozen tanned buffalo hides. The replica teepee is made of canvas.

An original **Homestead Shack** was built in 1908 near Buckingham, Colorado. According to the Homestead Act of 1862, a citizen could obtain 160 acres of government land if he agreed to live on the land for five years, make improvements, and begin cultivation. Eastern farmers who ventured to the Great Plains put up the simplest frame structures on their claims. The roof and walls of this shack are covered with tarpaper for weatherproofing. Inside walls are papered with 1908 *Greeley Tribune* newspapers.

An unusual exhibit is the **Wagon House,** which dates from 1917. It is a cabin on wheels that was used to transport an invalid from Lamar, Nebraska, to Kersey, Colorado. Lon White built the house on a wagon frame when he was advised to take his tubercular wife to a high, dry climate.

Adobe was a common building material in the high plains

area. The **Adobe Farm House** was built between 1905 and 1915, about twenty miles from Greeley as a farmhouse. Bricks were made from sun-dried clay.

The **Stone House** is a replica building modeled after a bunkhouse on a cattle ranch along the South Platte River.

Log cabins were not common in northwestern Colorado because there were almost no trees on the barren plains. One of the few native trees was the cottonwood, and the **Log Cabin Courthouse** built by Andrew Lumry in 1861 is built of that material. Cottonwood had a serious drawback as a building material in that the logs warped a great deal as they dried out. Although the courthouse is the oldest structure in Weld County, this cabin with its logs all askew and large gaps filled with mud is comical rather than venerable looking.

To commemorate the Hispanic heritage of northwestern Colorado, the Chicano Historical Society built the **Hispanic Heritage House** in 1976. It is an adobe brick house built in the Pueblo style. The first white men in the area were Spaniards, who taught the Indians the secret of making water-tight adobe bricks—adding manure to the mud, straw, and water. Inside the surprisingly cool adobe house is a tortilla oven.

Side Trips

The **Meeker Home Museum,** which is listed in the National Register of Historic Places, is a substantial, two-story adobe brick house built in 1870 for the Nathan C. Meeker family. Two-thirds of the Victorian furnishings in the house belonged to the Meeker family and were brought from New York by train.

During the Meeker Massacre on September 29, 1879, in which Nathan Meeker was killed, Mrs. Meeker and their daughter, Josephine, were taken captive by the Ute Indians. During captivity, Josephine, who must have been a remarkably self-possessed young lady, made herself a dress out of an army blanket. When the Utes released their prisoners in Denver twenty-three days later, Josephine had her picture taken in her army blanket dress at a Denver photography studio. Both the dress and the photograph are displayed in the Meeker house.

Located at 1324 Ninth Ave., Greeley, the Meeker Home Museum is open Memorial Day to Labor Day from Tuesday through Friday, 10 A.M. to 5 P.M., and Saturday, 1–5 P.M.; rest of year, Tuesday through Saturday, 12–5 P.M., except closed from January 15 to February 15. Admission is free. Tel. (303) 353-6123.

Fifty miles east of Greeley is the majestic **Rocky Mountain National Park,** a 417-square-mile national park which straddles the Continental Divide. This popular summer recreation area has 104 peaks over 10,000 feet high, hiking trails, lakes, canyons, picnic areas, campgrounds, fishing and horseback riding and is a wildlife sanctuary. For information, write to the Superintendent, Rocky Mountain National Park, Estes Park, CO 80517-8397 or call (303) 586-2371.

Georgetown Loop Historic Mining and Railroad Park

Restoration of a silver mine and narrow-gauge railroad and a historic district with two mid-nineteenth century mining towns; National Register, National Historic Landmark

ADDRESS: P.O. Box 217, Georgetown, CO 80444
TELEPHONE: (303) 569-2403, (303) 279-6101; (303) 670-1686
LOCATION: 50 miles west of Denver on I-70, exits 228 or 226
OPEN: Daily, Memorial Day to Labor Day for train ride and mine tour; Friday through Sunday during September for train ride only. Georgetown Terminal departures at 10:40 A.M., 12 noon, 1:20 P.M. 2:40 P.M., and 4 P.M.; Silver Plume Terminal

departures at 10 A.M., 11:20 A.M., 12:40 P.M., 2 P.M., 3:20
P.M., and 4:40 P.M.
ADMISSION: Railroad tickets (round-trip): adults $9.50, and
children 4–15, $5; Mine tour: adults, $2.50, and children 4–
15, $1.25; group rates available
FACILITIES: Gift shop in Silver Plume Depot
MOTELS/HOTELS: Comfort Inn, Box 278, 1600 Argentine,
Georgetown 80444, tel. (303) 569-3211
BED AND BREAKFAST: Brewery Inn, 246 Main St., P.O. Box
473, Silver Plume 80476, tel. (303) 571-1151 or (303)
569-2277
CAMPING: Arapaho National Forest: Clear Lake, Echo Lake,
and Guanella Pass Campgrounds, tel. (303) 567-2901

History

The Clear Creek Valley area of central Colorado, like so
many areas in the West, was settled because gold was discovered here. As soon as the word got out of a gold strike,
droves of people with get-rich-quick or gold fever appeared.
Almost overnight a town developed.

Gold was discovered around Central City and Idaho Springs
in late 1858 and early 1859. Two brothers from Kentucky,
George and David Griffith, arrived in Colorado in 1859.
Pushing further west from Idaho Springs along the main
branch of Clear Creek, they discovered gold at the confluence
of two streams near the corner of Eleventh and Rose streets in
present-day Georgetown. They immediately staked a claim
and the next year established the Griffith Mining District.
George Griffith became District Recorder, and the growing
cluster of prospectors' cabins became known as "George's
Town."

Because it was not gold but silver which was found in
abundance, a silver camp named Elizabethtown, named after
the Griffiths' sister, developed in 1864 just south of George's
Town. In 1868 the two towns merged into Georgetown. By

1870, Georgetown was a prosperous mining town of three thousand residents. There were many mines operating along with mills to crush the silver ore.

Georgetown became the commercial hub and service center of an extensive mining region. A newspaper, the *Colorado Miner*, began. Businesses sprang up. There were doctors and lawyers. A school was built in 1874. Several churches were established, including a Methodist, Congregational, Catholic, Lutheran, Episcopal, and Presbyterian. Hotels, opera houses, and saloons all did good business. Successful mine operators and businessmen built substantial Victorian houses, replacing the quickly erected log cabins and shanties that had been built by the first arrivals. Georgetown was a boom town; in 1877, its population reached five-thousand.

The Colorado Central Railroad, a narrow-gauge railroad, linked Georgetown with Denver. Although the railroad company planned to proceed westward from Georgetown, it did not do so until 1884. The problem was that southwest of Georgetown, Clear Creek Canyon narrowed into a rocky defile known as Devil's Gate, then climbed steeply for two miles to the mining town of Silver Plume, 638 feet higher than Georgetown. Even with the narrow-gauge railroad's three-foot spacing between the rails, which allowed the trains to turn tighter curves and climb steeper grades, narrow-gauge locomotives could pull no more than a 4 percent grade; the rise from Georgetown to Silver Plume was 6 percent.

Robert Blickensderfer, a Union Pacific enginer, designed a series of curves and one grand loop whereby the railroad crossed over itself via a 300-foot-long trestle almost 100 feet above Clear Creek. The problem solved, the railroad steamed into Silver Plume in March 1884.

Silver mining around Silver Plume began in the mid-1860s. Watson's Wagon Road brought miners and mine investors from Georgetown. Several major lodes were discovered directly north of present-day Silver Plume in the mid-1870s. The town began to develop as the number of producing mines increased.

In 1880 the town of Silver Plume incorporated; by the mid-1880s, it had a population of 1,120, including Cornish, Irish, English, Italian, German, and Scandinavian settlers.

In the mining tradition of boom and bust, silver mining fortunes dissolved in 1893 when Congress repealed the Sherman Silver Purchase Act, placing the country on a gold standard. As the value of silver plummeted, mines and mills closed. No longer able to make a living, miners and business people moved elsewhere, leaving the towns of Georgetown and Silver Plume behind. Abandoned buildings deteriorated. By 1930, only three thousand people lived in Georgetown and a smaller number in Silver Plume.

The Georgetown Loop Railroad, as the engineering marvel from Georgetown to Silver Plume was known, survived somewhat longer than the silver mining towns. Because of "that famous knot in a railroad" and magnificent mountain scenery, the Georgetown Loop became popular with tourists in the next two decades. By the fall of 1939, faced with declining revenues, the Colorado and Southern Railroad, the current owners, abandoned the Clear Creek line from Idaho Springs to Silver Plume. The high bridge across Devil's Gate was dismantled and sold for scrap.

The impetus for preservation of the silver mining towns and their railroad came from James Grafton Rogers of the Colorado Historical Society. In 1959 at Rogers urging, Stanley T. Wallbank donated almost one hundred acres of mine claims halfway between Georgetown and Silver Plume to the Colorado Historical Society. In 1966 the Georgetown–Silver Plume National Landmark District was created under the National Historic Preservation Act. In 1982 the Boettcher Foundation granted $1 million to reconstruct the Devil's Gate high bridge. The Georgetown Loop Historic Mining and Railroad Park is a property of the Colorado Historical Society.

Tour

Your tour of Georgetown Loop Historic Mining and Railroad Park consists of a round-trip narrow-gauge railroad ride between Georgetown and Silver Plume, plus a tour of the Lebanon Mine, the restored mill, and the reconstructed mining company buildings. In addition, you may walk through the Georgetown–Silver Plume Historic District, which includes more than two hundred nineteenth-century buildings in the two mining towns.

Purchase your train tickets at the **Morrison Valley Center,** the Georgetown depot, which features an interpretive slide show of the valley. (You may also board at the Silver Plume Depot for your round-trip train ride.) The scenic, six-mile round-trip takes you over the reconstructed Georgetown Loop, including the Devil's Gate high bridge. Reconstructed at a cost of almost $1 million in 1983, the high bridge is three hundred feet long, almost one hundred feet above Clear Creek, and built on a 2 percent grade from west to east.

Pulled by steam locomotives, trains consist of open wooden cars with benches along the side and roofed wooden cars. The narrow-gauge railroad tracks pass over four bridges, and through a tunnel, traveling by pine- and aspen-covered mountains.

The **Lebanon Mine and Mill Complex** is only accessible by train. Operated during the 1870s and 1880s, the Lebanon was a silver mine in Republican Mountain owned by the Lebanon Mining Company from New York, which began buying up individual claims in the 1870s.

Mining was a difficult and unhealthy job. Miners would start in the mines at age fourteen and were usually dead by forty-five of black lung disease. They breathed in silica, which cut up their lungs.

Tourists don hard hats to enter the **Lebanon and Everett Mine Tunnels,** which were mined heavily from 1872–94. Tunnels are approximately one thousand feet long. Entering the mine at the fourth level, a guide demonstrates and describes silver mining methods. The difficulty of being a miner is quickly sensed because of the darkness, the damp cold, the lack of fresh air, and the cramped quarters. Miners even ate their lunches in the mine in a small area with benches designated as the lunch room.

Guides also provide tours of the mining company buildings, which have been carefully reconstructed on their original foundations. The **dry room** is the building where miners changed their clothes. Miners walked to the mines from their homes in Silver Plume or Georgetown. Since the mine operated year-round, that would often mean a walk through deep snow. After changing into their work clothes, the miners would hang their street clothes to dry in the dry room, which had a furnace in the middle of the room. Work clothes consisted of long johns, since it was between 40° and 46° in the mines, a baggy pair of jeans cut off below the knees, heavy boots, denim jackets, and felt hats dipped in resin or linseed oil to make them hard.

The **manager's office** is a simple one-room wooden building with wide-plank, unfinished wooden flooring. Furnishings include a rolltop desk, chests for mining tools, lanterns, and an iron stove.

The **equipment shed** was used to store mining equipment, including drills, and barrels. There is also a restored **blacksmith shop** complete with tools and equipment.

Part of the **old mill** is original while part is reconstructed. The purpose of the mill is to crush rocks, making them cheaper to ship to the smelters. The two-story frame mill has a lower-level receiving room from which ore was carried by elevator to the second floor where it was crushed, sampled, and sacked. The mill was built in 1872 under the supervision of Julius G. Pohle, superintendent of the Lebanon Mining Company. It is one of the few remaining structures of its size and type in Colorado.

The **Silver Plume Depot** is a one-story, rectangular frame building with board and batten siding. The restored depot has a stationmaster's office, baggage room, and waiting room. A gift shop is operated here. Historic engines and railroad cars can be seen on sidings in the railroad yard.

The **Georgetown-Silver Plume Historic District** is composed of parts of two mining towns. They feature commercial, residential, and public buildings ranging from simple frame structures to elaborate stone and frame mansions in late nineteenth century styles.

The **Hamill House,** on Argentine and Third streets in Georgetown, was built in 1867. It has been restored by the Georgetown Society. Between 1879 and 1885, William Hamill, who was successful in the silver mining business, expanded the house. The one-and-one-half-story country style Gothic Revival house includes a solarium, parlor, dining room, library, kitchen, and butler's pantry on the first floor. The second floor has a nursery, master bedroom, three children's bedrooms, and a bathroom. The Hamill House also has central heating, gas lighting, four fireplaces, walnut woodwork, and bay windows. Also on the property are a stone carriage house and stable and a cut granite Hamill office building. It is open daily from 9 A.M. to 5 P.M. from Memorial Day through September 30 and noon to 4 P.M. Tuesday through Sunday from October through May. Admission for adults is $2.50; seniors, $1.50; children under 16, free. Tel. (303) 569-2840. It is listed in the National Register.

The **Hotel De Paris,** 409 Sixth Avenue, Georgetown, was a luxurious hotel and restaurant built by Louis Dupuy. Opened in 1875, it has been restored to the 1875–1900 era by the National Society of Colonial Dames of America.

The large hotel kitchen has brick ovens with iron doors, a very large wooden icebox, and a three-compartment sink. The elegant dining room has linen-covered tables set with Limoge china and silver. There is a wine celler with old barrels and bottles. The ten upstairs bedrooms are carpeted, have lace curtains, Victorian beds and dressers. It is open daily from

9:30 A.M. to 6 P.M., May 1 to October 31, and 12 to 4 P.M., Tuesday through Sunday, November to April. Admission for adults is $2.50. Tel. (303) 569-2311.

Side Trips

The **Arapaho National Forest** has 35 campgrounds, 26 picnic grounds, 7 winter sports areas on more than one million acres. Also in the forest is the 14,260-foot. Mt. Evans, which has the highest paved automobile road in the United States. Tel. (303) 224-1277

Mesa Verde National Park

Largest archeological site in the United States; large number of twelfth-century Anasazi cliff dwellings in addition to earlier pit houses and pueblos.

ADDRESS: Mesa Verde National Park, CO 81330
TELEPHONE: (303) 529-4461, (303) 529-4475
LOCATION: Southwestern Colorado, midway between Cortez and Mancos, off U.S. 160
OPEN: Daily all year. Archeological Museum, 8 A.M. to 5 P.M.; Ruins Road, 8 A.M. to sunset. Lodging, campgrounds, restaurants, and gas stations open mid-May to mid-October; full interpretive services available mid-June to Labor Day
ADMISSION: $5 per car
FACILITIES: Visitors' Center, Archeological Museum, slide shows, restaurant, cafeteria, snack bar, gift shops, campgrounds, hiking trails, guided tours, bicycle rentals, gas stations
HOTELS/MOTELS: Far View Motor Lodge (mid-May to mid-October), Box 277, Mancos, CO 81328, tel. (303) 529-4421 or (303) 533-7731; Cortez Inn, 2121 E. Main St., Cortez

81321, tel. (303) 565-6000; Ramada Inn, 666 S. Broadway, Cortez 81321, tel. (303) 565-3773
CAMPING: Morefield Campground, Mesa Verde National Park, CO 81330; San Juan National Forest: Thompson Park, U.S. 160, Mancos, tel. (303) 533-7716; Mesa Verde Point Kampark, 35303 U.S. 160, Mancos 81328, tel. (303) 533-7421

History

Mesa Verde is the largest archeological preserve in the United States and contains the greatest number of cliff dwellings ever found. Nearly 3,900 sites, including more than 600 cliff dwellings, have been located in the park. At an elevation of 7,000 feet, the park has a series of pine- and pinon-covered mesas separated by deep, narrow canyons.

Man first inhabited Mesa Verde about A.D. 500. These first residents, who were called Anasazi, a Navajo word meaning ancient strangers, had formerly been nomadic hunters and seed gatherers. By A.D. 500 they had become sedentary farmers who raised corn and squash. At Mesa Verde the Anasazi discovered that the mesas were a good place to farm because there was a long growing season, hot summer temperatures, a reliable water supply, fertile soil, and dependable rains. There was an abundant supply of wood for fires and house construction, and winters were relatively mild.

The first permanent dwellings at Mesa Verde were mesa-top semi-subterranean mud dwellings called pit houses. Built during the period of Anasazi development labeled by archeologists as the Modified Basketmaker period from A.D. 450–750, they followed the same pattern as other Anasazi in the Four Corners region. During this stage, the Anasazi, already known for their beautiful baskets, began producing pottery. Since pottery could be used for cooking, it changed their eating habits. They hunted using an *atlatl*, a spear thrower.

The next stage in the evolution of the Anasazi culture is called the Developmental Pueblo, A.D. 750–1100. During this period, pit houses were replaced by surface dwellings with vertical walls, flat roofs, and stone rather than mud construction. Sometimes joined together in long rows, the houses usually faced south or southwest to take advantage of the heat of the sun. Nearby would be dug a subterranean pit room, much like their former dwellings, to serve social and religious functions. Eventually, this developed into the kiva, the round, underground room used by Pueblo Indians for their religious ceremonies. The Anasazi now hunted with bow and arrow. Farmers grew corn, squash, melons, and beans. Dogs and turkeys were domesticated animals kept by the Anasazi.

In the Classic or Great Pueblo period, A.D. 1100–1300, the population at Mesa Verda grew to an estimated five thousand. Houses were built with walls two stones thick so they could support upper stories. Small pueblos were abandoned in favor of multistoried community houses with two- to three hundred rooms built on mesa tops.

Villages reflected a more complex social structure as complicated building projects required a good deal of organization and many laborers. Work was performed for the benefit of the community rather than just the small family unit. Farming was a group activity as water conservation and irrigation practices, necessary for the success of the crops, were established. Kivas, which became spacious enough to accommodate the growing community, required many construction workers.

During the Classic period, Anasazi reached their cultural heights. Food production was high enough so that food could be stored. Thus, time was available for more creative endeavors. Pottery became very finely shaped and well decorated. Clear, black geometric designs were painted on grayish white pots. Potters produced mugs, shallow bowls, ladles, pitchers, cooking jars, food storage jars, and kiva storage jars.

Buildings reflected a good deal of preplanning, and masonry techniques improved. Other products produced included stone tools, such as axes used for building. Because Mesa Verde rock is soft, craftsmen had to travel to the Mancos

River to obtain rock hard enough for tools. Animal bones were also used for tools for sewing and weaving. Jewelry and ornaments, often made of shells and turquoise obtained by trading, became abundant. Mesa Verdeans also began weaving, using cotton acquired by trading.

Although Mesa Verdeans followed the same housing patterns as other Anasazi during the pit house and pueblo stages, the housing they are most associated with is the cliff house. Cliff houses can be found at other locations in the Southwest but Mesa Verdeans are best known for them, not surprising given the fact that over six hundred cliff house sites have been located at the park by archeologists.

Around 1150, after six hundred years of living on the mesa tops, some Pueblo people moved into large alcoves under canyon rims. A major shift of population off the mesas took place around 1200. What caused the move is not really known, but it is speculated that there was some need for protection from either enemies or a drastically colder climate.

The majority of the cliff dwellings face south or southwest and were built in large alcoves. Building was difficult work since building stones, as well as the dirt and water needed for mortar, had to be carried into the inaccessible canyon-side caves. Some of the rock ledges had to be filled with stone to level them for construction.

After one hundred years of occupation, the unique cliff dwellings and the rest of Mesa Verde were abandoned in 1300. A drought from 1273–85 was undoubtedly a major factor as food production was essential to the survival of the large community.

After Mesa Verde's abandonment by the Anasazi, the high plateau was overlooked by the Spanish and Mexican explorers and travelers settling the Southwest. In the mid-1870s, surveyers from the U.S. Geological and Geographical Survey of the Territories saw a few of the Indian cliff houses. It was Richard Wetherill, a local rancher, who is usually credited with the "discovery" and initial archeological investigation of Mesa Verde.

Benjamin Wetherill and his sons were cattlemen in Mancos near the foot of the verdent plateau. Wetherill obtained permission from the Ute Indians, whose traditional lands encompassed Mesa Verde, to graze stock there. In December 1888, Richard Wetherill and his brother-in-law, Charles Mason, climbed the mesa on horseback to look for stray cattle. At the edge of a mesa, the ranchers found themselves looking across the canyon at a large masonry house perched on a rock ledge. They named it Cliff Palace.

Entering Cliff Palace, they found clay pots and stone tools laying around almost as if the residents expected to be returning soon. The Wetherills began searching for more cliff dwellings and by 1890 had examined one hundred eighty of them. They dug in many of them and accumulated three major collections of specimens and some pertinent data. As scientists and other interested individuals came to Mesa Verde, they used the Wetherill Alamo Ranch as their headquarters and the Wetherills as their guides.

Gustaf Nordenskiold, a Swede who came to the Southwest for his health, became interested in Mesa Verde. In 1891, with help from the Wetherills, he excavated several cliff sites. The first scientific descriptions of the remains were written by Nordenskiold. Artifacts he found in the sites were shipped to the National Museum in Helsinki, Finland.

As word spread about the Indian sites at Mesa Verde and the valuable artifacts found there, large numbers of pothunters continually rifled the sites. Agitation began for government protection of the ancient Indian sites, and in 1906 Mesa Verde National Park was established. Also in that year, the Federal Antiquities Act protecting archeological resources on government lands became law.

Archeological excavations were conducted by Jesse Walter Fewkes of the Smithsonian Bureau of American Ethnology from 1908–22. The National Park Service and the University of Colorado have also conducted archeological excavations. Repairs to, and stabilization of, ruins accessible to tourists have also been accomplished.

In September 1978 the World Heritage Convention of the United Nations Education, Scientific and Cultural Organization selected Mesa Verde National Park to be a World Heritage Cultural Site in recognition of the significance of the ancient Pueblo culture that flourished here between the sixth and thirteenth centuries.

Tour

Mesa Verde National Park fulfills all its promises and more. Multistoried Indian villages constructed of salmon-colored rock set in rock alcoves of deep, spectacular canyons surpass all expectations. The combination of the largest archeological site in the United States and the southwestern canyon and mesa splendor is unbeatable. You will not be disappointed with a visit to Mesa Verde. Allow a couple of days to see, savor, and appreciate the incredible remains of early Anasazi Indians in an extraordinary natural setting.

The National Park provides many services for tourists. There is a Visitors' Center at Far View, an archeological museum at Chapin Mesa, lots of films to see, books to purchase, and guided tours to take. Self-guided tours of the archeological sites along Ruins Road have signs and guidebooks giving full explanations.

The **Chapin Mesa Archaeological Museum,** which is open daily, is a good place to begin your visit to Mesa Verde. Here you can gain a perspective into the culture of the Mesa Verde Anasazi.

The following series of dioramas provides a historical overview of Mesa Verde: Early Man in the New World, from 10,000–15,000 years ago; the Basketmaker period of 1,600 years ago; the Modified Basketmaker period of 1,300 years ago;

the Developmental Pueblo period of 1,100 years ago; and the Classic Pueblo period of 700 years ago. An exhibit on dendrochronology describes the science of historical dating by using tree rings.

Displays of such artifacts as jewelry, tools, baskets, and pottery portray Anasazi craft skills at different periods of cultural development. An exhibit of models traces the development of Anasazi architecture from the shallow pit house to the above-ground masonry pueblo structures. Anasazi culture and economy are portrayed by exhibits on agriculture, religion, and handicraft production, such as basketmaking and weaving.

In addition to interpreting the life and culture of the Mesa Verde Anasazi, the story of the discovery of the ruins by the Wetherill brothers is told. The work of such professional archeologists as Dr. Jesse W. Fewkes and Jesse Nusbaum is illustrated. The museum also features displays on the contemporary Ute and Pueblo Indians. The museum bookstore has gifts, slides, and books about Mesa Verde.

After exploring the museum at Chapin Mesa, join a ranger-led walking tour which leaves from the museum to **Spruce Tree House,** the third largest cliff dwelling in the park. It was constructed between 1200 and 1276 and contains 114 rooms and 8 kivas. The cave occupied by Spruce Tree House is 216 feet wide and 89 feet deep. One hundred people lived in this village.

The major archeological sites on Chapin Mesa can be seen by taking the twelve-mile **Ruins Road,** which consists of two one-way driving loops. One loop leads to Cliff Palace and Balcony House and the other to the Mesa Top Ruins. The tours are either a self-guided tour in your own automobile or a commercially operated guided bus tour which leaves from the Far View Motor Lodge. Arrangements for the guided bus tour should be made in advance at the Lodge by calling (303) 529-4421. The fee for the bus tour, which leaves at 9:30 A.M. and 1:30 P.M. daily, is $7.50 for adults and $3.50 for children under 12. Ruins Road is open from 8 A.M. to sunset but may be closed in the winter months because of adverse weather conditions.

Cliff Palace, the largest cliff dwelling in Mesa Verde National Park, was sighted accidently and named by Richard Wetherill and Charles Mason on December 18, 1888. You, too, will be impressed with your first sight of this ancient village perched in a sandstone cave. The tour will take you into the cliff dwelling. Signs will indicate into what areas you can walk.

Constructed about A.D. 1200 and occupied until 1300, it contained more than 217 rooms and 23 kivas and housed a community of 200 to 250 people. The series of buildings fills the cave, which is 324 feet wide, 89 feet deep, and 59 feet high. Buildings were one, two, three, and four stories high. Some structures still standing are several stories high, giving them a towerlike appearance because most of the surrounding walls have disintegrated.

On the rock ledge above the buildings are the remains of fourteen storage rooms. Accessible only by ladder, food was probably stored in these cool, dry rooms to keep it away from the domestic animals, dogs and turkeys, and rodents.

Refuse from the village was thrown over the front of the cliff. Burials have also been found in the refuse heap, not out of disrespect but because it was the easiest place to dig.

Wooden beams seen in the structures are original. They were used as ceiling beams upon which another story was constructed.

Balcony House, located under a sandstone overhang above the floor of Soda Canyon, is named for the large balcony which served as a social and work area and provided access to the rooms on the second story. Built on a high ledge, it housed some fifty inhabitants in forty-five rooms. Two kivas are also located on the site. Balcony House features finely executed stone masonry, original plaster work and wooden timbers, and several courtyards. As is true of other cliff dwellings, the defensive security of the site was important. Today's visitors who enter by means of a ladder and a tunnel will appreciate the structure's security system. A wall, built along the north end of Balcony House, protected the front of the structures and prevented small children from falling into the canyon. This site also had easy access to water, which flowed from two nearby springs.

The second one-way loop on Ruins Road will take you to the **Mesa Top Ruins,** which features a sequence of archeological sites that are interpreted in chronological order of development. The Mesa Top sites interpret six hundred years of Anasazi history, from A.D. 600 to 1200, prior to the construction of the cliff dwellings.

By A.D. 500, the Anasazi, who were turning increasingly into a sedentary agricultural people, were making baskets and crude pottery. In the early sixth century, they entered the period of development known as Modified Basketmaking. The first site of the Mesa Top Ruins features a **pit house,** a dwelling of the Basketmaking period built around A.D. 575. A pit house was made by digging a shallow pit, or depression, in the earth, erecting four upright poles as roof supports, covering the structure with sticks and brush, and then plastering it with a layer of mud. Entry to the pit house was through a hole in the roof.

The second stop on the Mesa Top Ruins Road provides a scenic vista of the 700-foot deep **Navajo Canyon.** Below the canyon rims can be seen more than 60 cliff dwellings. Directly across the canyon from the scenic outlook is **Echo House,** which contains 20 rooms and two kivas.

Square House Tower, the third stop on Mesa Top Ruins, was discovered by Richard Wetherill and Charles Mason on December 18, 1888. The four-story tower that gives the site its name is actually a remnant of what was originally a multi-storied building complex that was occupied between 1200 and 1300. Today the remains of sixty rooms and seven kivas can be seen.

Stop four, **pithouses and early pueblo villages,** shows the progression in the Anasazi building techniques. In contrast to the shallow pit house of the first stop, these pit houses, built in A.D. 674, were dug deeper into the earth and had a bench built around the interior walls. These pit houses also featured the innovation of a vertical ventilator shaft that carried fresh air into the house.

At the fifth stop, a **pueblo village** illustrates a major change that occurred in Anasazi life. Around A.D. 850 the Anasazi entered the Developmental Pueblo period when the subterranean pit house was converted into a surface structure, the pueblo. This new construction technique involved setting up large support beams and weaving walls of sticks, branches, and brush between them. The structure would then be plastered with a layer of mud. Series of such rooms were built adjacent to each other to form the pueblo.

A small **village of A.D. 950** is featured at the sixth stop on the Mesa Top Ruins Road. The village consisted of surface structures in which the rooms were built of stone blocks cemented with mud. The kiva, shown at the site, is of the earliest type and includes such features as the bench, firepit, and ventilator shaft that were adapted from the pit house. In addition, four stone pillars supported the logs which formed the roof.

Stop seven, **three villages on the same site,** presents the traveler with some fascinating archeological problems. Excavations at this site indicate that three villages existed here during three different time periods. The archeological problem was to separate the ruins of one era from those of a later period. The first village established at this location was of post and adobe construction. The few remaining visual traces that indicate that a village once existed here are several charred posts and a kiva. The second village, a small masonary walled unit established around A.D. 1000, was built on and partially covered the first village. The archeological remnants of the second village are three attached rooms, a separate room, and a kiva. Improvements in construction and design can be noted at the second village. A third village was constructed at the site around A.D. 1075. The construction used in the third village had double stone foundations instead of the single style used in the second village. The ruins of the third village indicate that there were several circular rooms, two kivas, and a round lookout tower on the site. The change from single to double masonary construction and the presence of the lookout tower suggests that the inhabitants were experiencing a time of tension and were constructing more fortified buildings to protect their settlements from possible attack.

Sun Point Pueblo, stop eight on the Mesa Top Ruins Road, was a large village built around 1200. It consisted of thirty rooms and perhaps fifty inhabitants. It represents the last stage of mesa-top development prior to the movement of the Mesa Verde Anasazi to cliff dwellings. The site is significant because it foreshadows the more contemporary Indian pueblo settlement. The series of rooms was built in a rectangular fashion that enclosed a central plaza area in which the kiva was located. An unusual feature of this kiva was its round tower, which also served as a lookout station. The tower suggests that the thirteenth century was a period of anxiety for the Anasazi, who may have feared attack.

Point nine, the **Sun Point Overlook,** provides an excellent vista. From here, it is possible to view **Fewkes Canyon,** named for the archeologist Jesse Walter Fewkes, and to see the **Sun Temple,** the **Cliff Palace,** and **Sunset House.**

Oak Tree House, the tenth stop, is viewed from an overlook. The site, excavated by Dr. Jesse Fewkes, consists of fifty rooms and six kivas.

Stop eleven, an overlook, provides a view of the **Fire Temple** and **New Fire House.** The great kiva at Fire Temple contains drawings of men, animals, and geometrical designs.

Construction on the **Sun Temple,** stop twelve, began around 1200 but was left uncompleted when the Anasazi abandoned Mesa Verde around 1276. The large stone, fourteen-foot-high building was probably used for ceremonial rather than living and storage purposes. The concrete which was laid on top of the walls to stabilize the structure permits visitors to walk on them and enjoy a close view of its interior.

The sites located on the **Wetherill Mesa** are accessible only during the summer months by the Park Service bus. No private vehicles are permitted. The bus, which leaves from the parking lot of the Far View Visitors' Center, takes visitors on a twelve-mile tour with stops that include the impressive ruins of Step House and Long House. The bus tour, which takes four hours, leaves every half-hour; the first tour leaves at 9 A.M. and the last tour of the day at 3 P.M.

Step House features ruins from two periods: the subterranean dwellings of the Modified Basketmaker period of A.D. 600 and the surface structures of the Classic Pueblo period of A.D. 1200. The structure is named for the steps located on the southern slope that were used by the residents to climb to the canyon rim.

Long House, the second largest ruin at Mesa Verde, with its 150 rooms and 21 kivas, is believed to have housed 150 residents. The rooms are arranged more horizontally than in the clustered vertical fashion found at other cliff dwellings. An impressive feature of Long House is its large central plaza, which was used for social and religious ceremonies. Rows of small rooms were also built on ledges above the main structure.

Side Trips

Hovenweep National Monument, thirty-five miles west of Mesa Verde, contains remains of many-roomed pueblos, tiny cliff dwellings, and a large number of towers that are contemporaneous with Mesa Verde. Hovenweep is under the administration of Mesa Verde National Park, and additional information may be obtained from that source.

South Park City Museum

Recreation of a late nineteenth-century Colorado mining town, 1870–1900

ADDRESS: 4th and Front St., P.O. Box 460, Fairplay CO 80440
TELEPHONE: (719) 836-2387
LOCATION: On S.R. 285, 85 miles southwest of Denver
OPEN: Daily, 9 A.M. to 7 P.M., Memorial Day to Labor Day; daily, 9 A.M. to 5 P.M., May 15 to Memorial Day and Labor Day to October 15
ADMISSION: Adults, $2.50; seniors and children 5–12, $1.25
FACILITIES: Gift shop; audiovisual presentation, restaurant in adjacent Fairplay Hotel
MOTELS/HOTELS: Historic Fairplay Hotel, 500 Main St., Fairplay 80440, tel. (719) 836-2565;
CAMPING: Pike National Forest, Fourmile, Weston Pass, and Buffalo Springs Campgrounds, tel. (719) 836-2727

History

The area called South Park, a 900-square-mile section of central Colorado roughly equivalent to Park County, was a hunting area because of its abundant game. Ute Indians made the lush valley, surrounded on all sides by majestic mountain ranges, their summer camp. In the late sixteenth and early seventeenth centuries, this area was explored by the French and Spanish fur trappers and traders who established posts for trading with the Indians. The name South Park was derived from the French word for game preserve, *parc*.

Colorado was part of the Louisiana Purchase acquired by the United States in 1803. Zebulon Pike explored the area in 1806 and, on his return, reported the abundance of game. Fur trading became the dominant business as hunters and trappers were attracted to the area. In the mid-nineteenth century, cattle and sheep ranching developed.

The town of Fairplay was originally a gold mining camp. When gold was discovered in Tarryall Creek in 1859, prospectors poured into central Colorado. Gold miners who arrived in a second wave at the nearby Tarryall Creek diggings were turned away. These disgruntled folks renamed Tarryall "Grab-all" because of the greediness of its inhabitants. Moving on to the junction of Beaver Creek and the South Platte River to start their own camp, these prospectors named it "Fairplay" and promised everyone who came a fair deal.

As other prospectors before them had discovered, the gold was difficult to get to. Mining equipment was needed to extract it. Individual claims gave way to the larger and more stable placer and hard-rock mining operations, which flourished for thirty years. In later years, hydraulic and dredge mining occurred in the area. In addition to gold, silver, lead, and zinc were mined.

Business people provided the goods and services needed by the population of the mining camp. Because of economic diversity, the town of Fairplay was not abandoned when the gold rush ended.

Leon H. Snyder is the mentor of South Park City, a recreation of a Colorado mining town. Snyder, an attorney from Colorado Springs who spent his vacation time fishing in South Park, became interested in preserving the town's history. He, along with other interested parties, organized the South Park Historical Foundation in 1957. The foundation purchased land on the outskirts of Fairplay. Four buildings remaining on the land were restored while other buildings from Park County were moved to the site. Many of the artifacts in the buildings were donated by people in the area.

South Park City opened to the public in 1959, one hundred years after gold was first discovered in a South Park creek.

Tour

South Park City is a recreated Colorado gold mining town of the late nineteenth century located on the main street of the small town of Fairplay. Fairplay is located in South Park, a broad valley of flat green grasslands surrounded by Rocky Mountain peaks. Today, Fairplay is a central point for the fishing, hiking, camping, skiing, and other recreational activities in the area.

Tours of the mining camp are self-guided and take a couple of hours. The recreated town is laid out on a long main street and is fairly compact.

The **Dyer Memorial Chapel** is a two-room log cabin that Rev. John L. Dyer and Rev. W. F. Warren moved from Montgomery and reassembled log by log. Originally a hotel, it was converted into a Methodist Church by Dyer, a snowshoe itinerant preacher who served the mining camps in South Park from 1863–77.

The interior of the chapel features a pulpit, organ, and pews in one room while the other room contains displays of religious vestments and articles used in services.

The **South Park Brewery,** built in 1879, is one of the four buildings in South Park City on its original site. South Park Lager Beer was brewed on this site by Charles and Leonard Sumner since 1866, years before the present building was erected. Listed on the National Register of Historic Places, the one-and-a-half-story building constructed of native red sandstone is now used as a museum. Exhibits are on mining, railroads, ice cutting, logging, period crafts, and the Riley doll collection. A slide show on South Park is also shown here.

Mining equipment displayed at South Park City includes large steam compressors, a stamp mill, an arrastra, and an ore cart on tracks running to a railroad car. There is also a diorama of a mine.

An important link in the gold or silver mining chain was the

Assay Office. A miner brought his ore here for evaluation of its worth. Moved from the North London Mine near the top of Mosquito Pass, this 1890 log building displays original equipment used for testing ore samples, chemicals, and a smelter.

The **1895 Garo Cabin** has been restored as a wash house. Exhibited are a Lexington No. 110 rocker-type washing machine, a rotary sewing macahine, a mangle, and irons.

The **Park County Courthouse** is a log building constructed in Buckskin Joe in 1862. When Fairplay was made the new county seat in 1867, the courthouse was moved. Inside can be seen a large upright desk, voter tally sheets, and a collection of law books.

The **Burro Room** contains a display of photographs of the burros used in mining. It is in the Logenbaugh Ice and Coal Company office building, which is located on its original site. Burros were the only means of transportation to get supplies to the often inaccessible mine sites. The burro room is dedicated to "the lowly burro, the miners' faithful and loyal helper. Sure-footed, patient, trustworthy and long suffering."

Inside the **Transportation Shed** are a runabout carriage, road cart, two sleds, a hearse, farm wagons, steam engines, chuck wagons, and a sheep-herder's wagon.

The **South Park City Railroad Station** was originally the Buffalo Spring School, built in 1900. Inside are a stationmaster's office, a baggage room, a waiting room with pot-bellied iron stove, and photographs of the railroad trains.

A **narrow-gauge railroad train** includes a steam engine, coal car, water tank, cattle car, and caboose that can be walked through.

The **Homestead** is an example of the simple cabins lived in by early pioneers. This two-room log cabin, moved from Leavick, is wallpapered with the *Fairplay Flume* newspaper and has a large tin bathtub on wheels.

The **Star Livery** was moved from the corner of Sixth and Front Streets in Fairplay. The oxen-drawn freight wagon inside was used to haul freight between Nebraska and Leadville during the 1880s.

The **Stagecoach Inn** was built in 1879 near the top of Mosquito Pass on the stage road between Leadville and Fairplay.

The **August and Lew Hoffman Blacksmith Shop** is an authentically equipped blacksmith shop.

The **School House** is a State of Colorado approved standard school moved 9 miles from Garo. Built in 1879, the one-room schoolhouse contains desks patented in 1872 and 1885, a potbellied stove, an organ, school bell, water crock, and *McGuffey's Readers* from 1879.

Businesses that provided services to the miners are represented in South Park City. There is a **Morgue and Carpenter Shop** where coffins were made, fully-equipped **dentist and doctor's offices,** the newspaper, the **South Park Sentinel,** the **Simpkin's General Store** which also served as the Post Office, the **Bank of Alma,** which contains its original fixtures, and the **J.A. Merriam Drug Store** with a complete range of 1890 drugs and a soda fountain.

The **Pioneer Home,** built in 1879 of native red sandstone, is on its original site. Decorated throughout with Victorian furniture, it reflects the lifestyle of an affluent pioneer family. The parlor has a red velvet settee and a Windsor organ, while the kitchen has a hand water pump with wet sink. A child's bedroom displays late nineteenth-century toys.

Rache's Place is typical of that most important institution in every mining camp—the saloon. Brought from Alma, it was both gambling house and saloon. There are card tables, gaming tables, a private gaming room, cuspidors, a player piano, and a large Victorian bar.

The **Company Store** is the museum gift store.

Side Trips

Florissant Fossil Beds National Monument is a 6,000-acre park where a wealth of fossil insects, seeds, and leaves of the Oligocene period are preserved in remarkable detail. There is also an unusual display of standing petrified sequoia stumps. The park includes a picnic area, nature trail, and guided walks; it is open daily from 8 A.M. to 4:30 P.M. and until 7 P.M. in summer. Write P.O. Box 185, Florissant, CO 80816; tel. (719) 836-2727.

5

WYOMING

Fort Laramie National Historic Site

Restoration of a mid- to late-nineteenth century western frontier military post on the Oregon Trail; National Register

ADDRESS: Fort Laramie, WY 82212
TELEPHONE: (307) 837-2221
LOCATION: On U.S. 26, three miles southwest of town of Fort Laramie
OPEN: Daily, 8 A.M. to 7 P.M., June through Labor Day; 8 A.M. to 4:30 P.M., Labor Day through June 15; closed Christmas and New Year's Day
ADMISSION: Free
FACILITIES: Picnic area, Visitors' Center with gift shop, audiovisual presentation, handicapped accessible
MOTELS/HOTELS: Best Western Kings Inn, 1555 S. Main St., Torrington 82240, tel. (307) 532-4011; Western, S.R. 1, Box 318, Torrington 82240, tel. (307) 532-2104

CAMPING: Guernsey Lake State Park, Guernsey 82214; Chuckwagon Campground, Fort Laramie 82212, tel. (307) 837-2828; Fort Laramie City Park, Fort Laramie 82212, tel. (307) 837-2711; Pioneer Park, 350 W. 21, Torrington 82240, tel. (307) 532-3879

History

For thousands of pioneers heading west along the Oregon Trail in the mid-1800s, Fort Laramie was the first sign of civilization they encountered after leaving Nebraska. Although it would become one of the largest military posts in the West, Fort Laramie was originally a fur trading post built by William Sublette in 1834. The log stockade, which was called Fort William, was a gathering place for Indians, explorers, trappers, and missionaries. Beaver pelts were in demand, and Indian trappers exchanged their furs for food and supplies.

In 1836, Fort William was purchased by the American Fur Company. Since the original stockade built of cottonwood logs was already beginning to rot, the American Fur Company built a new fort of whitewashed adobe a short distance away. Located on the Laramie River, the new fort was named Fort John. There were eighteen rooms inside the rectangular stockade. In the 1840s, thousands of people enroute west stopped at the fort to trade tired animals for fresh ones and to obtain food and clothing. The declining demand for beaver skins along with the western migration changed the focus of the post from fur trading with Indians to supply station for pioneers. Because these pioneers were occasionally harassed by Indians along the trail, demand grew for military protection of white travelers.

In 1849, Fort John was purchased by the U.S. Army from the American Fur Company for $4,000. It was named Fort Laramie, which it has been called unofficially for many years. Major W.F. Sanderson and the sixty-three men of Company E, Mounted Rifleman, were the first troops posted at Fort

Laramie. Troops from Company O, Mounted Rifles, and Company G, Sixth Infantry, joined the post that summer.

Forts were established not only to provide military protection for the emigrants but also to be a source of fresh supplies for the pioneers. Located along the Oregon Trail, Fort Laramie saw as many as fifty thousand people heading west each year. Concern about the fate of whites traveling west through Indian lands led Congress to propose a treaty council with the Indians at Fort Laramie.

The Fort Laramie Treaty was signed September 17, 1851, between the government and the local Indian tribes—Sioux, Cheyenne, Crow, Araphoe, and Snake. The terms of the treaty were that whites could travel the roads west without harm from the Indians while the Indians would receive a government annuity of goods worth $50,000 each year.

Tens of thousands of people following the Oregon and Mormon trails continued to head west using the military forts as supply depots. An incident involving Mormons and Indians in late summer 1854 severely challenged the peaceful situation achieved by the Fort Laramie Treaty.

When a Mormon-owned cow entered a Brule Sioux camp, it was appropriated by a visiting Miniconjou named High Forehead. Although the Brule's chief offered to make restitution, a military party from Fort Laramie led by Brevet Second Lieutenant John Grattan was sent to arrest the brave. Fighting led to the deaths of Grattan's 29-man military party. To avenge the Grattan massacre, 600 soldiers led by General W. S. Harney attacked the Brule Sioux village in September 1855. This battle left 86 Indians dead and 70 women and children captured.

Trouble between the Indians and whites continued to occur, justifying the continued military presence at Fort Laramie. The Colorado gold rush of 1858 precipitated another wave of western migration. Troops were reduced during the Civil War, at which time Indians stepped up their raids on settlers. When the war ended, more military troops were dispatched to the fort. The buildup of troops necessitated new construction and removal of older buildings. By 1862, all Fort John buildings were gone.

Wars with the Indians of the Great Plains continued for over a decade after the Civil War as settlers encrouched on Indian lands. Not only did Fort Laramie troops participate in these wars, but the fort served as a supply station for troops from other forts engaged in the wars.

Indians particularly opposed the Bozeman Trail, a new emigrant road to the Montana gold fields that passed through their Powder River hunting ground. A result of that conflict was the Sioux massacre of an 80-man military party led by Captain William J. Fetterman from Fort Phil Kearney. The government later withdrew from the Bozeman Trail when the Union Pacific Railroad provided an alternate route to Montana.

Fort Laramie was used as a supply station in the Utah campaign, which ended without direct confrontation between the Mormon militia and the army. The problem stemmed from clashes between government officials sent to Utah and leaders of the Mormon Church. President James Buchanan believed that the Mormon Territory was in rebellion and ordered thousands of soldiers into Salt Lake City. The Mormons were able to thwart the troops' arrival, and peace terms were eventually arranged between the government and the Mormons.

Fort Laramie served as a Pony Express station, with the first rider arriving in April 1860. The telegraph, which reached Fort Laramie in September 1860 and was hooked up to the West Coast line in October 1861, marked the end of the short-lived Pony Express.

The U.S. Army abandoned Fort Laramie in 1890 and opened its 35,000 acres for homesteading. Many of the fort's buildings were sold to homesteaders for scrap. In 1937 the state of Wyoming purchased 214 acres of the former fort site for preservation purposes and in 1938 turned it over to the National Park Service for restoration. Named Fort Laramie National Monument in 1938, Fort Laramie was changed to a National Historic Site in 1960.

Tour

Fort Laramie was one of the largest frontier military posts, with at least one hundred eighty buildings constructed by the army between 1849 and 1885. Although some buildings were dismantled after the post was abandoned and others are in ruins, this is a large, impressive fort which gives a real sense of western military life.

Unlike the earlier adobe Indian trading post which disintegrated long ago, the restored fort was never enclosed. Twenty-one fort structures are arranged around an octagonal parade ground. In addition to the nine buildings restored to their nineteenth-century appearance, the stabilized ruins of approximately a dozen structures can also be seen. Foundations of still other buildings are visible.

Begin your tour at the Visitors' Center, which is located in the 1884 **Commissary Storehouse.** Inside this long, one-story building is a bookstore, museum, and an auditorium where a film on the fort is shown. The two large rooms were used to store food supplies, with meat in one storage room and flour, rice, and beans in the other. The two small offices were for the commissiary officers. Extra rations could be purchased at the commissiary by enlisted men and officers.

The **Old Bakery** consists of parts of two bakeries. The cement part of the bakery was built in 1876, used until 1884, and then converted into a school, while the brick portion was used from 1884–90. Five hundred loaves of bread could be baked in the two brick ovens, which measured 6 feet 5 inches by 8 feet. Each soldier was issued a daily ration of bread, an 18-ounce loaf. The enlisted men rotated as bakers, assigned to ten-day shifts, and lived in the bakery in a simply furnished bedroom during their tenures as bakers. Inside the bakery are large barrels of flour, large bread dough troughs, and the huge ovens.

Three guardhouses were built at Fort Laramie, one in 1850, a second in 1866, and a third in 1876. The restored **guardhouse** is the 1866 building. During its restoration in 1960, the foundations of the 1850 guardhouse were discovered as they were both built on the same site. The restored guardhouse is a two-story stone building. The main floor has quarters for the post guard and an office for the Officer of the Day. General confinement cells and solitary confinement cells are on the lower level. The foundation originally was five feet high and almost entirely beneath ground level, making it somewhat like a dungeon. Solitary confinement cells were five feet high and five feet long.

A two-story, white frame duplex with a porch built in 1870 served as the **Captain's Quarters.** Two officers and their families shared the house along with an enlisted man who was assigned as the cook. Each side of the house has a parlor, dining room, kitchen, and pantry on the first floor and two bedrooms upstairs.

Old Bedlam, built in 1849, is the oldest army structure surviving at Fort Laramie and is believed to be the oldest standing military structure in Wyoming. The two-story white frame building with green shutters has wide verandas on both floors. Used for forty-one years, it was originally intended to be the officers' quarters. It also served as post headquarters and bachelor quarters. Old Bedlam has been restored to two different periods: as bachelor officers' quarters in 1854–55 and as post headquarters and family quarters of Lieutenant Colonel William O. Collins in 1864.

The offices of the post headquarters on the first floor were used for official duties like daily record-keeping and court martials. There is also a conference room and a kitchen because it was often used as the officers' mess. Upstairs is

Lieutenant Colonel Collins' apartment consisting of a parlor, bedroom and laundry.

The bachelor officers' quarters in Old Bedlam was home to three commissioned officers. The masculine decor includes tables with playing cards and whiskey glasses and buffalo skins used as rugs and bed coverings. A section of the wall is exposed to show the construction methods used in Old Bedlam.

The **Post Surgeon's Quarters** is located on the west side of the parade ground known as Officers' Row. The two-story duplex is constructed of lime concrete. Because the post surgeon was an officer of independent means, his house is well decorated. The parlor has Victorian furniture upholstered in horsehair, velvet draperies, and an organ. There is also a dining room, a kitchen, and a study with stuffed animals and other scientific collections. Upstairs, the three bedrooms are for the post surgeon, his wife, and children.

Also on Officers' Row is the **Lieutenant Colonel's Quarters/ Burt House,** a single-family house. The two-story, lime-concrete house with dark red shutters was built in 1884 and has been restored to 1887, when it was occupied by Lieutenant Colonel Andrew Sheridan Burt and his family. Because Lieutenant Colonel Burt was the fort officer who was second in command, his well-decorated, comfortable home reflects his high rank. Furnishings are typical of the late Victorian era and include a number of original Burt family household items. There are horsehair upholstered pieces, wicker furniture, and kerosene hanging lamps. Upstairs bedrooms have iron beds and Victorian dressers.

The **Sutler's Store** building consists of an adobe portion built in 1849 which housed the post's sutler's store and a stone section added in 1852 which was used as the sutler's office, post office, and game room. An 1883 lime-concrete addition on the rear contains the enlisted men's bar, which was open to the public, and an officers' club.

The post sutler was a civilian trader licensed to do business on a military base. The goods at the store supplemented the bare necessities provided to soldiers by the army. The sutler also supplied the emigrants who passed through on the Oregon, California, and Mormon trails, as well as Indians and miners. The store has been restored to its 1876 appearance when campaigns against the northern Plains Indians were at their peak and the Black Hills gold rush was on. Merchandise includes tools, weapons, clothing, and household goods.

The officers' club, operated by the post trader, was restricted to officers, their wives, and a few high-ranking civilian employees. The officers could buy champagne, wine, beer, whiskey, ale, and brandy. Only beer and wine were sold in the enlisted men's club, but it was a very popular place with both soldiers and civilians who played cards and pool.

The only surviving enlisted men's barracks, the 1874 **Cavalry Barracks,** is a long, two-story building with verandas on both floors. The barracks housed two 60-man companies of troops. Sleeping quarters were on the second floor in two large dormitories, while the mess room, kitchen, washroom, cook's room, storage room, day room, library, armory room, and first sergeant's room were on the first floor. Restoration is to 1876 when Company K, Second U.S. Cavalry, under Captain James Egan lived in the barracks.

PART IV

NORTHWEST

6

OREGON

Mission Mill Village

Recreation of the first Protestant mission to the Indians west of the Rockies, an 1834 Methodist mission relocated to this site in 1841, and a textile museum housed in an 1889 woolen mill

ADDRESS: 1313 Mill St. SE, Salem OR 97301
TELEPHONE: (503) 585-7012
LOCATION: In Salem, near the state capitol; from I-5 take the north Santiam Highway exit, go west to 14th St., turn right, go to Mill St., and turn left
OPEN: Tuesday–Saturday, 10 A.M. to 4:30 P.M.; May–September: Sunday, 1–4:30 P.M.
ADMISSION: Adults, $3; senior citizens, $2.50; children, $1; group rates available
FACILITIES: Visitors' Center, cafeteria, craft shops, picnic area, fiber arts classes, library, handicapped accessible
HOTELS/MOTELS: Best Western New Kings Inn, 3858 Market St. NE, Salem 97301, tel. (503) 581-1559; Chumaree Comfortel, 3301 Market St. NE, Salem 97301, tel. (503) 370-7888

or (800) 248-6273; Shilo Inn, 1855 Hawthorne NE, Salem 97303, tel. (503) 581-9410 or (800) 222-2244; Travelodge, 1555 State St., Salem 97301, tel. (503) 581-2466

CAMPING: Silver Falls State Park, 15 miles southeast of Silverton on S.R. 214, tel. (503) 873-8681; Detroit Lake State Park, 50 miles east on S.R. 22, tel. (503) 854-3346; Champeog State Park, seven miles southeast of Newberg, tel. (503) 678-1251; Forest Glen RV Park, 8372 Enchanted Way, Turner 97392, tel. (503) 363-7616; KOA Salem, 1595 Lancaster Dr. SE, Salem 97301, tel. (503) 581-6736

History

Oregon in the early nineteenth century was much larger than the state we know today. An ill-defined region extended along the Pacific coast from the 42nd parallel, south of which was Mexican-held California, to the 54th parallel, north of which was Russian territory, and eastward to the Rocky Mountains.

The United States, Great Britain, Spain, and Russia all made claims to the area. Through the diplomatic efforts of U.S. Secretary of State John Quincy Adams, Russia and Spain were persuaded to drop their claims. That left the United States and Great Britain, both of whom alleged discovery of the region. In 1818 the two countries agreed to postpone a decision about the disputed property for a decade. Both governments would jointly occupy Oregon for ten years. In 1827 the agreement was extended for another decade.

At that time, fur traders and trappers were the region's only white occupants. The British company, the Hudson's Bay Company, dominated fur trading in the Pacific Northwest. Several American companies, including John Jacob Astor's American Fur Company, and many American mountain men tried to penetrate the Northwest's rich fur trading business but with limited success.

Missionaries were the precursors of the first American permanent settlements in Oregon. Between 1831 and 1842, they accounted for much of the American activity in Oregon. In 1831, four Flathead Indians traveled east to St. Louis asking for missionaries to minister in the Northwest. Among those answering the invitation were Jason and Daniel Lee, an uncle and nephew.

Jason, an ordained Methodist minister, had been a missionary in the British provinces of eastern Canada. In 1833 the Lees and three volunteers joined a pack train of fifty-eight men and eighty horses leaving Independence, Missouri. The leader of this expedition was Nathaniel J. Wyeth of Cambridge, Massachusetts, an organizer of a trading company. This was his second expedition to the Northwest. Although Wyeth's expedition did not prove to be economically successful, it was historically important. Wyeth built two trading posts which were helpful in establishing future American claims to the Northwest.

In September 1834 the missionaries reached Fort Vancouver, where they were warmly received by Dr. John McLoughlin, the chief factor of the Hudson's Bay Company. As the Lees began construction of their mission at French Prairie in the Willamette Valley, McLoughlin gave them livestock and assistance and provided them with a home at the fort. A ship sent from Boston with supplies for Wyeth also brought materials for the missionaries.

The mission established by the Lees on the east bank of the Willamette River was the first Protestant Christianizing attempt west of the Rocky Mountains and the first mission established by any denomination in Oregon. The missionary site was near the agricultural settlement of French Prairie, founded by former employees of the Hudson's Bay Company.

The Indians that the Lees had hoped to convert were plagued with disease and showed little enthusiasm for the new religion. Jason Lee began to see his endeavor as both a mission and colonization program. In 1838, Jason Lee returned to the East to recruit missionaries and settlers along with more money. His lectures, full of the glories of this little-known region, were the inspiration for many people to settle in the West, not to become missionaries but pioneers on the newest frontier.

In 1840, Jason Lee moved the Willamette Mission ten miles south to Salem, where water power was available. Fifty recruits from the East arrived to settle in the area. Within a couple of years, they had completed a gristmill, sawmill, Indian school, home for Jason Lee, and a parsonage.

Although the colony was successful, mission work among the Indians was not. The Methodist Mission Society suspended Lee in 1843 and sold the church property to settlers. A prosperous agricultural settlement called Chemeketa, later Salem, soon grew up at the site. The town was platted in 1846. With a population of 252, Salem was named territorial capital in 1850 and state capital in 1859.

In 1896, Thomas L. Kay, an English emigrant, built a red brick woolen mill to replace a wooden mill that had been destroyed by fire. The architect of the building was Walter D. Pugh; when built, the mill was the largest mill of its type in the state. It was in operation until 1965. Outbuildings on the mill site included a warehouse and dye and picker houses.

Adjoining Mission Mill Village is Willamette University, the oldest university in the Far West. Founded in 1842 as Oregon Institute, a literary and religious institution of learning, it was started originally to educate the children of the missionaries.

Tour

Mission Mill Village, located on a four-and-one-half-acre site in the center of Salem, contains buildings from the 1841 mission site and the Thomas Kay woolen mill which operated from 1889 until 1965. The setting is park-like, with picnic tables located near the millstream. There are herb and rose gardens. Begin your tour at the Visitors' Center located on the first floor of the **mill building.**

Buildings from the Methodist mission era include the **Jason Lee Home,** built in 1841, which was moved from a nearby site. The frame, two-and-one-half-story rectangular house features a two-tier veranda. The restored house is furnished with period furnishings.

Another mission building is the **Methodist Parsonage,** which also was built in 1841. The two-story frame house was built for the teachers who conducted school at the mission. Some classes were held in the parsonage. The furniture and books in the parsonage reflect its educational function.

The **John D. Boon Home** was built in 1847. Boon was an early pioneer in the Willamette Valley. The small, slab-style house was one of the first single-family homes in this area. It was moved to the village, restored, and furnished. John D. Boon was the first treasurer of the Oregon Territory.

The **Pioneer Presbyterian Church,** which was built in 1858, was moved to the village from nearby Pleasant Grove. The small church has been restored and is often used for weddings.

The largest building in the village is the **Thomas Kay Woolen Mill,** which was built in 1889. At that time, the three-and-one-half-story red brick building was the largest mill of its type in the state. Built on a native stone foundation, the building is noteworthy for the truss system for its roof. Of the forty-eight 12-by-16-inch beams which support the floors, only one of the 60-foot timbers is spliced. In the 1920s the 120-foot building was expanded to 180 feet.

Inside the Thomas Kay Woolen Mill are exhibits on Oregon's pioneer woolen industry. Demonstrations on working textile machinery show how raw fleece, primarily from Coos and Curry counties in Oregon, is transformed into yarn. On the first floor is the retail store, which features products from local craftspeople.

Originally the woolen mill was powered by water from the millstream. In later years, electric motors were added. Now, in the **wheelhouse,** the restored 1914 turbine and the shaft and pulley system run again.

Across the bridge from the mill building is the warehouse complex, which consists of three separate structures with common walls. In the **Rag House** and **Stock Warehouse** are a number of craft and antique stores.

Aurora Colony Museum

Restoration of a German religious communal society led by Dr. William Kiel, 1856–81

ADDRESS: Aurora Colony Historical Society, P.O. Box 202, Aurora, OR 97002
TELEPHONE: (503) 678-5754
LOCATION: On S.R. 99E, between Salem and Oregon City; Aurora-Donald exit from I-5
OPEN: 10 A.M. to 4:30 P.M., Wednesday–Saturday, and 1–4:30 P.M., Sunday, February through December; also Tuesday, 10 A.M. to 4:30 P.M., June through August; closed legal holidays and month of January.
ADMISSION: Adults, $1.50; children 6–18, $1.
FACILITIES: Audiovisual orientation film
HOTELS/MOTELS: International Dunes-Edgewater, 1900 Clackamette Dr. at McLoughlin Blvd., Oregon City 97045, tel. (503) 655-7141 or (800) 622-0211; Best Western Sherwood Inn, 15700 SW Upper Boones Ferry Rd., Lake Oswego, Portland 97034, tel. (503) 652-1500; Holiday Inn–South, 25425 SW Boones Ferry Rd., Wilsonville 97070, tel. (503) 682-2211; Allstar Inn, 17959 SW McEwan Rd., Portland 97224, tel. (503) 684-0760; Westin Benson, SW Broadway at Oak St., Oakland 97205, tel. (503) 228-2000

CAMPING: Champeog State Park, off S.R. 219, 7 miles south-east Newberg, tel. (503) 678-1251; Woodburn I-5 RV Park, 349 Amey Rd., Woodburn 97071, tel. (503) 981-0002; Isberg RV Park, 21599 Dolores Way NE, Aurora 97002, tel. (503) 678-2646

History

Communal societies are groups of people who live together, usually united by common religious or sometimes secular beliefs. They reject the notion of private property, and title to property is held jointly. Communal societies existed in the United States during the eighteenth and nineteenth centuries, with a few dating to the seventeenth century. Most of these communities were located in New England, the mid-Atlantic states, and Ohio, Indiana, and Kentucky. However, in the mid-nineteenth century, a communal group which began in Missouri immigrated to the Pacific Northwest to Oregon.

William Keil, the temporal and spiritual leader of the Missouri and Oregon communes, has been described as charismatic, magnetic, fanatical, autocratic, and a mystic. Obviously, it was Keil's personality as much as his religious principles which attracted followers. Keil was born in Germany in 1812 and immigrated to America in 1831. His occupations included tailoring and medicine. Not your typical medical practicioner and without formal medical training, Keil worked from a book of prescriptions written in human blood. Unfortunately for history, the German doctor destroyed his book.

Keil spent some time in Pennsylvania, where he had contact with the Rappites, a German religious community under the leadership of George Rapp, at Economy. A schism occurred at Economy in 1832 in which one-third of the Rappites left to follow a new leader. He was Count Maximilian de Leon, who had advocated marriage to the celibate Rappites. When De Leon died in 1833, some of the De Leonites joined Dr. Keil.

Keil preached a doctrine of communism based on the Bible. Every man and woman was to be brother and sister to every other man and woman in one family with God as their father. No matter what work they did or what initial contribution they made, every man was an equal partner in ownership of the communal property. A guiding principle was "From every man according to his capacity, to every man according to his needs."

Keil's first large communal experiment, designed along Rappite lines but without celibacy, was founded at Bethel, Missouri, in 1844. Beginning with 2,500 acres, the community and its businesses, which included a distillery, gristmills, sawmills, and woolen mills in addition to agriculture, prospered. After a decade, the community numbered 650 people and owned nearly 5,000 acres.

Keil envisioned an even larger community on the Pacific coast and sent a scouting party ahead to find an appropriate location. On May 25, 1855, Keil and a caravan consisting of 175 people in 35 wagons left Bethel to travel the Oregon Trail. Their departure had been delayed by the death of the leader's oldest son, Willie, who was to have driven the lead wagon. Since Willie had begged not to be left behind, the body of the 19-year-old traveled to the West in a lead-lined coffin filled with alcohol.

In the fall, Keil and the caravan arrived in the Willapa Bay area in Washington Territory, the site selected by the advance scouts. Willie Keil was buried there. However, the Washington site did not look promising to Keil and his followers. After spending the fall and winter in Washington, the group moved to a new location above the falls of the Willamette in Oregon Territory where they founded a settlement.

The colony's town was named Aurora Mills in honor of one of Keil's daughters. Property was purchased from earlier settlers, Dave Smith and George White. Although the colonists' first dwellings were built of logs, two to three-story frame structures followed quickly. In addition to homes, stores, and a church, the community built a large hotel to serve the needs of stage passengers. The food was reputed to be so good that it became a very popular stage stop.

Aurora grew into a prosperous community. For the next decade, the arrival of caravans of colonists from Bethel swelled the population of the town to 600. The settlers acquired 18,000 acres of land. Vineyards and orchards were planted. Shops produced furniture, clothes, baskets, and tools. Colonists' needs were filled from the general stores without cost. These German immigrants believed in hard work and plain living. They had no interest in decorations or intellectual or aesthetic concerns. Education, which was available to both sexes, was limited to the three R's. The colonists were known for their love of music. They believed that music was a celebration of faith. Band concerts were held frequently both in the community and throughout the area.

When Dr. Keil died suddenly in December 1877, there was no one to assume leadership. Members of the Aurora communal group decided to disband in 1881 as had the Bethel community in 1880. Each member received a share of the total property and holdings.

The Aurora Colony Historical Society is responsible for the preservation and restoration of the original colony buildings.

Tour

Buildings maintained by the Aurora Colony Historical Society as museums open to the public are just a few of the original colony buildings which remain in the small town of Aurora. Seventeen buildings are included in the National Historic District and are listed on the National Register of Historic Places. The non-museum buildings are privately owned and may only be viewed from the outside, except for those occupied by shops.

The Aurora Colony's main restored building is the **Ox Barn Museum,** which contains the bulk of the exhibits and artifacts related to the history of the Aurora Colony. Just as its name implies, it was a barn for oxen. There was another barn for horses. The ox barn was remodeled by the Fred Will family and used as a combination general store and residence. The building was purchased from Will descendents by the Aurora Colony Historical Society to be used as a museum.

One exhibit in the Ox Barn Museum focuses on the Aurora Colony church. Built in 1864–67, it was torn down in 1912. During the active period of the colony, services were usually held every other Sunday by Dr. Keil, who would preach on the theme of communal sharing. Services were discontinued after Keil's death. Artifacts displayed include an original chuch window, a German family Bible, and sketches of the church.

The Colony Hotel is another structure no longer standing which is the subject of an exhibit. Noted for its excellent food, it was a popular stage stop. View the sketches and photographs of the hotel.

The Keil family exhibit displays photographs of William, his wife Louisa, and their nine children. Their longest living child was Emmanuel Keil, who died in 1922.

The five migrations of colonists from Missouri to Oregon from 1855–67 are the focus of the Oregon Trail exhibit.

Many of the exhibits focus on the products made by the industrious Germans and the tools they used to produce them. There are fine quilts, samplers, rugs, lace, and pillow shams. There are workbenches, toolboxes, tools, lathe, cobbler's bench, crosscut saw, *schnitzbank* (shaving bench), loom, spinning wheels, sewing machines, apple pickers, sausage stuffer, and sauerkraut cutter.

Other exhibits feature the Aurora drugstore and doctor's office, the school, and the music of the colony.

The **Kraus House,** built in 1863, is a white, two-story frame house in the up and down board and batten style. It is furnished with handmade furniture made in the colony. Most colony furniture was made from Douglas fir and is noteworthy for its simple, but beautiful styling. The kitchen has a wood-burning stove and a baking oven. Both the corner cupboard and the dry sink were made in the colony.

The **Steinbach Cabin** is a three-room log cabin built in 1876 for George and Catherine Steinbach. It was constructed of peeled and hand-hewn timbers chinked with mud. Most of the furnishings, including tables, chairs, beds, dishes, and a quilt, belonged to the Steinbach family and were donated by their descendents.

The **Wash House** was a separate building serving several families. Many of the chores performed by women were done here, and several women usually worked together. In this simple, white frame building, soap was made, sausages were stuffed, clothes were washed, and fruit was canned.

There is also a display of nineteenth century buggies and steam-driven farm equipment.

7

WASHINGTON

Fort Vancouver National Historic Site

Reconstruction of an early nineteenth century Hudson's Bay Company fur trading post, the commercial and political center of the British Empire in the Pacific Northwest's Oregon Territory; National Register

ADDRESS: 1501 E. Evergreen Blvd., Vancouver WA 98661-3897
TELEPHONE: (206) 696-7655 or (206) 696-7618
LOCATION: In Vancouver; from I-5, turn east at the Mill Plain Boulevard exit; from I-205, exit at S.R. 14, go west about 5 miles, turn right on Grand Blvd.
FACILITIES: Visitors' Center with museum, audiovisual program, living history programs
OPEN: Daily 9:30 A.M. to 4 P.M. during Standard Time; 9:30 A.M. to 5:30 P.M. during Daylight Saving Time; closed holidays

CICERO

BOOKSHELF
at Hooligan Rocks
Gateway Plaza
Truckee, CA 96161
(916) 582-0515
(800) 959-5083

MADE IN U.S.A.

ADMISSION: $1 per person; $3 per family

HOTELS/MOTELS: Shilo Inn Downtown, 401 E. 13th St., Vancouver 98660, tel. (206) 696-0411 or (800) 222-2244; Travelodge, 601 Broadway, Vancouver 98660, tel (206) 693-3668; Red Lion Inn at the Quay, 100 Columbia St., Vancouver 98660, tel. (206) 694-8341 or (800) 547-8010

CAMPING: Jantzen Beach R.V., 1503 Hayden Island Dr., Portland, OR, tel. (503) 289-7626 or (800) 443-7248; Battle Ground Lake State Park, 20 miles northeast of Vancouver, 3 miles east of S.R. 503, tel. (206) 687-4621 or (800) 562-0990; Paradise Point State Park, off I-5, 5 miles south of Woodland, tel. (206) 263-2350 or (800) 562-0990

History

Fort Vancouver was a British fur trading post operated by the Hudson's Bay Company. Toward the end of the eighteenth century, British seamen became aware of the magnitude of the Pacific Northwest's fur resources when they traded with coastal Indians for fur. The sailors were able to sell the furs in China for fantastic prices. Soon a race developed between European, Canadian, and American traders for control of the lucrative fur trading business; after a struggle, Britain's Hudson's Bay Company became dominant.

In 1818, America and Britain agreed to occupy the Oregon Territory jointly until they could resolve their boundary dispute in that region. To strengthen British claims to Oregon, which consisted of present-day British Columbia, Washington, Oregon, and Idaho, in 1824 the Hudson's Bay Company moved its western headquarters one hundred miles upstream on the Columbia River. It had been located at Fort George at the mouth of the Columbia River.

The imposing fur trading fort was a 325-by-732-foot log stockade guarded by one bastion. It was named for Captain George Vancouver, an English navigator and explorer, in

March 1825. The fort became the visible symbol of the British Empire in the Pacific Northwest.

For the next two decades, the Fort Vancouver trading post was the economic, political, social, and cultural center of a large, virtually uninhabited wilderness. In addition to the two dozen major buildings inside the stockade, a village of thirty to fifty wooden houses, employees' residences, developed next to the fort.

The chief factor of the Hudson's Bay Company post was Dr. John McLoughlin, who was born in Quebec and served as a physician for the North West Company. When the North West and the Hudson's Bay companies merged in 1821, McLoughlin was named head of the Columbia Department, the company's headquarters in the Pacific Northwest.

McLoughlin was a sophisticated, urbane man who entertained elegantly with silver, china, crystal, and bagpipe music, a significant feat in the wilderness. The over six-foot-tall white-haired doctor was a hospitable host and an excellent businessman who was highly respected by the Indians. The successful trading post was the center of a vast commercial empire that ranged from the Rockies to the Pacific and from Russian Alaska to Mexican California. Furs from all the company's stations were gathered at Vancouver for shipment to England.

Fort Vancouver was also an agricultural center, with its 2,000 acres of farmland producing crops of peas, oats, barley, wheat, and garden vegetables. Large herds of livestock included cattle, horses, hogs, sheep, and goats. Apples, pears, peaches, plums, and cherries grew in the orchards. The fort also had fisheries, salt works, shipyards, flour mills, and sawmills.

Two- to three-hundred people were employed at the fort. As a self-sustaining community, the residents had to supply all their own services. There were blacksmiths, carpenters, coopers, bakers, millers, farmers, and herders. The active fur trading business employed many accounting clerks. Clerks and officers, who came from the British Isles, formed the upper class at the post. Most of the fort workers, who represented many nationalities—Iroquis, Cree, Canadians, and Sandwich Islanders—were illiterate and made up the lower class. They lived on the land outside the stockade.

When American pioneers, lured by the fertile land of the Willamette River Valley, began arriving at the fort after traveling the Oregon Trail, McLoughlin cordially received them. He offered them supplies, lent them seed grains and provisions, provided passage for them in company boats, protected them from hostile natives, entertained them in his home, and extended them credit. His encouragement fostered the growth of an American population in the Willamette Valley, and he is often referred to as the "Father of Oregon."

In 1846 the United States and Great Britain resolved the Oregon Territory boundary dispute by establishing the 49th parallel as the southern boundary of Canada. This had a negative impact on Fort Vancouver as it was now located in United States territory. The influence of the fort and the Hudson's Bay Company declined as United States settlers began taking over the land near the fort.

Three years after the United States acquired this region, an army fort called Camp Vancouver was established adjacent to the Fort Vancouver trading post. The military base was garrisoned by a regiment of mounted riflemen and troops.

Hudson's Bay Company officials welcomed the U.S. Army's presence as they hoped the soldiers would prevent American settlers from taking over their land. This did not happen and relations between the British and the Americans became strained. The fur trade declined and the Hudson's Bay Company landholdings and livestock dwindled. In 1860 the fur trading company evacuated the post, turning over the buildings and land to the U.S. Army. All these buildings burned in 1866.

Fort Vancouver, as the military base was designated in 1853, was at the center of the campaigns against the Indians in the

Pacific Northwest. A troop marshalling point and major command post, it was the headquarters of the 11th Military District in 1850–51. Fort Vancouver troops saw action in the 1877 Nez Perce War.

During the Spanish War and World Wars I and II, Vancouver was a mobilization and training center. Called Vancouver Barracks in 1879, it was a key military headquarters and supply depot during World War II. Famous officers who served there during their careers include Ulysses S. Grant, Philip H. Sheridan, George Crook, Oliver O. Howard, and George C. Marshall.

The historic post was retired by the army in 1947. The next year the Vancouver Barracks parade ground and the site of the Hudson's Bay Company post were established as a national monument administered by the National Park District. In 1961 the 208-acre site became the Fort Vancouver National Historic Site.

Tour

Fort Vancouver National Historic Site, a 208-acre property administered by the National Park Service, is a reconstruction of the British Hudson's Bay Company trading post which was built in the 1820s. Archeological surveys of the site have located the foundations of the post's buildings. Reconstructed buildings have been placed on their original foundations. A **Visitors' Center** has exhibits which interpret the role of the Hudson's Bay Company and the participants in the fur trade in the development of the Pacific Northwest. Artifacts found during archeological excavations are displayed.

The wooden **stockade** has been rebuilt along with the one **bastion**. Built in 1845, the bastion was built to protect the fort against American threats. The three-story corner structure had eight 3-pounder cannons which were sometimes used to fire salutes to ships arriving at the fort.

Buildings include the **blacksmith's shop** where a vast variety of iron and steel items needed by the fur traders was produced. This shop also produced items needed at the twenty to thirty other Hudson's Bay posts in the Columbia District. The interior is a fully equipped blacksmith shop.

The **bakery,** a two-story structure located in the east wall of the stockade, contained two fire-brick ovens. Bread for the two- to three-hundred fort employees was baked here. The bakery also provided biscuits for ship crews and the brigade.

One of the larger buildings was the **Indian Trade Shop and Dispensary.** It housed the fur trading operations at Fort Vancouver. Indians would bring in their furs and trade them for goods, most of which were imported from or through Britain. There was often a two-year lapse between ordering and receiving. The Indian Trade Shop was the center of the fort's operation as it was the pelts trapped by the Indians which were the basis of the business. This building also housed the hospital, the doctor's office, and his residence.

The **Chief Factor's Residence** was the home of Dr. John McLoughlin, the man credited with the phenomenal success of the fur trading business at Fort Vancouver. As a chief factor of the Hudson's Bay Company, Dr. McLoughlin's authority was second only to that of Governor George Simpson, the direct representative of the London governor and committee of the Hudson's Bay Company.

That there were few Indian outbreaks during his administration from 1824–46 is indicative of Dr. McLoughlin's executive genius and strong control over the region. In addition to managing the fur trading business, he developed agriculture and husbandry and opened up markets for the exportation of lumber, salmon, and flour.

Dr. McLoughlin was a kindly man, well known for his hospitality to all visitors. His commodious and elegant home was the social center of the post. The white clapboard house had a large front porch. There was a large mess hall inside where clerks and officers ate their meals and where parties and dances were held.

The **kitchen** provided meals for the officers and clerks at the fort and their guests. The building contained a cooking area, pantry, larder, and living quarters for the kitchen staff.

Side Trips

The **McLoughlin House National Historic Site** contains the restoration of the house that Dr. John McLoughlin lived in after retiring from the Hudson's Bay Company. Built by McLoughlin with lumber from sawmills he had established, the McLoughlin family moved to the house in 1846. McLoughlin occupied the house until his death in 1857, his widow until 1860, and his daughter and son-in-law, Mr. and Mrs. Daniel Harvey, until 1867. The house was moved from its original site at Third and Main streets to McLoughlin Park, which is on land donated to Oregon City by Dr. McLoughlin in 1850. The McLoughlins' graves were also moved to this site. Located in Oregon City, McLoughlin Park is between Seventh and Eighth streets, four blocks east of Pacific Highway, U.S. 99. Open Tuesday–Saturday, 10 A.M. to 5 P.M., and Sunday, 1–4 P.M., in summer. In winter, open Tuesday–Saturday, 10 A.M. to 4 P.M., and Sunday, 1–4 P.M. An admission is charged.

Fort Walla Walla Museum Complex

Recreation of a pioneer village and agricultural museum housed on the 1858 military reservation of Fort Walla Walla

ADDRESS: P.O. Box 1616, Myra Road, Walla Walla, WA 99362
TELEPHONE: (509) 525-7703

LOCATION: In southeastern Washington, 6 miles north of the Washington-Oregon border and 158 miles south of Spokane; on Myra Road in Walla Walla
FACILITIES: Handicapped accessible
OPEN: Tuesday–Sunday, 1–5 P.M., June through September; Saturday and Sunday, 1–5 P.M. in May and October; closed rest of year
ADMISSION: Adults, $2; children $1

Whitman Mission National Historic Site

Site of second Protestant mission to the Indians in Oregon country founded in 1836

ADDRESS: S.R. 2, Box 247, Walla Walla, WA 99362
TELEPHONE: (509) 522-6360
LOCATION: 8 miles west of Walla Walla on U.S. 12
FACILITIES: Visitors' Center, audiovisual program, handicapped accessible
OPEN: Daily, 8 A.M. to 5 P.M.; 8 A.M. to 8 P.M. in summer
ADMISSION: Adults $1
HOTELS/MOTELS: Best Western Pony Soldier, 325 E. Main St., Walla Walla 99362, tel. (509) 529-4360; Imperial Inn, 305 N. 2nd Ave. at Main St., Walla Walla 99362, tel. (509) 529-4410; Whitman Motor Inn, 107 N. 2nd Ave., Walla Walla 99362, tel. (509) 525-2200
CAMPING: Fort Walla Walla Park, Dalles Military Road, Walla Walla 99362, tel. (509) 525-3700; Lewis and Clark Trail State Park, R.R. 1, Dayton, tel. (509) 337-6457; Godman Campground, Umatilla National Forest, Dayton, tel. (509) 843-1891

History

Fort Walla Walla, a U.S. Army military base, was founded in 1856 during a series of Indian outbreaks. Almost half a century earlier, in 1818, the North West Company, a British fur trading company, built a trading post which was also named Fort Walla Walla. When the North West Company was forced to merge with Hudson's Bay Company in 1821, the fort became an outpost of that powerful British fur trading company. This trading post was destroyed by floods in the early 1840s, rebuilt, and eventually abandoned in 1855. The Hudson's Bay Company site is now under the water of Lake Wallula behind McNary Dam.

The army base named Fort Walla Walla was located about thirty miles east of the trading post of the same name. Initially, it was situated north of Mill Creek, but in spring 1858 it was relocated a mile south to its present location.

Although fur traders were the first whites in Oregon country, which was jointly controlled by Britain and America, American Protestant missionaries to the Indians arrived in the mid-1830s. The first Protestant mission was the Willamette Mission founded by Jason and Daniel Lee in 1834. (See Mission Mill, Oregon.) The Whitman Mission was the second Protestant mission in the Oregon country.

Marcus Whitman was a Presbyterian elder and a physician. He and Rev. Samuel Parker had been sent to the Northwest in 1835 by the interdenominational American Board of Commissioners for Foreign Missions to investigate the possibility of starting missions among the Indians. After talking with the Flatheads and Nez Perce, Whitman returned with enthusiastic reports.

Whitman, along with his new bride, Narcissa Prentiss, a devout Presbyterian, were natives of New York. Accompanied by Henry and Eliza Spalding and William Gray, they departed from Liberty, Missouri, in April 1836 and arrived at Fort Vancouver, the Hudson's Bay Company heaquarters, the following September. Narcissa Whitman and Eliza Spalding were the first American women to travel across the continent.

The Whitman Mission to the Cayuse was established on Mill Creek, on the north bank of the Walla Walla River, twenty-two miles above its junction with the Columbia and the Hudson's Bay Company post of Fort Walla Walla. Spalding's Mission to the Nez Perce was one hundred ten miles further east.

The Cayuse were a nomadic tribe who hunted and gathered their food. Acquiring the horse in the mid-eighteenth century, they quickly became expert horsemen. They had good relations with the English fur traders. A Cayuse chief, Umtippe, gave the Whitmans some of his land for their mission, which was named Waiilatpu, which means Place of the Rye Grass in the Cayuse language.

Despite their friendly welcome, the Whitmans were not very successful in converting the Indians to Christianity. Most of the Cayuse continued practicing their own religion. The Whitmans introduced agricultural practices and cattle raising but most of the mission Indians preferred hunting.

On March 14, 1837, Narcissa Whitman gave birth to a daughter, Alica Clarissa, the first white child born of American parents west of the Rockies. Unfortunately, a little more than two years later, little Alicia drowned in the Walla Walla River.

As other missionaries arrived and established separate missions, the Whitman Mission became the informal headquarters of the mission field. Improving on the first, quickly erected structures, the mission included a large adobe mission house, an adobe residence for William Gray, a gristmill, a blacksmith shop, and a sawmill. Despite the Whitmans' hard work and devotion, their Christianizing efforts met with little success. The missionaries also engaged in constant quarrels with each other.

Because of the limited success and great expense of maintaining the northwestern missions, the American Board ordered the closing of the Whitman and Spalding missions in 1842. During the winter of 1842–43, Marcus Whitman returned to Boston to try to get that decision overturned, which he succeeded in doing.

On his return trip in 1843, Whitman encountered a wagon train of one thousand settlers at Independence, Missouri, traveling west on the Oregon Trail. Because of his experience, Whitman became their guide and physician and brought them to Waiilatpu. As emigration on the Oregon Trail increased, more and more people found their way to the Whitman Mission. A family of seven children orphaned enroute was adopted by the Whitmans.

The Whitmans became preoccupied with tending to the pioneers rather than the Indians. Relations with the Indians deteriorated as more Indian hunting grounds were invaded by whites who grazed their livestock on them and fished out their streams. They also carried fatal diseases. A measles epidemic in 1847 spread by the pioneers killed half of the Cayuse. The Indians noticed that Whitman was able to cure many of the whites but that the Indians, who had no immunity to the disease, invariably died. The Cayuse suspected that Dr. Whitman was poisoning them.

On November 29, 1847, a small group of Cayuse attacked the seventy-five people living at the mission. They killed Dr. and Mrs. Whitman, two of their adopted sons, and nine others. Seven mission residents managed to escape, three halfbreed boys were released by the Indians, and two adult halfbreeds participated in the attack. Fifty people were taken captive by the Indians; three of them, children sick with the measles, died. The remaining forty-seven were ransomed on December 29, 1847, by Peter Skene Ogden of the Hudson's Bay Company. After the massacre, the Indians burned all the mission buildings to the ground. The Whitman Massacre temporarily ended Protestant mission efforts in the Oregon country.

The year before the massacre, Great Britain and the United

States had reached an agreement on the disputed Northwest boundary. The Whitman Massacre had occurred in American territory. A U.S. Army expedition spent the next two years pursuing the Cayuse who had committed the hideous crime. When five Cayuse presented themselves to army officials as the perpetrators of the massacre, they were hung. Only then did the army drop its pursuit of the Cayuse.

In the spring of 1849, a territorial government was established over the Oregon country. In 1853, it was divided by an east/west line into the territories of Oregon and Washington. Emigration into the new territories increased rapidly.

Isaac Stevens, the first territorial governor of Washington, called a council with the Indians of the Walla Walla Valley in May 1855. Gold had been discovered in eastern Washington, and Governor Stevens was eager to negotiate settlements with the Indians before news got out.

Three treaties were negotiated. The Nez Perce ceded some of their outer grazing land in central Idaho and southeastern Washington for $200,000 in goods along with promises to provide schools, shops, mills, and a hospital and to keep whites off Indian lands. The Yakimas ceded nearly ten million acres in Washington east of the Cascades, retaining only a small Yakima Reservation in exchange for goods and promises. The third treaty established the Umatilla Reservation in Oregon in exchange for large areas in southeastern Washington and northeastern Oregon which were ceded to the United States.

Although the Indians were told they would not have to vacate the ceded lands until the treaties were ratified by the U.S. Congress—a process that would take years—in less than two weeks, Governor Stevens and Joel Palmer, superintendent of Indian Affairs for Oregon, published notices that the area was open to settlement. When land hunters and gold miners rushed in and moved across Indian lands to the Colville mining district, angry Spokan, Coeur d'Alene, and Palouse Indians felt betrayed and attacked and killed the intruders.

Also feeling angry and betrayed, the coastal tribes went on the warpath in 1855–56. This prompted the establishment of Fort Walla Walla, a U.S. Army post, in fall 1856 by Major Edward J. Steptoe. In addition to controlling the area's hostile Indians, the fort was to protect settlers and the crews constructing the Mullan Road.

In the Coeur d'Alene War of 1858 between the Indians and the army, 164 men from Fort Walla Walla commanded by Major Steptoe were attacked by 1,000 Indians near the present city of Rosalia. After a day of heavy fighting, Steptoe and the surviving troops marched 85 miles to the Snake River where some friendly Nez Perce helped them to cross the river to safety. Soldiers who died in this battle are buried in Fort Walla Walla's military cemetery.

Using Fort Walla Walla as his base, Colonel George Wright sought revenge for Steptoe's defeat. Battles between the Indians and the army troops lasted four days. Commencing on September 1, 1858, in the Battle of Four Lakes and the Battle of Spokane Plain, Wright's 600 cavalry and infantry troops killed 60 Indians without incurring a single casualty. Colonel Wright ended the 1858 campaign in eastern Washington by hanging 15 Indian war leaders and taking others prisoner.

The opening of the Walla Walla Valley to settlement in fall 1858 created new friction with the Indians, and the Fort Walla Walla troops were kept busy protecting these new settlers from Indian attacks. From 1859–62 the fort also helped protect crews constructing the Mullan Road.

The fort was closed in 1911. The military reservation was converted to a Veterans Hospital in 1921 which occupied original fort buildings. The Fort Walla Walla Museum Complex is administered by the Walla Walla Valley Pioneer and Historical Society.

Tour

The Fort Walla Walla Museum Complex features a pioneer village which contains original buildings moved to the site, recreated structures, and a large horse-era agricultural display in five display buildings.

The **Ransom Clark Cabin** was built in Walla Walla in 1859 by a pioneer settler. Clark had first entered the Walla Walla Valley in 1843 as a member of a surveying party. After an unsuccessful gold mining venture in Canada, he returned to the valley in 1855 but was forced to leave again as all settlers were ordered out because of the Indian uprising. When white settlers were permitted to return in 1859, Clark began construction of his log cabin. It consisted of a living room and a kitchen separated by a breezeway. Children slept in upstairs sleeping lofts reached by ladders. Clark died before his cabin was completed, and Mrs. Clark married a neighbor, Almos Reynolds. Many of the furnishings and artifacts in the cabin belonged to family members.

The **One-Room Union Schoolhouse** was built in 1867 west of Dixie. School was held in the District 26 building until 1930, when it was closed. Furnishings, including desks and pictures, were obtained from other Washington schools, but the blackboards are original.

The **Country Store** log cabin was built by A. J. Isitt on the northeast corner of Fort Walla Walla. In addition to carrying all the items needed by the settlers, it was also the post office.

The **Babcock Railroad Depot,** built in 1880 on the Northern Pacific Railway, was located near Eureka, thirty miles northwest of Walla Walla. Items from both the Union Pacific, formerly the Oregon-Washington Railroad and Navigation Co., the Northern Pacific, and the Wallula–Walla Walla Railroad are displayed. Chinese laborers were employed to build the railroads, and Walla Walla once had eight hundred Chinese residents. An exhibit of Chinese artifacts is also in the depot.

The **Prescott Jail** was built in 1903 in Prescott. The 10-by-14-foot structure is made of 2-by-6-inch planks spiked together for the walls and 2-inch planks for the floor and ceiling. Windowless, the only opening is a small barred hole in the door.

The **Umapine Cabin** was built in 1878 near College Place in an area that was a favorite wintering place of Chief Umapine and his tribe. Now an Indian museum, it displays photographs of local Indians, petroglyphs, baskets, and many other items.

Built around 1900 in Walla Walla, the **Elliotts' Carriage Barn** was used to house the family's horse and buggy and a sleigh. It contains saddles, harnesses, buggies, and sleighs of the early twentieth century.

A small cabin built by Henry Jacky in 1925 was often used as a children's playhouse. Now a children's museum, the **Jacky Family's Play Cabin** houses antique toys including dolls and stuffed animals.

The **Pioneers' Clinic,** built in 1890 on Mill Creek by the Klicker family, is a combination barber shop and doctor's office. The doctor's office in the small frame building contains a desk used by Governor Isaac Stevens, the first territorial governor of Washington. In the barber shop are an 1870 barber chair and a 1900 shoe shine stand.

Among the reconstructed buildings is the **blockhouse,** which is designed like the blockhouses built at the first Fort Walla Walla military base. The two-story blockhouse is made of logs with rifle openings facing in all four directions.

Another reconstruction is the **blacksmith shop,** which contains original tools and equipment used in the 1870s. Note the large collection of branding irons, which were used to identify cattle that roamed the open range.

The **Cabin of the Pioneers** was constructed of hand-hewn logs from an 1877 cabin built by W. W. Davies near Mill Creek. The cabin is furnished as it would have been by the Davies family. Items found in the cabin include homemade soap, candle molds, butter churn, flour bin, cast-iron waffle iron, flatirons, iron kettle, and spinning wheel.

In addition to the pioneer village, there is a large exhibit on horse-era agriculture in the Walla Walla area which is contained in five modern exhibit buildings. One building houses a stationary grain threshing outfit; a second, a large 1919 side hill combine used for threshing wheat pulled by a team of thirty-three life-sized fiberglass mules, fully harnessed and hooked up to the Shenandoah hitch that is driven by one man. Another building holds vehicles pulled by horses or mules, and a fourth building is filled with farm machinery. Pioneer tools and household items fill the fifth building.

Nearby is the **Fort Walla Walla Military Cemetery** where soldiers who took part in the Indian wars are buried.

Eight miles west of Walla Walla is the **Whitman Mission National Historic Site.** No original structures remain here since the Indians burned the entire mission after killing its inhabitants. The National Park Service has established a nearly one-mile long, self-guiding trail which has interpretive signs and audio stations at each of the significant historic sites.

Start your visit at the **Visitors' Center,** which shows orientation films and displays a large model of the mission as it was in 1847. Exhibits in the museum relate to Marcus and Narcissa Whitman and the Cayuse Indians and include many items found by archeologists at the mission.

The self-guiding trail begins outside the Visitors' Center. At the first stop is a section of the **Oregon Trail,** the two-thousand-mile route from Missouri to Oregon which thousands of pioneers in covered wagons traveled. Many emigrants stayed at the mission, where they were warmly received. The mission became a way station for those who were too ill to go on.

Although Marcus Whitman was not very successful in cultivating Christianity, he was very successful in cultivating the land. Watered by the **irrigation ditch,** the mission fields grew abundant quantities of wheat, potatoes, peas, and other vegetables.

The **mission orchard** has been restored. The original orchard was started by Narcissa. Apple and peach seeds gathered during her stay at Fort Vancouver became the basis for the orchard.

The site of the **first house** built by Marcus Whitman for his bride is marked. It was a small log lean-to that provided scant shelter during the first winter. In the spring of 1837, Whitman added a larger section of sun-dried adobe bricks.

Three mills have stood at the **Gristmill Site.** After the second mill burned down, a third mill with forty-inch millstones was built. Because the Cayuse had become dependent on the mill, it was the only building at the mission which was not destroyed after the massacre.

The **millpond** built by Marcus Whitman has been restored. Whitman built the millpond to provide water power for the grist mill and to irrigate the fields. A millrace from the river carried the water to the pond.

The site of **Emigrant House,** which name does not reflect the house's original use, is indicated. The house was originally built as a home for William Gray, the mission mechanic who traveled west with the Whitmans and Spaldings. After Gray left in 1842, the house was used as a shelter for Oregon Trail emigrants.

Another stop on the trail is the site of the **Mission House.** Built in 1838, it was much larger than the Whitmans' first home. The one-and-one-half-story whitewashed house was T-shaped. This is where Marcus and Narcissa were killed; the doctor died in the house and his wife in the yard.

Fifty years after the Whitman Massacre, in 1897, the **Memorial Shaft** commemorating those who died was erected. The twenty-seven-foot shaft was placed on top of the hill that Narcissa used to climb to catch sight of her husband returning after ministering to the ill.

One of the most moving sites is the **Great Grave** where the massacre victims are buried. As if they hadn't suffered enough, the bodies which had been interred in a shallow grave two days after the attack were disturbed by wolves. When the Oregon Volunteers arrived three months later, the soldiers reburied the bodies which were strewn throughout the area. In 1897 the remains were placed in a marble vault and the names of the slain carved into the marble.